THE
TAKING

CELESTE CASTRO

BELLA
BOOKS
2019

Bella Books, Inc.
P.O. Box 10543
Tallahassee, FL 32302

Printed in the United States of America on acid-free paper.

First Bella Books Edition 2019

Editor: Ann Roberts
Cover Designer: Sandy Knowles

ISBN: 978-1-64247-079-6

Other Bella Books by Celeste Castro

Homecoming
Lex Files

Acknowledgments

My wife: Thank you so much for supporting me every step of the way. Thank you for all the pep talks and spanks on the butt—which I totally earned and very much enjoyed.

My sister: I love that you ALWAYS dress as a slutty fairy for Halloween and that you repeat the same story of how the mean lumberjack cut down your tree and took you home. Thanks for the story idea.

My readers: Thanks for taking a leap of faith every time you read one of my books. I sincerely appreciate your support.

Treena Colby: Thanks for reminding me that I *can* command a huge cult if I wanted.

Bella Books: Linda and Jessica Hill and everyone that make Bella Books happen. Thank you for investing in my writing.

Bella Books Sister Authors: Thanks for including me and for collaborating with me. I am enjoying getting to know you and reading your work.

Ann Roberts the Only: Thank you for helping me be a better writer. Thanks for sweating through this one with me.

Saint Sandy Knowles: Thank you for working with me on creating a kick-ass cover that I am proud of.

The best beta readers in the history of beta readers:

Amelia Green: Thanks for being honest about the direction, rather misdirection, of this story, and ideas for course-correcting.

Cade Haddock Strong: Thanks for talking through this story with me over and over and over. Thanks for letting me step outside of the story and being a listening ear when I needed it.

Catherine Lane: Thanks for the manuscript critique! Thanks for taking the time from your own writing to help me with mine. You're right, Peachy is a cry-cry bitch. I've knocked some sense into her.

Christina Alger: Thanks for helping me realize I used the word fuck 192 times! Thanks for pointing out other similar patterns that got in the way of my story.

Devon Sweeting: Thanks so much for the NOLA history lesson and ideas to better set the stage of my story. I loved that you loved my malleable minded made to order meat hunks of men. Thanks for also being a cheerleader, telling me what parts you liked, adding encouraging commentary throughout my manuscript.

Frances, my mother-in-law: Thank you for helping me create vivid imagery through better descriptions of people and places. Thank you for being one of my biggest supporters.

Genevieve Dallmeyer: Thanks for your help on world-building, identifying character motivations, your guidance on style and suggestions for the story's timeline, the chapter-by-chapter comments, your honesty, phew! Good call on the less crying on the couch and more ass-kicking! P.S. Hope you like Minette. She's for you.

Michael Quevedo: The craft of writing is an art form and I'm at the finger painting stage. Actually, I'm learning how to take the caps off the tubes of paint and making a complete mess while doing so. Thanks for your guidance in helping me understand how I can be a better writer.

About the Author

Celeste is an American Mexican from small-town, rural Idaho, where most of her stories take place; she's populating the conservative state with even more lesbians one story at a time. In addition to fiction, Celeste writes for Hispanecdotes, an online magazine for LatinX writers, where she publishes essays and poetry. After thirteen years in Seattle, she and her wife recently moved to Chicago.

PROLOGUE

Louisiana, 1811

"Is everyone here?" Lisette asked. "I am eager to begin."
Someone lit another candle giving her better light to count the
heads in attendance. They hadn't much time before their slave
masters noticed that the majority of their fifteen slaves were
unaccounted for. "Where are the others?"

The creak of the door hinges answered her question. Adèle
and Lisette's twin, Beatriz, along with two other slave members
of their household, Marie and Pauline, descended the steps into
the underground passageway, their rendezvous spot. Here they
planned the details of their participation in the revolt that was
to take place later that evening. Marie handed Lisette a tightly
folded piece of paper.

"From Charles."

"Wonderful work, Marie." Lisette unfolded the note and
moved closer to someone with a candle to read it.

"What does it say?" several people asked. "Tell us. We are
eager."

Lisette, along with her sisters, were among the few slaves who
could read. "We are to meet Charles Deslandes at the Andrey

Plantation at dusk. We are to wait in the field by the armory until his signal. We are to use whatever measures possible, be it gun, blade, or club to kill." Lisette felt a collective hush befall the darkened corridor.

"Lisette?"

"Yes, child." Lisette handed the correspondence to her sister and came closer to the young slave woman. "Speak freely, Marie."

"I do not mean to question, for your heroic deeds in Saint-Domingue are known as is the success of your alignment with Toussaint L'Ouverture."

"You are in a safe place, child. Tell us what is on your mind."

"We are scared." Similar sentiments trickled amongst the people.

"As am I. As are my sisters. But we have a message to send, no matter the cost. Some of us *will* die—maybe not tonight, maybe not tomorrow. And those who do not die will carry with them the treasure of knowing that they fought when it mattered, that they stood up and did not back down." Lisette stepped through her comrades, placing her hand upon the shoulders of her people as she walked, offering a tender rub of their hands when she took them in her own, or a nod of her head, acknowledging the fear in their eyes. "Please, someone remind us what today is about?"

"We are not happy," a brave soul murmured.

"Say it with your heart! What is today about?"

"We are not happy!"

"What else?"

"This life is not of our choosing," said another.

"Pauline, what have you to say?"

"Why are we fit enough to raise their children, but only permitted to travel underground to tend to them?"

"Marie? Claire, and all of you, tell me. Shout it from your lungs."

"Why are we treated as less because of the color of our skin? It is not fair that we are not their equal!"

"What do we want?"

"We want freedom."

"What else?"

"We want equality! We want freedom! We want equality!"

Their chants grew louder and their collective energy echoed within the small area, but Lisette was not concerned by the volume of their chorus. They were fifteen feet under rock and soil. No one would hear them, but soon enough, their white masters would hear. Everyone would hear what they wanted. They would feel it in their bones and in their hearts.

"Then who is here to fight for it?"

The small crowd chanted their assurances.

"Then we must fight to the death to send that message. Who here is prepared to die?"

No one said a word.

"No one here is ready to trade their life for freedom?"

"I am," said a brave voice.

"What about you, Marie?"

"I am."

"Claire?"

"Yes'm."

"Pauline?"

"Yes. Yes!"

Others proclaimed their willingness to lay down their lives and fight. Their voices became lost in a chorus of more chanting. "Who else?" Lisette asked, but she didn't need any more assurances. They were ready. She felt their desire to trade their lives for their freedom in her veins.

"Freedom or death! We are ready! Yes, we are ready, but let us further prepare. We have a gift for you. Gris-gris for protection in times of war." Beatriz and Adèle circulated around the room with the gris-gris, small cloth bags filled with bone, feather, and bread. "These are sacred, blessed by our queen mama in Saint-Domingue, to ensure our success this night."

The members of the group helped each other pin the gris-gris to the inside of their clothing and they did so without question. In addition to their tales of heroic deeds, fighting alongside L'Ouverture in their quest to abolish slavery for a sovereign Haiti, the sisters were well known for their practice of the voodoo religion. "I am proud to call you *all* my sisters this day and hereafter. Now, let us meet Deslandes and his men. Let us carry to him the feeling we harbor inside ourselves at this very moment." She kissed the cheek of each of her comrades as they climbed the steps out of the underground corridor to the stable where they would wait for her command.

Lisette turned to Beatriz and Adèle for her last set of orders. "Do you have everything you need to secure the big house?"

The sisters shared a look between them. "Yes," they said in unison. "We are ready."

Lisette knew from the look on her twin's face that they were hiding something. She reached for her twin's hand and held it tightly in her own. "What are you thinking?" She hushed her question.

"Do not question my tactics," Beatriz whispered as she yanked her hand from Lisette's grasp.

"You have your role in this quest, and we have ours," Adèle added. "Off. Be with your people. They are waiting for your command."

Lisette looked to the top of the stairs to where one of her devoted followers stood waiting for her.

"Trust that when you return, we will have the big house under our control in a most advantageous way."

"We should avoid drawing unnecessary attention to our existence. Sisters, we've talked about this."

"Every action that we will take tonight is necessary." Beatriz pushed her way past Lisette. "Come now! We want freedom! We want equality! Go and lead your people. With caution all of my sisters!"

"With caution," Lisette echoed through gritted teeth.

CHAPTER ONE

Present Day

"I *am* listening." Peachy put her phone in her back pocket as to appear totally invested in the conversation that was about to take place. "Tell me what to do," Peachy asked of Lisette, her mentor and role model, who took her in as a down-and-out twelve-year-old going on thirty-five, a troublemaker living on couches and boasting an impressive rap sheet, including two minor charges of possession and a grand theft auto.

"It will be dangerous," Lisette warned. "But you are ready, child, and no longer stupid." Though on the cusp of her twenty-fifth birthday, Peachy tolerated Lisette calling her a child, but not being called stupid.

Danger wasn't a foreign concept to her. She still ran jobs for money—favors and blackmail—but she operated in a more sophisticated way. "Are we talking like a five out of ten on the danger scale, or like a nine?"

"Do not test me."

"That was a legit question."

"Failure would mean your death and mine."

"Okay, I'm listening."

"There is an amulet that we must have."

"How much is it worth?"

"It is priceless."

"Are we stealing the crown fuckin' jewels?"

"Do not make me doubt my decision to include you," Lisette said in her signature stern voice that made Peachy sit straighter or stand taller. "It has been in my family for generations. My mother's ancestors brought it with them from Saint-Domingue and handed it down from woman to woman to use in her own unique way."

"Used how?"

"An energy lives within this amulet."

"That does what exactly?"

"Anything you want it to do."

"What do you mean?"

"I will explain it to you in due time, child. What's important right now is that the amulet is deep inside the walls of the *Spanish Rose*. My sister Adèle has had it in her possession for far too long. She has misused it, and she no longer deserves it."

"Who does deserve it?"

"Me."

"And what's in it for me?"

"I choose to hand it to you."

"What? No, I can't—"

"You are and will always be the closest to family I will ever have."

"I am honored, Lisette, really, but I didn't say that because I wanted it."

"It will be yours and you will honor and protect it. I will tell you everything once we have it in our possession."

"I don't know what to say."

"You will not say anything right now. Ninety percent of voodoo is listening. Wherever you are, listen more than talk. For when you rattle your mouth, you do not learn. This job has many moving parts, one of which is my sister Adèle."

Peachy had only met Adèle a couple of times, and both times left her feeling like she was in a room with something otherworldly. Her hair would stand on end, and she would get physically ill. Worse, Adèle had an awful scent to her, how a person would smell if they rose from the dead—like dirt and lilies and the encounter always left Peachy with a feeling of dread.

Adèle's reputation preceded her. She built her vast fortune trading in the black market. She could get anyone anything at any time for the right price. Adèle was the person you called when you wanted someone to disappear; she was the person you called when you were in the market for a baby. Adèle stopped at nothing because she couldn't be stopped. She owned the town—the police, politicians, and judges—because she knew their secrets and blackmailed them to get what she wanted.

Adèle and Lisette could not be more different. Granted, Peachy and Lisette weren't always on the up-and-up, but they never hurt innocent people, never killed anyone, or stole children. People knew Lisette for her healing abilities. She practiced patience and kindness and people respected her. Aside from Adèle, Peachy hadn't met any of Lisette's other relatives. As far as Peachy knew, it was just the two of them.

"If Adèle finds out we're behind this, even I will not be able to protect you," Lisette warned.

"Don't you think it will be obvious that we are involved when she realizes the all-powerful amulet is missing? I mean, besides you, who else knows about it?"

"I have a plan for that too," Lisette said. "This…" she handed Peachy a replica amulet, "…has been enchanted."

"A swipe and swap." Peachy had done it a hundred times.

"Not just any swipe and swap, Peachy. Remember that our lives are in danger and hinge on our success. The replica will buy us some time until she realizes that it is a fake and puts two and two together."

"Then what happens?"

"We will go into hiding and your training will begin."

"Hiding? Training?"

"Are you having second thoughts?"

"I don't even have first thoughts. You won't tell me anything."

"It must be this way. Do you trust me?"

"Of course."

"Then know that once the amulet is in our possession, you will have all the answers your big heart desires. Are you okay with that?"

"Do I have a choice?"

"You always have a choice."

As much as the voice in Peachy's head yelled at her, told her to push back, demand answers, and decline the job, she went along willingly. "I'm okay with it."

"Good. Do you have any other questions about the *plan*?"

"No. Wait. Yes. Won't Adèle be wearing the amulet?"

"The amulet is not meant to be worn for extended periods of time. It is a means to an end. It is worn when needed. My sister has grown careless with it; she has forgotten its powers and I have insured that carelessness."

"How?"

"Greed. I have paid off her dry cleaner to ensure that a few drops of my Mix of Mayhem will come into contact with a certain fur coat that she favors this time of the year."

"Ouch." Peachy knew about Lisette's Mix of Mayhem, a simple mixture that caused painful blisters when it got on the skin.

"Putting anything remotely close to her neckline will be absurd," Lisette said with a hint of pride to her voice. "Again, child, once you're within Adèle's quarters, take caution, and do not touch anything if you can avoid it. All inside is vile, tainted and tied to truly hopeless souls. Don't let their pain and sorrow attach to you. People act out of desperation when they hurt for money. You know this as well as I."

"Then let us do good with that money. Let me also rob her blind."

"That is out of the question."

"But why?"

"Because it was built from suffering. My sister knows not of the riches of love and how several hundred doors can open, compared to the divisiveness of the door handles she chooses to turn. Remember that always."

"But we can do good with it, help a lot of people, even ourselves." Peachy looked around their tiny dwelling, a couple of rooms and a kitchenette tucked behind *Lisette's House of Voodoo* tourist trap in the heart of the French Quarter.

"We will not talk about this again."

Peachy sighed and left it at that. She always left it at that and never took it too far, preferring to wait for Lisette to share when she decided the time was right. But after this job, with the priceless amulet in hand, Peachy would shift the narrative.

"Once inside the big house, your last set of challenges includes accessing Adèle's workroom and then hacking her safe."

"Can I involve my own person?"

"Can they be trusted?"

"With my life."

"Then I trust this person too."

"Good, because she's the best when it comes to hacking safes."

"The biggest challenge, Peachy, won't be the safe."

"What do you mean?"

"Taking the amulet into your possession is the most challenging part of this entire job. The bearer needs practice and training to wield it safely. Do not let it rest against your heart, and do not touch it without gloves."

"Why? What does that mean?"

"The amulet's power will manifest from the heart of the bearer its deepest desires and fears. You cannot control what it chooses to represent. It could take what is in your heart and morph you into someone we would not recognize. Are you prepared for this?"

"I guess."

"You guess?" Lisette looked at her wide-eyed.

"I wish I had more answers to my questions, but yes. I'm prepared."

"This is how it must be."

"Then I know what I need to do. I'll be ready."

"Good. Take my hand. Let us say a prayer and light a candle, ensuring us a successful outcome."

Lisette swore that Adèle would be gone by seven. It was fifteen past and still no sign of her. Peachy took a last draw from her hand-rolled smoke then sent it sailing. It floated in the air and sizzled out in a puddle of water left over from a recent rain that hurricane season had brought to New Orleans. Peachy pulled her leather gloves from her back pocket, slid her hands into them, and enjoyed the feel of the leather. Her fingers sat snug within the second skin.

She risked a glance around the corner to ensure that her lookout girl, Minette, was in position. She looked sexy as hell suited and booted in black leather, straddling her motorcycle, awaiting her role: ensure Peachy at least three hours of uninterrupted thieving by tailing Adèle and guaranteeing her an unfortunate collision. Peachy stole another look to the house, an architectural treasure, a living, breathing thing, complete with feelings, secrets, and needs.

The *Spanish Rose*. A pristine, white, three-story, twenty-thousand-square-foot landmark, one of the finest examples of antebellum architecture in all the city. Forty Ionic and Corinthian fluted cypress columns and expansive verandas circled the exterior, and leaded floor-to-ceiling windows acted as the *Rose's* ever watchful eyes. Fleur-de-lis motif iron fencing and stone pillars sat along its perimeter, ensuring no one entered or exited without its permission. That is except for Peachy.

The *Spanish Rose* was also the kind of place that tour groups would occasionally visit, to marvel at its sheer beauty and learn of its sordid, morbid, and well-deserved place in history.

Peachy knew the nearly forgotten story of the most successful slave revolt in American history. In 1811 some five hundred slaves revolted against their owners, killing many of them with clubs, axes, and pitchforks after their ammunition ran out, burning plantations along the way, shattering the white-perpetuated myth of the happy slave. The story didn't have a happy ending for the slaves involved. Hundreds died for their cause, their mutilated and defiled heads were mounted on stakes and placed along the river. Tour groups stopped at the *Spanish Rose* because therein existed another side to the story. A sect of slaves, sisters from Saint-Domingue, who were successful in a revolt of their own kind, set into motion a series of events that led to the eventual overtaking of their white masters.

The sisters murdered the family's children on that fateful night, sending the owners into a grief so deep that they agreed to do anything the sisters asked—if they would bring back their dead children. When the sisters supposedly made true on their promise, the family spiraled further into insanity and murdered each other, but not before signing over their entire estate to the sisters.

Peachy's only issue with the story is that the tour guide attributed the success of the sisters to the rumors that they were powerful witches, rather than intelligent women with a mastery of a unique form of voodoo. The tour guide would even go as far as to pass around a laminated sheet with side-by-side images, a faded silhouette photo of the sisters from the revolt and recent photos of their descendants, claiming that the descendants were in fact the actual sisters from way back when, immortals, that walked and talked among the living. One was Adèle Blanque, the great Voodooieanne who lived in the *Spanish Rose*.

The only identifying resemblance that Peachy could discern was their tignons, a decorative head covering, a popular fashion accessory that the sisters wore then and now. In addition, the sisters had the same names as their great-great-great grandmothers. None of it meant a thing. As far as Peachy was concerned, the rest was utter bullshit because Peachy lived with one of the supposed *immortals* from Saint-Domingue—Lisette Blanque—another powerful, far from immortal Voodooieanne, whose seventy-third birthday they celebrated together the week before.

A flicker of light drew Peachy's attention to the old carriage house. Adèle was moments away from making her exit.

Showtime! Peachy texted to Minette.

She got into position and heard the unmistakable sound of someone's voice projected through a bullhorn. A tour bus!

What the hell! she texted. *You said you talked to Jean? No tours tonight!*

I did!

Do something! They're blocking the exit!

The carriage house's door opened in tandem with the electronic gate around the perimeter, and unless the tour bus moved now, Peachy wasn't going to get in without being seen.

Distract her! Peachy urged Minette.

Peachy zipped her black Windbreaker, and she smoothed her hair inside her hood. She sprinted toward the Mercedes and began pounding on Adèle's window, asking for her autograph, flashing her phone's camera. Minette, along with other members of the tour group, joined her as well in overtaking the car. It was an all-out circus! The distraction caused Adèle to lay on her horn, squeal her tires and hop the curb in the opposite direction. In her agitation, she failed to close the perimeter gate. Peachy strolled through and sprinted toward the carriage house door, her lungs burning as she ran. She slid underneath the rolling metal door as if she were sliding into home plate, just as it closed. She popped up, pressed herself against a wall, and looked out the window. The tour bus still blocked the driveway with frenzied tourists snapping photos of Adèle's taillights. Peachy spotted Minette jumping on her bike and everything was back on track. Peachy took a calming breath and pulled out her phone to check the time.

She had a text from Minette. *U In? Good luck. I <3 U!*

In! U were brilliant! B together soon.☺

Peachy's training over the past month culminated in this very moment. She closed her eyes, saying a Voodoo prayer that she wouldn't forget a single detail of the series of dangerous challenges she was about to perform. Peachy had been in the *Spanish Rose* once with Lisette. One could say that the inside was immaculate, flawless, impeccable. A mere look at an item of furniture or a glance at a gilded mirror would leave a smudge. Peachy wondered how many cleaning staff Adèle employed. The inside of the carriage house, on the other hand, still showed signs of its past: the decaying structure of a horse stable with brittle leather tack, rusty tins, wooden crates, and the smell of oil and dust.

Peachy shone her flashlight as often as she could risk. She spotted an oddly placed tool chest not quite flush against the wall. Before rolling it out of her way, she rummaged inside for things she might need, like a flathead screwdriver and a hammer. With the tool chest out of her way, she spotted the wall with the door to the underground corridor. A thick slab of metal was screwed diagonally across the small wooden door. Using her newly found tools, she hammered away until she worked loose the rusty metal screws. She jimmied the old iron key that Lisette had given her into the lock before she got it to work. She twisted the small doorknob and bit her lip when the door wailed on its hinges. She covered her nose and mouth, smelling the musty bloom and pungent dank and damp dirt.

She shone her flashlight through the doorway toward rotting wooden planks. She tested one and found it secure enough to hold her hundred-and-twenty-five pounds. She shone her flashlight about the narrow corridor. The void swallowed the beam of light whole.

"I ask that you permit me to travel in peace." The void absorbed her words. "I mean no harm, and it is with respect that I enter this place and with permission from Lisette Blanque." Peachy pulled her Zippo from her pocket, and from the other, dried leaves of sage. She lit the end, blowing sweet white smoke into the air. She pushed onward, her outstretched arms clearing cobwebs as she descended.

At the end of the tunnel, Peachy spotted the next set of steps—solid concrete this time. Surefooted, she reached a door. She used the key again, putting her shoulder into it as it creaked and groaned, disrupting years of neglect before letting her inside. Her flashlight illuminated the long-forgotten underground world of the slave quarters of the *Spanish Rose* for the first time in over a half a century.

Peachy brushed herself free of cobwebs and made for the upper levels and to Adèle's quarters, navigating through a maze of hallways and rooms with vases of white lilies. Up two flights of polished marble stairs, her steps grew heavy with dread, which caused a dull ache in her chest and behind her eyes.

She winced as she turned the door handle into Adèle's quarters. She spotted the white bookcase with gold trim that Lisette said disguised the entrance to the secret room. She found the hidden mechanism and popped open the false bookcase. Behind the false door was a metal door with a more sophisticated lock. It proved no match for Peachy and her tried-and-true lock pick set, a gift from Lisette on her sixteenth birthday. She put her flashlight in her mouth, illuminating her workspace. She worked the lock's pins until they shifted into place, and she opened the door to Adèle's private and sacred workroom.

Cluttered shelves held strange objects like baskets full of dried plants, herbs, sticks, bone, balls of wax, and burlap cuttings. Organic material like chicken feet and goat hooves floated in jars. A scavenger's nest that felt odd that it existed within the expansive pristine mansion with its marble floors, wrought-iron windows, and lilies in every room.

Peachy eyed the safe. She and Minette had studied it well. A $90,000 custom Knox luxury safe by Boca do Lobo, a six-by-three gleaming rectangle that looked more like a bar of gold than an actual safe. Adèle's first mistake: opting for the digital override. Peachy's girl Minette was a black hat hacker, a genius literally responsible for developing infectious malware capable of crippling financial systems. Peachy wouldn't need to cut cords or splice wires. She ran her gloved fingers on the safe's burnished finish and found the safe's brain. She inserted the USB drive that Minette had given her. Three shrill beeps and the flash of three bright green lights, three muted clicks, and one rewarding pop indicated that she could turn the handle and open the door.

"Damn," she whispered, eyeing stacks of money in various currencies, gold bars, passports, weapons, jewelry, diamonds, strange notes written in a language Peachy didn't recognize, and more jars of biological matter. Peachy gasped when she saw the severed hand of a child floating in one of the jars. She closed her eyes and said a prayer for the desperate souls that had traded or had been forced to deal with the likes of Adèle.

Lisette had said that the amulet would pull Peachy toward it. At the time Peachy failed to understand what she was talking about but felt the energy that Lisette warned her of. The amulet wanted her to find it. It told her which objects to inch out of the way, helped her steady her hand and avoid disturbing as little as possible. A small gold velvet box seemed to radiate energy. She reached for it, and a tiny jolt of electricity coursed through her veins and swirled in her mind, telling her to pick it up. She held it in her hand, then opened the lid. The amulet! Such a serious term for a thin and pale silver necklace, its delicate links woven together. The amulet itself was oval-shaped and no bigger than a quarter, multifaceted, with a blue, almost black jewel at the center. She cast the beam of her flashlight directly upon it to an unfolding world where she didn't *see* images or *hear* words, but rather she *felt* the images and the words were sensations in her mind, as if a cloud settled on her and she swam through it. Emotions like anger, desire, love, and betrayal were imprinted upon the surface of the jewel and it pulsated in her hand.

"Daughter."

Peachy twisted around, expecting to see someone standing there, but she was alone. "Long have I waited—"

She shut the box. The snapping sound startled her. She caught her breath and looked behind her, feeling again as though someone was watching.

She summoned the courage to open the box again. With utmost care, she lifted the amulet from its velvet bed. She said the words Lisette told her to say and placed the enchanted replica inside. She placed the real amulet into the inner pocket of her Windbreaker, a pocket within a pocket that even the greatest Voodoo trickery couldn't find. She closed the safe door and pulled the USB drive from the device. Green lights blinked three times, signaling an online connection, and a thump told her that it had locked. She closed the door to the workroom, reset the bookshelf latch, and headed out of the room and down the hall.

She knew the imposter would not fool Adèle. The real thing felt alive with thought and breath. It emanated energy from within her pocket, warmed her chest, and she felt like she could fly if she wanted.

CHAPTER TWO

"Oaf." Peachy ran into a tower of a man, all muscle. "Who the hell are you?" she asked. He grinned, his mouth a dark void. "Look!" She pointed behind him.

He took the bait, which bought her enough time to dart in the opposite direction—smack into another meat-wall of a man. A similar grin spread upon his face too. "Shit," she said. "You got me." She held her hands out and slapped them against her thighs. "What do you want?"

"Well, well," came a voice Peachy thought she recognized. The speaker remained shrouded in darkness, shapeless and ownerless. "We meet at last."

"If you call talking to a disembodied voice *meeting*, then sure, nice to make your acquaintance."

"Such sarcasm." The woman ticked her tongue. "I like you already."

"I wish I could say the same about you."

"Maybe when you get to know me."

"I basically judge people on their looks alone, so I'm going to need to see you first before jumping into a relationship."

"There will be plenty of time to get acquainted, but how that introduction goes depends on one little thing."

"And what would that be?"

"Oh, I think you know."

"Oh, I really don't."

"Do you need me to spell it out for you?"

"Yes, and slowly, please. I never finished high school."

The fact that two giant men stood within grabbing distance didn't shake her in the slightest. She knew the larger the man, the smaller the brain. The fact that one of the two fell for her *hey look* trick almost guaranteed her a decent probability of escaping.

Fingers snapped and a meaty hand wrapped around her neck and pinned her against the wall while the other hand searched her coat pockets, her jean pockets, in between her legs, and under her arms. Her phone, the USB drive, her lock pick set, a few dollars, her smokes, and her lighter spilled onto the floor. Her throat burned. Her vision blurred. Tears streamed from her eyes. Her world faded to black, then reappeared slowly, like a paint by number. It took time to make sense of the world coming into focus. When he let go, she crumpled to the ground—sputtering, coughing, and burning inside.

"Have you a better understanding now that I have spelled it out for you?" the woman in the shadows asked.

Peachy couldn't answer if she wanted. She grabbed at her injured throat. She desperately needed to catch her breath.

"The amulet," the woman said as she came into focus and knelt at Peachy's level. She grabbed hold of Peachy's face and turned her head from side to side, inspecting her like an object for sale. She stood and brushed off her hands, as if touching Peachy had dirtied her.

"Lisette?" Peachy croaked.

At first glance, the woman looked like Lisette, thin and tall with the same slim eyebrows, long neck, and high cheekbones. Upon further exploration, though, the woman's hollow pits for eyes gave her away. They appeared void of color, lacking Lisette's warmth, love, and overall spirit. Peachy had never seen Lisette without her tignon. This woman had a great head of hair with mud and twigs in it. She wore old, soiled and stained clothing with holes, and no shoes on her feet. This most certainly was not Peachy's trusted friend. She had to be a sister, a twin that Peachy had never heard of before.

"Lisette 2.0. Isn't that what kids say these days? Everything computer this and computer that." She picked up Peachy's phone. "I've always wanted one of these. It is strange, these little things." She held the phone as if it were a complicated puzzle. "Everywhere you look, these are looking right back at you."

Peachy cursed herself for not setting a passcode. It was no problem if the woman kept it. She had a burner in the bushes outside. She could only hope that Lisette 2.0 didn't know how to use it. She handed the phone over to the goon, and he took several photos of Peachy—the flash blinding her—and stuck the phone in his pocket.

"Why are you looking at me with such confusion?" The woman offered a shrill laugh that bounced off the marble floors and skipped around like a mischievous little girl with muddy shoes. "I am saddened that my sister never mentioned she had a twin."

"Never heard of you," Peachy croaked.

"I am Beatriz." She smiled a big toothy grin. Though she possessed both teeth and tongue, her mouth appeared an endless void. "And I assure you, you will know me after the night is over. I guarantee it."

Peachy covered her ears for the sound that came from the woman's mouth, a shrill, high-pitched reverberation. It was her horrendous laughter. It caused pulsating beats to shatter the inside of Peachy's head. "Fuck you—" Beatriz snapped her fingers again—louder this time—and Peachy felt a boot to her ribs that took the air from her once again. Another snap and another boot in the back. The woman continued snapping and laughing, the sound worse than the blinding crack to her ribs.

"Stop!"

"Why?" She held her hand inches from Peachy's face, about to snap her fingers once again.

"Because I don't have it!"

"Liar! What do we do with liars, boys?"

A goon went for Peachy, and in an attempt to get a head start, she scrambled on the floor, her efforts no match for the combination of slick marble flooring and two-hundred-fifty pounds of muscle fueled by Beatriz's snapping. Peachy thrashed about, kicking her limbs every which way, as if one of those actions—or all of them combined—would give her a small advantage. The goon picked her up as if she weighed nothing and tossed her. She heard a dull crack at the nape of her neck, then double vision disoriented her and slowed her from getting to her feet.

"I will not ask nicely again," Beatriz said as she hovered over Peachy.

"I don't have it. The hack didn't work." The man picked her up by her arm and twisted it behind her back. Peachy wondered how she managed to scream so loudly with her terribly damaged vocal cords. "I couldn't!" she rasped. "Please! I couldn't get into the safe! I'm telling the—" He bent her arm until white lightning and a snap!

"Goon!" Beatriz yelled.

Peachy fell to her knees, her entire left side of her body limp and useless. She cradled her injured arm on the verge of passing out from the pain.

"She does not respond to pain. Maybe a game then?" Beatriz brandished a pistol. "You will try again to open the safe and for every time you fail, kapow! It's a game called Russian Roulette. You kids still play this game, yes? Oh, it's fun. You get one more chance, or not. Get her up."

Peachy howled as he lifted her aching body and pushed her forward, escorting her up the stairs toward Adèle's quarters. "Wait. Stop," she cried.

"Change of heart, dear?"

"I need the thing, the USB, from my pocket," she whined as they passed her belongings that littered the floor. "I can't try again without it." The goon pushed her to her knees. She failed to focus on any one object, but she found the tiny white bit of plastic. With the drive in hand, she prayed that Minette's hack would get her back into the safe and then Lisette's enchanted replica would save her. They ascended the stairs to Adèle's quarters. Peachy realized the stench of death emanated from Beatriz. She wondered how long Beatriz had been inside the *Spanish Rose.*

"Ready to play?" Beatriz gave the pistol to her goon. He took it into his meaty hand, slid a single bullet into the chamber, spun it, and held it to Peachy's head as he cocked the hammer. "Prove to me now that you are not a liar."

Minette said that the USB drive would work at least once. After that she couldn't guarantee it would work again. Peachy had cracked her fair share of safes before, but nothing like the Boca do Lobo. She never doubted herself as much as she did in this moment, but still she couldn't relinquish the amulet. It was hers. She felt it in her heart. No way would she hand it over.

"Do it!"

Peachy felt Beatriz's spittle upon her face. She winced in pain as she crouched behind the safe and popped in the chip, activating a series of shrill beeps and an odd thumping sound. She tried the handle. Click, click, click…clunk! Fail! A pull of the trigger and Peachy shrieked. Her legs gave out and she trembled uncontrollably.

"Aren't you the lady luck? You got four more chances. Best focus now. Goon! Help her focus."

The next thing Peachy knew, her head felt enormous, wet and warm, but she didn't feel pain. In fact she felt wonderfully cool. She couldn't see, but then her world came into focus—shuffling black boots, smeared bright red paint everywhere, and she heard mumbling that echoed as if she were in a tunnel.

She coughed, retched and vomited. Her pain came roaring back. Her lungs burned and she tasted blood. Why hadn't she given Beatriz the amulet? She'd had a short life and nothing to show for it but a handful of jobs and a few dollars to her name. Why had she chosen pain and a broken body before death? Lisette wasn't her mother; she wasn't even related. Who cared if she carried on some stupid voodoo tradition? Peachy would sleep on it. Sort this whole thing out later, perhaps after dinner and a smoke.

"This is worth your life, child. It cannot fall into the wrong hands." Lisette's words jolted her to life.

"You idiot! Why did you do that? Get her up! Come on Peachy, little sweet Peachy, the game's not over yet! You got at least three more chances."

The goon propped her up against the safe. She gripped it like an oversize body pillow, but she felt no comfort. She still held on and wished and pleaded, playing the bargaining game that this would be the last job she'd run if she could just open the safe and make it out alive. *Please. Open.*

She pulled the drive out and shoved it back it. *Let me in.* She heard a series of beeps and clicks before a single pop. She tried the handle again and success! Beatriz shoved her back to the floor. She lay in her own blood and vomit while Beatriz rummaged inside the safe, chucking the contents that Peachy had previously spent considerable time moving so as not to raise suspicion.

She held her breath as Beatriz, mad with intent, clutched the gold velvet box that Peachy had moments ago raided. Beatriz's laughter worked its way into Peachy's broken brain, further degrading it.

"Lisette's powers are at a new low. She has grown weak, focusing on healing and taking care of the likes of rats like you! Where's the real amulet?" She threw the replica at Peachy, missing her by a fraction. "Where is it?" Beatriz hovered over her, lifting her by her jacket, shaking her like a rag doll. "Give it to me! It was mine to begin with!" She yelled and frothed like a rabid dog, ripping Peachy's clothes in search of it.

"Oka…kay, lease. Don't ill, m' sorry…" Peachy pleaded and sobbed, stuttering through the blinding pain.

"There is nothing to be sorry for, child. Just hand it over and all this will go away." Beatriz managed to sound soothing. "I am pleased that you have responded well to a bit of discipline. You and I will get along well; I can feel it. Don't worry. You don't look that bad. Nothing that can't be fixed."

"M'sorry," Peachy cried.

"There, there, child."

"Yo can ave, I don't know...why I..." She reached into her Windbreaker, into her hidden pocket within a pocket, and grasped the amulet. She felt it in her hands, felt it take over her mind. "Take it. Take it!" She dangled it inches from Beatriz's face.

"Hello again, lovely." Beatriz inspected the treasure from all angles, as if entranced by it. Her black eyes filled with life when she reached for it, but she pulled back and her face contorted as if in pain. "Now, now, be good...long have I waited..." She continued to eye it. Peachy knew of the feeling that it caused from her own short inspection of it. The amulet held the answers to all of her problems, unlocked every door, supplied her with unlimited everything. Why had Lisette failed to mention that she had a twin sister? Now Peachy was the one who lay destroyed on the ground, suffering with what felt like a shattered head and broken body. Lisette wanted her to have the amulet, so Peachy gripped it tighter, her anger giving her life, and when Beatriz reached for it, Peachy pulled her knife from her boot and drove it into the woman's neck.

Beatriz screamed. Her face turned white, her eyes grew huge, and she dug her own nails into her face. Her shrill voice caused all within earshot to cower in pain. Peachy had no choice but to fight through the agony or die in that room.

"Get her!"

With the last burst of energy Peachy had, she scrambled to her feet through a blinding scarlet veil that clouded her vision. She stumbled through the door to the hallway. Next were the stairs with the thunderous footfalls of the goons pounding after her.

"*Do not place it upon your neck. Do not let it rest against your heart*" Lisette reminded her. Peachy hadn't any other choice. She needed help. "*It will take from you. We would not recognize you.*" She put the amulet around her neck. It burned her like a hot knife, branding her skin. She wailed and fell to her knees, trying to take it off, though a boot to her back sent her into the arms of a goon. He held her so tightly she couldn't scream. She bit his arm and he pushed her away.

Only one way out. Over the banister. A three-story drop. She'd rather take her chances there. She hurried toward the railing. She swung one leg over the edge and then the other, and jumped. Beatriz grabbed her from behind, and they struggled before Beatriz managed to grab hold of one of Peachy's wrists. With her free hand, Peachy clasped a wooden banister spindle and pulled with all her might, hoping to take Beatriz down with her, but she was no match. The woman exuded immeasurable strength.

"Where do you think you're going?" Beatriz asked, her iron grip holding Peachy in place, the knife still protruding from her neck. Peachy cringed in horror when the crazed woman slid it out. Blood spurted from the gaping wound, but it didn't seem to faze her. "Do you know what I am?"

"A...fffucking cunttttt!"

Beatriz stabbed the knife through Peachy's hand, pinning her to the banister. Falling to her death couldn't come soon enough, but she couldn't move. The pain of the knife reinforced every poor decision she had made that night—maybe in her life—a sorry ending to a sorrier story. She had lost. It was over. But something inside gave her strength and helped her hang on.

"Do you think it was a coincidence that Lisette happened to find you in the alley that day?" Beatriz sneered. "That out of the kindness of her heart she shared her home with you? And how fitting that you would stab me in the neck, and now here I am, using your blade against you." She laughed and slowly drew the blade from Peachy's hand. Beatriz grasped Peachy's wrists and pulled her upon the ledge of the railing.

"No!" Peachy moaned and tried to wiggle her way out. Her legs dangled over the edge, while her torso was upon the ledge. It was still anyone's game. She felt a dose of energy from within. *The amulet.*

"This is poetic justice, or maybe a clever coincidence. I killed your mother this exact way. I stuck one of my beautiful enchanted blades into her neck, into her entire body, over and over and over. You would have loved it. She screamed just like you did, and the heavens opened and swallowed her whole. Where she went, I don't know. Where you came from, I haven't a clue. Maybe Lisette and you talked about it? The look on your face says otherwise, though it is quite swollen. I can't tell. Do you want to know more?"

Yes! Please tell me. I'll do anything. Anything! That's what Peachy wanted to say, but she couldn't form the words. All that came out sounded distorted, like dumbfounded mumbles.

"Give me the amulet and I'll tell you everything."

But she couldn't. It wouldn't let her have it. She tried for more words but only managed to spray blood upon Beatriz's face.

"You two are very much the same. She was our traitorous bitch of a sister."

"Li… r."

"I do not lie, little Peachy. I'll never lie to you, as my twin has done for so long. Haven't you ever felt it, felt power inside of yourself? Haven't you ever felt someone's words before they said them? Felt other people's feelings inside your heart as if they were your own? You have much to learn. I can teach you."

"Fff…" Peachy whispered, still struggling to focus. Her tongue felt swollen. She wanted water and a last smoke of her hand-rolled cigarettes.

"I'll make this offer one time only." Beatriz leaned toward her, close enough that Peachy smelled that suffocating death upon her breath as she spoke. "Depending on your answer, here is what will happen. I cut your hand off. When you fall, my goon will cut the amulet off your head, and I will feed your pathetic broken body to tourists looking for Voodoo trash. Or…join me, Peachy. I've been watching you. You have greatness inside you that my stupid sister has hidden from you, preferring to squander your abilities in favor of running jobs, stealing petty little shit. She fears you. Why do you think she wants the amulet? She needs you. With that power against your heart, you could be great. Anything you want can be so. All you need to do is desire it. Be here or there, or anywhere, or nowhere at all. The power is already yours." Beatriz made another unsuccessful attempt to pull Peachy the rest of the way up.

Peachy's gloves served two purposes: to cover her prints and avoid anyone's firm grip on her. Through mind-shattering agony, she worked herself free from Beatriz's hold.

She thought about home, let go and fell.

CHAPTER THREE

Noomi parked her sled with the other sleds of those who were already inside The Forge, one of her village's trading posts that supplied necessities such as herbs, oils, unique foods, fabrics, maps, and baskets. The latter two Noomi created for trade. She prayed to her goddesses for a fair deal so she could afford an array of items to tide her family over the long winter.

"Wish us luck," she said to her sister Gabin, who would stay behind and keep watch of their belongings. Noomi walked toward the mercantile's entrance; however her gaze was pulled toward a small crowd. She smiled when she saw what they were observing. She heard the lyrics of one of her favorite stories of the birth of her people. From the looks of it, the elder, Manon the Only, was working with another of her town's elders, training her to one day carry forth the tradition of performing the story.

"Go ahead and speak," Manon instructed her pupil.

"We are Heathers, named aft' our foundin' mothers, five divine women, each one unique and powerful. One born o' creative thought possessed the ability to foresee, to anticipate, and to counsel through connections o' the mind. This Heather was a Seer. Another was born o' wild instinct. Her gift allowed her to shift at will, to empathize with creatures great and small. She was a Shifter. The third was uprooted from the earth, covered in soil and fragrant foliage. Her gift was mastery o' plants, minerals, and elements. She was skilled in alchemy with the ability to heal with her touch. This Heather was a Healer. The fourth, shaped through strategic thinkin' and leadership, possessed the ability to call willin' minds to order. She was a Protector. The fifth, the last, was born o' the sky, a celestial wonder with the ability to conjure, not to foresee, but to shape the future to her will. She was a Teller.

Together these foundin' Heathers brought peace and structure. Their rule ensured a thrivin' realm. Through their inhabitants, they sealed their immortality. Every living Heather was proof that their plan was sound. Upon a Heather's death, he or she would bestow their gifts to others for the betterment and protection o' the realm."

"Very well said," Manon replied. "Ye are ready to learn the endin'."

Noomi moved along. She knew the story well, as did every one of her realm's people. This story was told when it was green about and they held a great festival. All young Heathers would attend with their loved ones as was their custom, and they would bestow their precious gifts. While the story hadn't changed much from when it was told in the beginning those thousands of years ago, the Heathers of today expressed their gifts differently than their founding mothers. A Heather could possess the ability to shift into anything that flew. Another Shifter could transform into *any* animal. Alternatively, a Shifter might only possess the ability to communicate with animal kind and without the ability to shift at all.

Very few Heathers possessed multiple gifts. Only a few Heathers could be a Seer and a Shifter, or a Healer and a Protector. Noomi was one of those blessed few. She was a Seer who was also a Shifter. Her sister Gabin, on the other hand, was a Shifter only and preferred her powerful animal form—a two-hundred-pound mountain cat—as opposed to an upright walking and talking member of their realm. In addition, Heathers lived very long lives. Some reached the age of seven hundred. Noomi and her sister were young, both were in their seventies, though they appeared youthful, which was another trait of her kind.

Not all the inhabitants of the great realm were born to bestow gifts. Some possessed equally important skills and trades. Some Heathers were farmers, merchants, builders, shapers of stone, fire, and metal. Others fed the masses, and a few enriched the minds through the creation of artwork, music, and the telling of stories. Most every soul that lived within the great realm of Heatherton and all her surrounding villages, lived in harmony, but like any other thriving city, there also existed villains, robbers, and mercenaries, who intermixed and lived in disguise. All inhabitants needed to exercise caution, and such was the life where Noomi was from.

She went about her business and on to her trading. The snow had picked up over the morning, and she needed to get a move on.

"Hours I invested in that particular basket," Noomi said upon presenting her woven creations to the shopkeeper Mer. She hunched over the trading bar, as she had already clanked her head once on a particular pot and twice on a cauldron, not because she towered above other people. In fact, she needed the assistance of a good and solid three-step lift to reach most things. She vied for elbow space and head space in the bustling mercantile, which was packed with other traders, who also looked for the best return on their wares. "'Tis me favorite one," she said. "I nearly left it behind, for I spent more'n me fair share o' time over firelight and into several dawns, softenin' and shapin' strips o' wood to me will."

Mer ran his fingers over the wood of the basket. "'Tis a work o' art, no lyin'." He was a big man with a great bushy beard that he combed his fingers through when he thought. He turned the basket over and inspected the intricate weave that she had perfected since her last visit to the village several months ago.

"Like the skin o' a Winterberry at peak harvest," he said and held the basket toward the bit of light that streamed in through the diamond-shaped windows of his shop. "How'd ye get the wood to take this color?"

"Trial and error."

"Fine, don't tell me." His great belly shook when he laughed.

"Aye, I will not." A smile spread upon Noomi's face, pleased with her work and more pleased that Mer thought so too. If he bought one more basket, she would have enough to purchase the remaining materials needed to finish the construction of her reading room at home that she was eager to get back to after her nearly fortnight stay in the village.

"I can't pass this one up. I will take it too," he said. "N'fact…" He placed his hand over the entire stock of her baskets. "I'll take 'em all, but this one is comin' home with me for personal use." He secured the indigo treasure under his arm. "Me lady will love it."

"Her lands!" Noomi said. She popped up and clanked her head on a cauldron. "Ack!" She laughed and rubbed her head. "I am pleased that ye like 'em."

"I love 'em," he said and steadied the swinging pot. "As do me customers. I wish ye'd visit us more oft'. Your baskets are popular with the villagers and handy 'round the shop as well. I cannot keep 'em on me shelves to save me life."

"With thanks, Mer. I get here when I can and to ye first."

"I am thankful," he added while inspecting his new stock of baskets. "How do ye prefer payment for today?"

"Part trade and part talents, if it will please ye."

"Ye have yourself a deal, friend." He extended his hand, palm down, and she placed hers on top of his to confirm their agreement. "What can we prepare for ye?"

Mer rang a bell to summon one of the several assistants running about the commotion of the mercantile. A new one Noomi hadn't seen before hurried to the counter as she pulled her list from her pocket and smoothed it on the countertop.

"A standard mix o' cookin' herbs. I favor the southern blend. A standard mix o' herbs for healin', three treated wolf hides, the squarer the better, and preferably black. Three full measures o' cookin' oil, four boxes o' bee's wax, four measures o' fire oil, five bound books o' parchment, one pound o' charcoal, four wells o' scribin' stain, three steel pens and three jars o' that fine fig jam if you're still in stock. And…" Noomi pointed to a heavy animal fur garment. "I am badly in need o' that beautiful garment, before winter takes her hold."

"I noticed your eye upon it the moment ye walked in and am glad that it will be yours," he said. "I am sorry to say that I've only two fig jams left. Will ye take a jar o' Honeyberry and a surprise on the house?"

"'Tis more'n fair. What is this surprise?"

"A new spirit type." Mer reached under the cabinet. "I am curious as to your opinion. A new potential supplier from Heather's Edge has a specialty process that turns wine into a thousand bubbles." He handed her a green glass bottle. "It comes with a warnin'. Don't shake before openin'. I learnt the hard way. It burst out o' the bottle all over the place and in me beard."

Noomi smiled. "I will avoid tasselin' it too much and with thanks, Mer." Noomi smiled and inspected her new treasure. "I will let ye know me thoughts next time I visit, for now I am curious."

"I trust your honesty." He sent the apprentice Jaxi off to compile Noomi's order while he saw to counting the talents he owed her. She watched them work, gathering her goods from baskets, boxes, tubes, jars, and cabinet doors stuffed with the necessities that Noomi lacked living in her remote cottage, which was a two-day journey on sled at this time of the year.

"Are ye comin' to the grand play tonight?" Jaxi asked. "I've a lead role."

"I am afraid I cannot."

"Are ye certain?" Mer asked. "I've discounted tickets, best seats in the hall. N'fact, buy one and I'll throw in a ticket for your sister."

"Her lands, that's a great deal, but I must be on me way home. That snow doesn't look to be lettin' up, does it?" She leaned her hip against the counter, joining Mer in his observation of the falling snow that had begun to obstruct the view out the glass window.

"Aye. Ye will need to keep ahead o' this one." He handed her a cloth bag fat with the talents he owed her. "Better get on."

"Tis me plan." She slid the cloth bag into her pocket. "With thanks, Mer. Tis always a pleasure tradin' at The Forge." She pushed off the counter, seeing that Jaxi had made for the door with her parcels.

"Always a pleasure, Noomi, and with caution, me friend."

"Nothin' out o' the ordinary am I expectin' on me journey home."

"Still, with caution. I hear stories o' travelers ill with intent, and they always seem to be fallin' from the sky." He laughed.

"Then I shall ride lookin' upward and downward, and sideways too." She laughed. "With caution, Mer." She gave him a parting glance and placed two fingers, her index and middle fingers upon her forehead and then extended outward. A customary sign of respect among her kind for saying goodbye to an elder and trusted friend. "Until next time."

"With more o' these baskets, yes?" he asked, waving one of them in the air.

"With plenty more, Mer, and a few other goods I've been craftin'."

She headed through the door and into a blast of snow that had picked up over the hour. She quickened her pace, reaffirmed herself into her animal skins, and lowered her fur hat to stay warm while they walked to her sled.

"Are ye sure ye cannot stay for one more night and for the play?" Jaxi yelled to compete with the howl of the wind as he helped Noomi secure her goods on her sled. "I thought ye might want to join me aft'. We could talk about actin' and the theatre."

"I am quite positive I cannot delay leavin' at this very moment."

"We could talk about your map makin', or way findin', or, or your baskets if ye want," he said and gave a last hearty tug on a strap.

"Not a good idea."

"Moments before ye came in to trade, we received notice, a storm warnin' for tonight."

Noomi smiled at the young apprentice's interest in her company, but it was never going to happen. "Well then, I must be on me way to stay ahead o' the storm, do ye not think?"

He nodded. "Next time." He added, "I shall share with ye the accolades and letters that I am sure to receive. Tis a date?"

"The only date I am makin' at this moment is me date with Mer for tradin' when it is green about, and besides, me friend Jaxi, male Fae kind do not interest me in that way."

"What way?"

She thought about how to say her next piece in a way that wouldn't let him down too hard. "They do not bring me enjoyment."

"I am full o' enjoyment. I promise, I will not disappoint."

"Let me try this again. I do not dream about male Fae kind or think about 'em physically or with arousal."

The boy wore a confused look before he said, "Oooh." Even through the falling snow and scarf around his face, she could see disappointment and embarrassment painted upon his cheeks.

She paid him a half a talent, more than she would normally pay someone for help with such a task, but she felt for him and she admired his eagerness. She gave her sled a hearty push to get it going. "With caution, friend."

"With caution," he replied and limply waved his hand.

That took longer'n it should've, Gabin said. Only Noomi heard her sister's voice, for Gabin sent it through their thoughts, as was how some Shifters communicated with each other. They only needed to think the words in order to understand each other. Their bond was special, as were most familial bonds between Shifters of the same family. At times, Noomi preferred to voice her responses to her sister, and no one thought anything of it. The Realm of the Heathers was home to a great many Shifters, some of whom, like Gabin, preferred their animal form. Heathers that appeared to be talking to no one, could, in fact, be talking to their mothers, their brothers, or someone who was close by.

"Poor dalt. If it weren't for his good looks, he'd be hopeless," Gabin observed. *"How'd we fare?"*

"We've earned enough to purchase the remainin' materials needed to finish the readin' room."

"That's wonderful."

"Yes. Now on to the next place." They followed the groomed village pathway toward the next merchant, one that sold building supplies. Gabin again watched their goods, while Noomi went inside to trade, returning a time later with two apprentices carrying her packages. One of the workers, a young female named Isl, helped Noomi rebalance her sled, which was already at capacity. Any more weight or volume, upward or outward, and she would not be able to guide it safely.

"I hope this is your final stop," Isl said.

"We are off immediately aft' this to keep ahead o' the storm."

"Good, for I suspect it will touch earlier'n what has been forecasted." She motioned into the distance. "What exit are ye usin'?"

"The northern exit will put us on the fastest path."

"Please, use our merchant route."

"I have not the talents."

"Free o' charge this time. With a load like that, ye risk inspection and unneeded delay."

"With gratitude, friend." Noomi smiled, noticing for the first time Isl's beauty. Rich copper skin with faint golden markings. Each Heather, gifted or not, bore a unique pattern, an identifying mark of their kind.

"A harsh winter is expected. Please, with caution, friend."

"With caution."

"Will ye call for me when ye return when it is green about?" Isl asked, running her hand along Noomi's shoulder.

"I promise," Noomi said, and she bid her new friend farewell. *"Come, Gab. Let us be off."*

"With caution, Noomi!" Isl helped give the sled a push through the prime access of the merchant's route, one reserved for shop proprietors or those with talents to spare for easy access without the delays of inspections and questions.

"*I think someone likes ye,*" Gabin said.
"*Maybe we* can *stay another day?*"
"*Fine see ye at home!*"
Noomi only smiled. "*Let's go.*"

CHAPTER FOUR

"*Yes, Gab, Isl was very generous to offer us the merchant route. I know exactly what she'll expect next time I see her, and I will gladly give it.*"

"*Tis a word for that.*"

"*And what word would that be?*"

"*Do I need to spell it out?*"

"*I needn't explain meself.*"

"*Yet, here ye are, explainin', in great detail, I might add.*"

"I like her." Noomi rolled her eyes as she gave her sled a push, hopped on the runners and let gravity fuel her momentum. "Why are ye laughin' at me? Shouldn't ye be scoutin' for danger instead o' pointin' out me weakness for women? We have a long ride north. We need to concentrate. Go. Scout. Now."

Noomi smiled only after shooing Gabin away. The cat plowed ahead, her gray-and-white fur blended with the winter white and made traversing the path difficult to follow at times. Luckily, hundreds of ancient red trees with their always-green branches lined their path and kept them on course. Noomi's heart filled with joy because she knew that the Heathers smiled upon their journey and had blessed them thus far with good trades, the merchant route, and a possible new friendship to explore.

"Gab, I need your help." Noomi's thoughts called her sister back to her side. A growing incline slowed her momentum. She needed the combined mix of Gabin pulling and herself pushing to negotiate the stretch. Over the next hour they trekked through drifts of snow, out of luck now, avoiding being dumped on by the large tufts of snow from the bent branches of the always-green trees.

"How much longer can ye go, Gab? I am gettin' hungry."

"Can we have some jam?" asked the cat, who did her own hunting but liked to indulge in Fae food from time to time.

"Great idea. I'm thinkin' a hot stew followed by bread and—" Noomi's thoughts were cut short by a severe gust of wind that grew more aggressive. Tendrils of energy sizzled through the air and nipped at her cheeks and nose, raising the hair on her arms despite the several layers of winter clothing she wore. *"Gab! Do ye feel that?"* The look in Gab's eyes confirmed that she did. *"Let us slow our pace, proceed with caution."*

Proceeding with caution only worked some of the time. Swirling, growing waves of magnificent indigo reached across the horizon, as if the heavens descended upon them. Thin as a spider's silk fragments of blinding white shards, the snow crackled and spread overhead.

"Voices? Gab, do ye hear? Voices. Faint, but gettin' louder, rage-filled!" Noomi placed her hand upon her heart, stilling pain mixed with sorrow and anger that flooded through her body and forced her to her knees. A calm in that next moment made her think it was over, but it was only the dead calm of heavy silence that proceeded a thousand claps of lightning that shook both earth and sky.

An indigo veil of light impressed upon her vision, blinding her, disorienting her. *"Gab!"* She used the reins to guide her toward her sister, reaching her in time to set her free from the harness and burden of the load. *"Get away!"*

Another harsh clap, this time directly above them, sent Noomi flying. She thudded to the ground. Time passed but when she came to, her sister lay next to her, nudging her, impatient for her to reanimate. "Her lands! What happened?" Noomi shook off her confusion along with the snow. "Our trades!" Their sled sat tilted on its side and buried under a significant amount of snow. *"Oh Gab! Help me!"* Noomi stood, though on unsteady footing, and trudged toward the overturned sled, holding her arms outward, to steady each step. *"Gab! We shouldn't linger. That did not sound friendly."* Noomi used her hands, arms, and legs to free their sled from the piles of heavy wet snow. "Gab?"

Gabin appeared petrified. Her fur stood on end. Noomi walked back to her, not knowing what to expect. "Oh sister, your poor whiskers are singed." Noomi held her sister's head in her hands and nudged her forehead against her sister's before following Gabin's line of sight, through mangled, warped and burnt tree branches. "What is that?"

"I don't know." Gabin slinked toward the form on the ground.

"With caution, sister." Noomi joined Gabin in assessing the crumpled mound. *"I do not advise that we…easy. Easy…"* The cat pawed the pile of snow to reveal a body. *"Her lands. Is it alive?"* Noomi looked to the sky above, unbelieving that it had opened and from it dropped this creature.

Gabin nudged the small form again with the very tip of her paw. She jolted backward when the creature's moan startled her. "Easy, Gab." Noomi ran her gloved hand through Gabin's fur. "Strange is our realm, full o' ancient and odd creatures and travelers who do not have names and are dangerous." She whispered as she knelt. The creature moaned again, this time louder. Both Noomi and Gabin froze. Noomi dug the creature from under the snow and rolled it onto its back.

"A Heather?" Gabin asked, locking eyes with Noomi.

"I do not think so." Noomi brushed more snow from its body, particularly its face. "Well, maybe. Its skin is dark, but… Hard to tell if it bears the markin's o' our kind."

"Elf-kind?"

"No." Noomi tucked the creature's hair behind its ears. *"It bears not the features, the elongated ears and fine hair. This creature's*

hair is thick. Besides, from what I can tell, this creature is too short, too small to be Elf-kind. It looks so helpless."

"Let me remind ye, sister, that danger comes in numerous sizes and forms, not to mention that it's dirty. Look at its clothes."

"Yes, they are torn, and…" Noomi leaned in. *"…smells o' vomit, and blood, fire."* The remnant crackling sound and electrical sensation drew Noomi's gaze upward to traces of smoke in the air. Noomi smoothed the creature's hair from its face and continued freeing it from under the snow. *"Her lands, Gab, there are bruises upon its neck; its clothin' is torn, tis strange…"* Noomi inspected the creature's face—eyebrows knitted in pain, and its breathing labored. She picked up the thing's hand and it oozed blood. *"Gabin, this blood, tis the oddest shade o' red. Her lands…"* A deep crimson discharged from an open gash that went clean through. *"This poor…"* She placed a hand on the creature's cheek. *"Cold, very cold. Its temperature is declinin'."* She placed both her hands upon the fallen oddity and gave it the warmth of her own body, a temporary solution as it left her cold, though she could take it at her present strength. With a tender touch, she opened the creature's eyes to see them filled with blood. *"This creature needs help."*

Gabin growled her opposition.

"We cannot leave it. We have room on the sled, if we make—"

"I do not think this is wise."

"Why?"

"We do not even know what it is. It fell from the heavens, for Heather's sake!"

"What kind o' Heather would I be, would ye be, if we left a creature in need? And so what if it fell from the sky?"

"Where would we put it, not to mention, would ye really risk our safety?"

"We can stay ahead o' the storm and balance the load, if ye help. So help me."

With a snarl, Gabin used her massive paws to dig the creature out, and with the creature mostly unburied, Noomi hoisted it into her arms. *"It is light in me arms, Gab. I am also certain that it is a woman."* Noomi inspected the form of the creature. It was most definitely a female. She walked with the creature and propped her against their sled. *"Keep her warm while I finish uncoverin' our sled."*

Gabin sat with a thud and nestled her body around the small being. *"We should leave it in that tree over there. Doesn't it look cozy?"*

"I am takin' her." Noomi sighed. *"For an enlightened mountain cat, ye are resistant to anythin' new and strange."*

"Ye are ill possessed to take a creature that has fallen from nowhere."

"Sometimes we have to take risks, and this is a risk we must take!"

With the sled free of snow and back onto its runners, through shifting and sorting and resorting, Noomi cleared an area adequate to place the injured woman. She lifted the being into her arms and set her upon an area padded with skins, covering her body with the new traded tunic from Mer's. They resumed their journey and continued until it grew darker and colder, and the creature's moans grew louder and more pained.

"Gabin, we need to stop for the night. She cannot take anymore. We should try to feed her and warm her up, and I want to look at her injuries." Gabin whipped her head around, showed her teeth and growled. *"We have no other choice,"* Noomi said. *"Please sister, I am worried."*

"Fine. Cut me loose and I'll scout out some places."

"Thanks, Gab! With caution. Keep northbound. Call me when ye spot somethin'."

The Heathers were favorable once again and showed them a space with a barrier on three sides that would protect them from the growing winds and under the cover of the always-green branches of a massive ancient red tree. It protected them from snowfall and provided ample room to hide their goods from robbers or malevolent-kind when they convalesced. With a fire providing both light and heat, and with the night set in, Noomi dug out her cooking gear and made a simple stew.

The creature moaned, coughed, and stuttered when Noomi propped her head up to feed her the warm broth, and she mumbled odd, incoherent words, which made it impossible for Noomi to really know what she said.

"Does she speak our tongue, Gab? I cannot tell."

"I am tired." The cat shifted so her backside faced them, huffed and puffed, and then curled into a ball and hid her face behind her massive tail.

Noomi rolled her eyes, continuing to feed the woman until her cheeks took more color and she warmed significantly. Upon Noomi's satisfaction that her belly could take no more, she inspected her injuries, starting with her hand. It had stopped bleeding, likely from the frigid conditions. Noomi mixed a small pot of healing herbs into a paste. She made cuts of cloth and cleaned the wound, which sizzled and bubbled and caused her to fret even more.

"Gab, look," she whispered upon uncovering the woman from the layers of fur covers. Gabin lay still, though her perked ears gave her away. "Fine. Ye can ignore me, but do not insult me intelligence by pretendin' to sleep. Her lands. Strange indigo material is wrapped tightly upon each leg with a hard and cold woven strip o' metal at her middle." Noomi grazed her finger over the odd material, pulling back sharply when the woman stirred. "A strip o' leather 'round her waist, but it is not any leather I have ever seen. There are markin's on it and strange walkers at her feet and not made o' wolf hide. I have never..."

Noomi covered the woman with the blankets again and shook her head in confusion, but her curiosity won. She took another glance, longer this time. The woman's tunic had round stones that held one side to the other, and underneath, a material wrapped around her torso—a sheer cloth of a color she had not seen before, and too thin to be useful. She wore an amulet around her neck that had burned her. Noomi kept that observation to herself, not giving Gabin another reason to abandon the woman in the snow.

Noomi lifted the woman's strange-colored tunic, noticing deep red and purple bruises on her entire torso. "Gab, this woman has taken a beatin'. Who would do this to her?" She rubbed healing paste around the bruised areas.

Despite the bruising on her face and neck, Noomi knew she was young. She had thick, long and wavy black hair. Her skin was olive but bore no pattern of the Heathers of Noomi's realm.

Her lips were full, dry and brittle. "Poor creature." There were purple and red markings on her neck. She moaned when Noomi touched her. Noomi covered her with the furs and woolen tunic and moved her closer to the warmth of the fire. As Seer, she possessed the ability to read the emotions of other beings, but only at the acceptance of the other person. Delving into an unsuspecting person's mind, especially one that bore no gifts, was an abuse of power. In this case, the woman couldn't give her consent, and in this case, to help her further, Noomi needed to know more about how she had endured. Noomi closed her eyes and placed both hands on the poor broken body. A flash of anger, confusion, and sorrow flooded her mind. She pulled back as if burned by the sensation. The emotions within the woman were too intense even for a Seer as skilled as Noomi. She'd try again when the woman was free from the threat of death. She still had no doubt that helping the woman was the right thing.

"Gabin, please help us."

The cat perked her ears and turned, and she lay her head on the ground and opened only one eye to look at the woman.

"She *will* die tonight if we don't help her."

Gabin rolled her eyes, sighed and then snorted as she readjusted her position to fully surround the woman.

Gabin and Noomi lent the stranger their warmth that night, but Noomi sensed both of them had failed at bringing her comfort from her horror-filled dreams and pained sobs, which filled Noomi's soul with a more haunting feeling than the sounds of the lost spirits and wild beasts that normally filled the lands at night.

CHAPTER FIVE

In the past when a job went south, Peachy would disappear for days at a time, but it had been four days and Lisette hadn't heard a word. She checked her phone again. No cryptic text messages, no phone calls from a friend of a friend, no hidden messages slipped under the door. Nothing. She asked herself why, as if asking again differently would glean her an answer. She should have stressed the danger of the job and the stakes. She threw around cheap sayings like *your life is in danger*, and *our lives are at risk*, but people said things like that all the time. These days, cheap phrases said to someone as young and fearless as Peachy didn't carry the weight that they used to.

Lisette should have told her everything beforehand, but she had good reasons to wait. Lisette did what she had to do in order to protect Peachy from knowing too much too soon. Every little detail would have been open for discussion. The amulet needed to be in hand before she gave answers, then training, then everything else. Besides, Peachy wasn't ready at the time, far from it.

Lisette rested her head in her hands, her elbows on the kitchen table. She rubbed her eyes too hard and they burned. She needn't look in the mirror to know that they were bloodshot. She took another drink of her coffee, forgoing sugar and cream. She needed strong and bitter to keep going. She scrolled through the photos on her phone, photos of Peachy, posing with food, dressed up for Halloween, and smiling at Lisette's birthday dinner. Peachy had taken her to the Commander's Palace for brunch. Lisette wore the beautiful silk tignon that Peachy had purchased for her, a stunning wrap of gold and blue, big with a tie, and an even bigger bow on the side.

She was all the envy at their lunch, with her matching goldthread laced blouse and skirt, accentuated by her gold hoop earrings and dramatic makeup. Everyone always stared at her wherever she went, always paid her compliments, telling her that she embodied the image of a living breathing Voodoo queen from yesteryear. When she went downtown, all the lovely tourists wanted photos with her. She never said yes, but she always invited them into her store for a reading.

She felt like a queen that day at Commander's sitting at the chef's table, enjoying dinner with her beautiful friend, who everyone thought was her daughter. And Peachy never corrected them. They shared copper skin, cleft chins, and long necks. Peachy would have known they also shared blood, if she had only returned with the amulet.

Peachy had only recently matured. She had come from horror, living on the streets, mistrusting as little as a glance of a smile her way. She was a smart-mouth delinquent with an array of bad habits by the time Lisette found her. Now, she made fewer poor decisions and had grown into a resourceful, intellectual woman. Her dyed green and pink dreads had been shaved off long ago, and in their place, wavy black curls reached the middle of her back. She no longer ate food from the trash, and her terrible acne had been replaced by a healthy complexion that made it seem as though she was made of gold, especially in the summertime with the Louisiana sun coloring her skin. She had grown into a beautiful woman, but one thing remained constant: she was and would perpetually be a smart-mouth, stubborn thing to tame. Lisette wondered if she'd ever settle down. Peachy was still young with years of growing to do, not to mention training—if Lisette ever had that chance again.

She ran through the scenarios, wondering if Peachy had even made it inside the big house, hacked the safe, and swapped the replica for the real one. She sorted through the various moving parts, trying to pinpoint where Peachy had met difficulty. Lisette should have given her something to defend herself with, something more than that *trusty* knife Peachy insisted on stuffing in her boot. She should have started training her a year beforehand. She shook her head at her stupidity. From what horror had Peachy found that warranted her to hide for nearly four days?

That had to be it. Peachy saw trouble before it found her; she was covering her tracks, diverting attention, and protecting the mission. Lisette floated on the thought and let it take her somewhere safe, someplace where she could avoid the constant reminder that she had spent the past few months planning the girl's death. On the other hand, the thought of Peachy taking the amulet for her own crossed Lisette's mind. It stood to fetch thousands of dollars on the black market. Lisette wouldn't put it past Peachy to take it to a pawn shop just to see how much it was worth. But if she had placed it around her neck… What if the power within the amulet decided to take her right then and there? Lisette hadn't planned for that. The amulet spoke to people in ways that were complex and maniacal. It drove their kind to stand on ledges, as if death was a welcomed solace, if they lacked the skills to possess it. The amulet beheld the bearer. In this case, this amulet was Peachy's, forged for her, and if she placed it on her neck, it would have, should have, submitted to her will.

Lisette jumped at the ringing of her phone, knocking the chair in which she sat to the floor. "Child, is that—"

"The *Spanish Rose* is utterly trashed," said Adèle, "and to make it worse, her stench lingers everywhere."

"Of whom do you speak?" Lisette placed her hand over her mouth and she closed her eyes and waited for the answer, confirmation that Peachy had, had…

"Who else reeks of death? Beatriz is back."

"How can you be certain?"

"She left a dead thing in my foyer."

"You are certain this dead thing is hers?" Lisette ground her teeth, pushed down nausea and waited for the answer.

"Three hundred pounds of rotting meat with no teeth and tongue. Who else is keen on seducing large men and hijacking their brains?"

"She left her trash. Why didn't she come for you?" Lisette asked and rubbed at her temples.

"I thought you might be able to shed light upon this unfortunate situation."

"What makes you think I want anything to do with *your* unfortunate situation?"

"Does it not concern you that Beatriz is alive?"

"Of course." Of course it concerned her that her twin had surfaced, breathed air and now crawled about New Orleans picking up where she had left off. "But I am ill-equipped to do anything about it."

"You share sight. Why not start there?"

"I haven't heard a word from her, not so much as a thought, in fifteen years since she stopped communicating. I thought she'd died."

"We would be so lucky."

They had been lucky, blessed to avoid the plague of their most demented sister for as long as they had. Beatriz's thirst for war, pain, and sorrow finally ended when she met a demon of her own, one that wielded more power than she could handle. It showed her so when it tired of her and encased her in cement and buried her so far underground that she'd been lost to eternity. It took Lisette over a year to locate where her cries were coming from and when she found where her body was buried, she said good riddance, ignored them and eventually, they stopped.

"I'd have cherished these past thirty-some years a little more if I knew she'd resurface," Adèle said.

"It seems to me you've cherished enough for infinite lifetimes."

"It isn't my fault you reverted to a pious do-gooder and left it all behind."

"I made a choice to stop hurting people." Lisette's decision to leave depravity behind had nothing to do with making amends and everything to do with Peachy's existence in her life.

"You make it seem like you're Mother Theresa incarnate the way you talk, as if decades of niceties have negated a century of—"

"Enough with this nonsensical back and forth waste of words. What is it you need from me?"

"We need to find Beatriz, and we need to talk."

"I have nothing to say to either of you. Why are you so desperate?"

"I am hardly—"

"Did she take anything from you?" Lisette asked.

"Nothing that concerns you."

"Then why do you concern me?"

"She is your twin. Find her!" Adèle ended the call.

With Beatriz in the picture, Peachy needed help. The fact that Lisette no longer felt the girl in her mind's eye could only mean one thing: Peachy no longer existed in *this* world and Peachy needed guidance.

CHAPTER SIX

The woman's moaning grew in intensity. They needed to move now as there was no better time than a break in the snowfall. Another positive sign from the Heathers. "We must make for home where I can properly care for her."

"And what happens when she regains her strength?"

"Ask me that when she regains her strength!" Noomi retorted. She had spent the greater part of the night and morning defending her decision to take the injured woman with them. "Keep her warm while I pack," Noomi ordered and began shoving their belongings where they would fit, not bothering to dry them, being more forceful than necessary, and tuning out Gabin's incessant objections. She fed the woman as much as she could, covered her under every available layer, and gave the woman as much warmth and strength from her own body as she could spare. There was no doubt that this next part of their journey would be painful.

Finally, with their sled dug out from under the piles of overnight snowfall, and with Gabin harnessed, they were ready.

At their pace, giving more than every bit of their combined effort, stopping only to check on the status of the woman, they would arrive home safely by nightfall. When they passed into Noomi's lands, they slowed their pace. By this time, the woman's sobs were constant and she stirred and thrashed with more energy than someone under duress should expend. Noomi saw her actions as a testament to her will. Her spirit was strong and vibrant, all of which would help her recover faster.

"Her lands!" Noomi gasped with the little bit of breath she could spare from her intense ride. "Finally home!" She stumbled off the sleigh and unharnessed Gabin. Both dropped to their knees and caught their breath.

"*Let us never travel at that pace again*," Gabin said.

"You have me word." Noomi panted and pushed through her door. She removed her wet and heavy layers, her walkers down to bare feet, and stripped off her sweaty clothing, letting it all lay where it landed—not a normal practice, but she cared not this time. She retrieved well-worn work clothes, a loose-fitting tunic and soft breeches, and set to lighting her home's great fireplace, her cooking fire, and several sconces along the walls to illuminate her path to rooms of supplies she might need. She readied several pots with water for care of the woman. The warmth, light, and comforting roar of the fire filled her home in a matter of moments.

"*Noomi! You're home! Sooner'n expected.*"

"Missy, Sissy, hello little ones." Noomi opened her hands and her wee mice friends climbed into them. They rubbed their noses against her cheek. "We found somethin'."

Her friends chirped, jumped, and clapped their tiny paws.

"Tisn't sweets from Mer's this time, darlin's. Stay put. I will need help," she said as she darted down a corridor and returned with several pelts and blankets in her arms that she layered and placed near the great fireplace where she would work. Missy and Sissy joined Noomi in smoothing out the edges of the pelt covers. "Be right back," she assured and headed out for the woman. She mustered her strength and hoisted the woman into her arms. "Hold on. I promise I'll help ye to the best of me ability." Noomi struggled, managing the woman and the door that had since blown shut from a gust of wind, all of which she did still frozen to her core.

"Gabin!"

The large cat's tail thwapped the fresh pelts that Noomi had moments ago laid down.

"Move." Noomi motioned with a flick of her head. "Look what you've done!" The cat left a wet patch on the pelt, and with a snarky growl, Gabin moved slightly and plopped down. "Was that so hard?" Noomi lay the woman down and gave Gabin a kiss upon her head. "With thanks, love. Ye helped me, helped her, more'n ye know."

"I am quite aware o' the role that I played." The cat punctuated her comment with an enormous sigh. *"I'll want a whole jar o' preserves to meself."*

"Ye can have both jars o' the fig, Gab. I know they are your favorite."

The cat started purring in response and began licking her paws, cleaning and drying her matted wet fur.

"Her lands," Noomi said. She stood rooted in place and scratched her head and rubbed her face. She looked upon the woman, as if seeing her state for the first time, realizing the attention she would demand from Noomi, from all of them. A mere look upon the broken body caused Noomi to tremble. "I know not where to start," she said to her companions. She secured her long black hair behind her head with a string of pelt and took a deep breath.

"What are her injuries?" Sissy asked.

Noomi shook her head.

"Let's take a look."

"Good idea." Noomi knelt next to the woman and began digging her out from under the soggy, sodden, soiled pelts to reveal her strange torn clothing and fabric walkers.

"She is a Heather?"

"We do not know who or what she is, but she looks like she might be. Her skin is similar to ours but lacks a distinct pattern that is common for our kind."

"Perhaps when she is healthy her markin's will return."

"Perhaps, but for the style o' her clothes, there is no doubt, she's not from 'round here." With better lighting, Noomi saw the difference in clothing between herself and the woman. Clothing worn by her own kind was simpler, of basic colors and patterns, and clasped with string, not small round shells. Even the breeches were different. They were tight and hugged each leg, while the style in Heatherton was loose and flowy, and secured with string instead of cold hard metal.

Missy and Sissy climbed upon the table, which Noomi knew to be their preferred and best vantage point to see the entire picture. They gasped when they saw the nature of their guest's injuries, and they busied themselves as they saw fit, rounding up clean rags and rolling over jars of Noomi's healing herbs and several small bowls that she would need. *"What happened?"*

"This was how we found her," Noomi said. The woman's left eye was swollen shut and the rest of her face was covered in caked, dark red blood that stained the collar of her lightweight tunic, accenting the bruising around her neck. Noomi lifted an eyelid. Blood surrounded the woman's chestnut-colored iris. Noomi smoothed her hair out of the way and gave her entire body a once-over. "'Here goes," she said, starting with the strange outer tunic. She easily figured it out, pulling a lone metal tab and opening the teeth. "What are these? I have never seen these sorts o' clasps. Usually the sides are fastened with string. These are round, precisely trimmed and soft, with the smallest bit o' string I have ever seen. How does she get out?"

"Let me try." Missy hopped down and climbed upon the woman's chest. She figured it out easily, showing Noomi how to unhook the round clasps to separate the sides of the fabric.

"'Tis ill-designed." Noomi caught on and worked the rest of them apart, revealing the woman's torso. Vivid blooms of red, purple, and green swelled on the woman's chest. "Horrible."

"I think her ribs are broken," said Sissy.

"I think ye are correct. Aye, friend. This might hurt a bit." Noomi bit her own lip as she eased the woman's arm out from the tunic and shirt, careful to avoid bumping the mauled hand.

All went well, and then she went for the other arm. The woman wailed in pain and animated suddenly. Her outburst paralyzed the others. She thrashed about trying to get up, knocking over the bowls the mice had set out, and then she fell back as fast as she jumped, yelling and crying.

"Easy, woman," Noomi said, taking hold of her hand, bracing her body against her own, until the woman calmed, and her eyes closed again. "There we go." Noomi smoothed the woman's hair from her face and lay her back down, realizing that her own fingertips were bloodied. "Her skull is bleedin' too. Girls, please get me the Elixir o' the Mountain. She cannot be allowed to do that again. Her injuries are too vast. She is far from stable. Get me gut and me needles. With haste!"

With the elixir in hand, she poured a hearty sip of it into the woman's mouth. "Tis the finest pain reliever in all the realm, friend. Ye will feel nothin' soon." Noomi let a few moments pass until the woman's breathing slowed before again attempting to slip the woman out of her tunic. Noomi was successful this time, and she pushed the soiled clothing away.

The woman wore a strange brace around her breasts with straps over her shoulders. The fabric was the brightest shade of red Noomi had ever seen. "I don't know how to get this off. Sissy, get me blade."

"Wait, I have an idea. Lift her."

"Are ye mad?"

"Just do it."

Noomi followed Sissy's orders and pulled the woman into her arms.

"As I suspected, the back, her back."

"What? Oh." Noomi felt the tiny clasps in the middle of the woman's back. "How does she do this every single day? Tis a terrible bear." She nearly gave up, but she finally succeeded in working the tiny clasps apart and pulling the brace off. "Too much work." She held the item at the tip of her finger and tossed it to the side. She lay the woman back down, careful to mind her broken arm, split skull, mauled hand, and broken ribs.

Next were the tight indigo leg wraps, which ended up being easier to remove than the woman's upper half. Noomi figured out the strange woven metal at the woman's middle. It was just like the mechanism of the thin tunic, only shorter. The woman wore another strange cloth not so different from what Noomi wore over the most sensitive parts of her body, though different, smaller, and of material that Noomi associated with royalty. She inched those off as well and added it to the growing pile of bloodied clothing.

"*She will struggle in her healin'*," Sissy said.

"Indeed she will," Noomi agreed, finally getting a look at the woman in her entirety. "But let us hope that her spirit is strong." The woman was small framed, in fact, quite similar to Noomi, about the same height and build, long neck, full breasts, broad shoulders, flat stomach, but she had longer legs than Noomi. Her muscles weren't as defined as Noomi's and her ribs stuck out. She was too skinny to ensure a speedy recovery.

"No," Noomi said, seeing that her mice friends were working the amulet off the woman's neck. "Leave it." Amulets were sources of power, enigma, and nobility in the Realm of the Heathers, beheld by a certain few, but that wasn't to say there weren't amulets in the hands of regular Heathers. There were several amulets in her realm that harbored powers Noomi did not have control over, nor was she privy to understanding.

"*But it has burned her.*"

"I do not want to risk further damage by removin' it."

"*Look! There are words.*"

Noomi leaned in. "Her lands." She popped up and looked for Gabin, thankful that her sister had retreated long ago to her favored sleeping spot in the other room. Noomi realized that the amulet bore ancient script of the Realm of the Heathers.

"*Can ye read it?*"

"I can't quite make it out," she whispered. "'Tis old, very old. I think it says, 'daughter, or child...' Ack, I don't know. Let it be for now and let us not tell Gabin right this second. When I can, I will consult me mentor, Nefertari, for guidance."

After stabilizing the woman, after nursing her to health, after the woman's strength returned considerably, only then would Noomi leave her in search of answers. In the meantime, the fact that the woman possessed an amulet with ancient script caused anxiety within Noomi's heart.

"*I feel sorry for her,*" Missy said. She took hold of Sissy's hands. "*We both do.*"

"As do I," Noomi agreed. The woman shivered constantly, her lips muttered, and her brow furrowed.

"*What will happen?*"

"We will nurse her to health and then send her on her way with rations to sustain her for the next part of her journey, whatever it may be." Noomi sighed, feeling her tears build at the sorry sight of the broken woman. "Come on, girls. There will be time to think about all that later. Come now. We have much to do. Help me clean her up. Is the water at peak heat?"

"*'Tis ready,*" said Sissy.

"Good. Please measure out me herbs for healin'."

Noomi filled a large bowl with steaming water fragrant with healing herbs that released a soothing aroma. She dipped a soft cloth in her bowl and began smoothing away the caked blood, dirt, and scorch marks, relieved that the woman hadn't also been burned from her descent through the heavens. Her skin felt soft to Noomi's touch and color returned to her body. She shivered less, and her breathing slowed as if she were in a peaceful slumber and not living a nightmare.

"More elixir, Missy." Noomi fed the woman a double dose and began setting the woman's broken arm. After that she stitched her skull and her hand. She finished by smoothing healing salve all over the woman's body, eliciting soft moans from her touch. "'Her ribs will require tight strips and a brace, but let's see how she does this night. I don't want her to wake up frightened because she is bound."

"*What about ye?*"

"What about me?" Noomi asked, taking residence in a nearby chair after washing her hands.

"*Do ye want somethin' to eat, or tea?*"

"I am too tired to eat." Noomi yawned and stretched her legs, placing them on the stone ledge and crossed her arms. "Tis up to ye now, stranger." She closed her eyes and had crossed into a dream when a nagging feeling took over that wouldn't quit. It was the girls. They were trying to wake her up.

"Go to bed. Tis too early to make breakfast..." Noomi folded her arms and readjusted herself into the seat. "Her lands, me back... Please, be quiet. I just laid down..." Noomi yawned and could scarcely open her eyes. She nearly fell off the chair and everything flooded back. The woman of the sky!

"There is a deadly heat upon her body."

Noomi darted awake, shaking off sleep, cracking as she stood from her hunched position. She knelt, placing her hand upon the woman's forehead. "She's ablaze." Noomi pulled the woman into her arms. "Gab, get up!" The cat growled and tucked her head into herself. "Quit ignorin' me, please. Missy, Sissy ready more strips o' cloth. We will need to reapply her bandages after what I am about to do, and clean tunics for us both! Gab bring the girls and the elixir when they are ready."

Noomi carried the fretting woman down the hall toward her bathing pools and straight toward the frigid cold basin fresh with snow runoff. "This will not feel good, friend; I can guarantee that, but tis necessary if ye are to live."

Noomi sat the woman on a wooden bench and supported her limp body with her own as she removed her fever-soaked gown. "Brace yourself." With the woman back in her arms, she inched her into the basin, and upon meeting the frigid bath, the stranger animated at once! Noomi's warnings were no good, for the woman jumped and screamed and thrashed about, yelling foreign and odd words that Noomi could not make out.

"Stop. Please. Ye are safe..." But the more she tried to soothe the woman, the more the woman fretted, cried, and yelled. Her eyes grew wide and her sobs grew louder. "Stranger, please...I do not understand ye. Please conserve your energy. *Gab! Come quick!* Ye are gravely injured but are safe. This I promise." Noomi hushed her tone and soothed her words, and it seemed to help, though now the woman shivered and darted her eyes to every corner of the room. She needed to stop moving, for her wounds were not stable and began coloring the clear water with her deep crimson blood. "Easy, friend." Noomi held her in place, even as she tried to push her away and stand. "I am Noomi. This is me home. Ye are under me care. I will not harm ye." Noomi's words did little to console her. It was obvious now that the woman did not understand her language. Nonetheless, Noomi whispered words into her ear, hoping she would derive comfort from her soothing tone.

"*Oh girls, Gabin, hurry. I need help.*" Gabin arrived with a basket in her teeth. Inside were Missy and Sissy and the bottle of the elixir. Gabin dropped the basket and must have felt it timely to also interrogate Noomi.

"*What is that?*"

"*Tis not the time, Gab.*" Noomi held the woman with one arm and reached for the elixir. "Drink," she said, but the woman would not do anything she asked. Noomi would have to force her because the woman appeared to have much more fight left, fight that would tear open her wounds even more. With a better grip on the bottle, Noomi succeeded in getting her to drink a little, spilling most of the elixir, but she finally felt she'd gotten enough of it in her, for the woman slowed her fight considerably. Noomi smoothed the stranger's hair out of her face and held her until she went limp again and passed out. "Her lands she is strong for how she looks."

"*She cannot stay here.*"

"*Why not?*"

"*Are you really askin' me that question? Look what is 'round her neck.*"

"*Tis a trinket.*"

"*With ancient script o' our realm!*"

"*I...*"

"*You knew this didn't ye. The whole time, even when we were campin' you knew this and still brought her into our home?*"

"*She would have died.*"

"*That is not our concern.*"

"*She is our concern now.*"

"*Takin' her is the illest thing that you have done in your seventy-two years.*"

"*I assure ye that she is only in need o' me healin', nothin' more.*"

"*How can ye be certain. Have you seen what is inside her heart and mind?*"

"*I will not delve into her mind without her consent.*"

"*There are a few times when there are exceptions to the rules.*"

"*I will consult Nefatari when the time is right.*"

"*The longer she is here, the quicker harm will find us.*"

"*How can ye assume that this amulet is evil and she bears ill intentions?*"

"*How can ye be certain?*"

"Look at her!" Noomi's shouts roused the woman, but she only moaned. "Shhh," she whispered and then turned her thoughts inward. "*She came into our lives for a reason. Do ye not believe—*" Noomi looked to her concerned friends as they studied the woman in her arms. "*She might not even make it through the night.*"

"*It will be a blessin' to her,*" Gabin said as she left the pool room.

Noomi continued to bathe her charge with palmfuls of frigid water until she was satisfied that the woman's temperature had lowered and she was free from danger. She dried her body, rewrapped her wounds and dressed her in a clean tunic. When Noomi was satisfied the woman could manage, it was already dawn. When Noomi tried to take her leave for a few hours of slumber in her own bed, the woman thrashed and moaned all over again, so Noomi stayed with her, laid next to her, held her hand, and gave her warmth and comfort—for two days and two nights. And all creatures, animal kind, Fae kind, and the stranger, slept and recovered from their ordeal.

CHAPTER SEVEN

Everything hurt when Peachy attempted to get up, so she lay there instead, which hurt even more. She tried again, straining her stomach muscles. Getting up no longer felt like a good idea. *What the hell did I do last night?* Partying excessively wasn't anything foreign, but she didn't party like *that* anymore. She couldn't remember a single detail. Her eyes felt heavy. She couldn't even open them. *Probably a good thing.* She didn't want to lay witness to the after-party fallout, gluttonous evidence of whatever she had done. Every inch ached! The moaning she heard from her own body, sounded off, not like her at all; it sounded weak. She needed something to drink. Damn, she wanted a smoke. This didn't feel like a killer hangover. Someone roofied her! She attempted to move but felt strapped in place. "Lisette," she croaked. She needed to cough but didn't have the strength.

She replayed her day, afternoon, and night for something to go on, but nothing came to her, only fog. She sifted through partial memories, one after another. A job...she and Minette.

Lisette. The swipe and swap. The carriage house. The *Spanish Rose* and the safe. The amulet! Beatriz and a pistol against her brain! Boom! Peachy's instincts fueled her next move, to get the hell on her feet, but she couldn't. Nothing worked—not her arms, her legs, not her little fucking finger!

Her captor…captors… Where were they? The huge men who beat her senseless. Images of the deranged woman snapping her fingers filled her mind. She felt their boots against her back, breaking her ribs. Her breath had escaped and it hadn't returned. That was why she couldn't breathe, couldn't move, couldn't think! She froze when she felt faint wind on her hair.

Move your legs! Mild relief when she wiggled her toes. She tried for her legs. Nothing happened. *Am I paralyzed?* There was a great weight upon her chest, around her ribs. Bound. Tied up. Chained for torture. She took what she could from each short spurt of breath she was able to draw. Her breathing sounded too loud. She was making too much of a commotion. She slowed each breath, focusing on the in and the out, the good and the bad, and she caught a scent of paper and herbs, fragrant notes, floral scents…and paint? It soothed her, and after she calmed herself, she tried again. She lifted her head as far as she could, but her neck burned and itched, and from the center of her chest, radiating energy throbbed against her heart, a dull ache, then a calming presence…maybe morphine. The amulet.

"I cut your hand off. When you fall, my goon then cuts the amulet off your head, and I feed your pathetic broken body to tourists looking for Voodoo trash."

Tears came to her aid, illuminating her world, moving her beyond the horror of her imagination. One eye and then two, a dull glow of light, the undersides of furniture, gray stone, heat, sparks and wood, open flame. She wasn't in a hospital, but where was she? Strings of dried herbs or flowers swung to and fro from the ceiling. She envied their leisurely movements. Shelves held jars and pots and metal objects hung on a wall, stained woods and baskets, so many woven baskets, and boxes and bowls. Every other space held books and stacks of paper, curled at the edges. Suddenly heat, too much heat, and crackling sounds. She turned

to her left, inches away from a great stone firepit. A window…
and did she hear voices?

She groaned and gritted her teeth. She still couldn't move
her legs. She started with her toes, clenching and curling them,
waking her body. Finally she was able to sit. Success! She wasn't
able to move one of her arms. It was held in place, bound against
her chest. Her other hand was wrapped in strips of fabric. She
scratched her head at a bandage over a pulsating beat that
throbbed and stung like nothing she'd ever felt. She groaned,
trying to be patient as she worked up her nerve and her energy
to get up the rest of the way. She kneeled and grabbed hold of
the wooden table. A bead of sweat rolled down her brow, and
she closed her eyes to slow the spinning and quiet the sound of
the blood swooshing around in her head.

She eyed a plate. Fruit, bread, and a cup, a rudimentary-
looking cup. She didn't care what the cup held inside. She would
drink anything. She reached for it but couldn't grasp it with one
arm braced against her chest and the other swollen twice its size.
She tried again, though, when she reached for it, she knocked
it over, making a loud ruckus and spilling all over herself. That
simple task took much more energy than she could spare.

She sat in the chair, knowing she might not be able to get
up again, but she needed to catch her breath. In doing so, she
noticed her clothing for the first time, or lack thereof. She only
wore an odd oversize man's dress shirt sans the buttons. She
heard a voice again, and it drew her back to her task.

Time to try again. She lifted her foot with the care that one
would take when a foot had fallen asleep, overwhelmed by the
sensation of tiny pinpricks. Getting to the window proved too
much work. It seemed miles away, and the voice grew louder.
It sounded like it was having a one-sided argument with his or
herself. She suddenly felt entirely spent. She forced herself to
stay upright and hugged the wall, rolled her forehead against it,
glad for the stability. At last, she had made it!

The wonder of the window. The beautiful and cleansing feel
of snow. Snow! Where was she and how long had she had been
out? Her wounds indicated not long, so why did it look like she

was at a clubhouse at a ski resort? She took a long and painful breath and focused on the voice, for clues as to where she was being held. She froze. The voice grew louder, as did shuffling of boots, maybe heavy combat boots.

She spotted her clothing folded on a bench along with her shoes and jacket. She hobbled toward them. Each step hurt from her teeth to her toenails. Her elbow got stuck trying to get out of the billowy shirt. The spinning of the room didn't help either. She stumbled backward and dropped onto a bench, failing to suppress overwhelming nausea. "Damn it." She moaned. She vomited water that smelled like tree bark and herbs. She wet her shirt, her bare feet and the floor. She wiped her mouth with her cuff. She'd have to change later after she escaped.

With clothing in hand, she worked one foot halfway in a shoe, but she'd shoved her left foot into her right shoe. None of that mattered. The door. They were here. She had to get out before they got in! She headed for it, but game over and no more quarters. A blast of frigid air hit her hard. The tunnel of wind knocked her on her back, and she hit her head and bit her tongue coming face-to-face with her captor—a woman.

A strange woman. Dark and perceptive, and yelling at her, but the words Peachy registered didn't make sense. It wasn't Creole or French, not Haitian French or a Caribbean version, not Spanish or Portuguese. Peachy wasn't a language expert, but she had heard enough to know that the woman wasn't from America, Europe, or Africa. Her clothing looked archaic, basic, and oddly colored with bright tones, as if she made them herself. Everything seemed oversize—huge boots, gloves, and a hat that the woman removed along with her gloves, discarded on the floor, which gave Peachy a better look at who she was dealing with. The woman's skin was olive, her hair tied behind her head. Wild and wavy, it seemed to be black with copper and gold. Her cheekbones were high, and her eyes were earnest and gentle, concerned, but also menacing, which Peachy took as an invitation to fight. Peachy thanked her adrenaline for fueling her to her feet. She could take her. The woman looked to be about Peachy's height and weight, probably Peachy's build— maybe—underneath all those layers.

"You wanna play, lady? Huh? I can take you. Come on! Come on!" Peachy yelled, but the closer the woman got, the more *off* she appeared. Her eyes reminded Peachy of cat's eyes, huge black pits inside rings of green and copper. The woman approached her with cat-like quickness that made Peachy think better of her ability to take her on. "Hey look!" Peachy screamed and she held out her bandaged hand pointing behind the crazed lunatic, but the woman didn't fall for it. Few women ever did. Peachy resorted to another tactic. She chucked one of her shoes. She nailed the woman, sending her back but a step, but the woman slinked toward her again, just like a cat. "Don't take another step, bitch!"

Yet the woman kept advancing and talking to someone over her shoulder. Peachy expected Beatriz and her goons to arrive any minute. A throbbing pain in her head felt like it originated in her soul, within her memory. She strained to see around the imposing woman's form to verify her fears. All the while the woman kept talking. She wouldn't shut up. She kept saying what sounded like *pa, pa, pa*, and nothing else she said made any sense whatsoever.

"Not one more step!" Peachy said and backed away. "I'm warning you…"

"Pa."

"What are you talking about?" Peachy backed up, even though it put her farther away from the door that would set her free. "What part of 'leave me alone' don't you understand?" she shouted, but the woman still wore that confused look as if she truly didn't understand.

"Kudo. Kudo Pa." The woman held out her hands in front of her.

"No, please!" Peachy had nowhere else to go. Her back was against the wall. The woman's outstretched hands were mere inches from her body. "No!" She screamed and pressed herself into it harder, hoping the wall would somehow absorb her. She closed her eyes. Maybe this was all a dream.

"Kudo," said the woman, her tone softer this time. "Kudo." She pointed to Peachy's bandaged hand.

Peachy followed the woman's line of sight to her own hand, dripping red, wet, and warm onto the crude hardwood floor that drank it up as if it needed blood. "Please, stay away…" Peachy muttered, her face puffy and swollen. She licked her dry lips. "Please—"

From behind the woman appeared a massive beast. "Jesus Christ!" Peachy screamed and barreled toward her, pushing her over, but she didn't get far. A bench tripped her up and sent her flying. The woman made her move. Peachy thrashed her arms and legs, hoping to get free, expecting to get stabbed or beaten, but the woman only held her against herself. Peachy had lost another fight.

"Kudo. Kudo…" her captor said over and over into her ear. Her words were soothing, as if putting her into a trance.

"The animal will kill us!" Peachy eyed the chair and made one last attempt to get the hell away. She kicked it with all her might, nailing the beast. The thing lunged toward her and bared its large teeth. Peachy screamed again and her captor's arms held her tight and whispered into her ear. The woman shouted at the cat, and as if the cat could understand her words, it backed off as flippantly as a housecat would. It plopped on the floor in front of the fireplace and started licking its paws.

Upon seeing this utter domestic display, Peachy passed out.

CHAPTER EIGHT

Lisette let it ring and ring again, and even after muting the volume and turning off the phone altogether, she felt the ringing, the calling of her twin pulsating in her brain. She couldn't ignore her anymore. "You're alive," she said, making no mistake that she really wasn't surprised and really couldn't care less.

"I thought I might have to leave a dreaded voice mail, but I guess the joke is on you to listen to it," Beatriz said. "I left Adèle a nine-minute message earlier. I wonder, do you think she listened to the whole thing? I made a joke at the end, one I think she would have appreciated." Beatriz laughed.

Lisette hated her sister's boisterous laugh. At one point she had loved it about her, loved how opposite it was from her own laugh—short, punctuated, and breathy. Aside from the way they looked, near mirror images of each other, their laugh was one of the few identifying differences between them, as was their manner of walking, and the way they spoke. Lisette had a more direct manner of speaking versus her twin's flowery long-windedness. Their taste in clothing also varied quite drastically.

Beatriz always favored whatever sophisticated style was vogue, while Lisette, also elegant in her own way, favored older, classic fashions. Their biggest distinction: Beatriz's proclivity for stirring up war, trouble, and the killing of innocent creatures.

At one point Lisette had loved her sister and would have done anything for her. She reveled in the thrill of war, but that desire flared only because she loved her sister. In her heart, she favored peace, creation, and art.

"What do you want?"

"Is that any way to talk to your twin?" Beatriz sweetened her voice. "After so long, sister?"

"Speaking of, where have you been?"

"Don't come at me with that. You heard my calls for help and did nothing. Did you know that while I lay in wait, my only hope was that you, my beautiful twin sister, would hear me and come to me if only for—"

"What do you want?" Lisette asked again, this time harsher.

"How rude to cut me off, your elder by two minutes."

"I do not have time to talk to you."

"Surely you can find a few moments to spare. Besides," Beatriz said, drawling her words, "I have images and fun video clips I think you will find interesting. This strange little device...so odd that it makes phone calls *and* takes photos *and* brings anything your heart desires right to your doorstep in under two days. One needn't go far for anything with this in their possession. I now have a new wardrobe. I'm loving the footwear. I have Louboutins in every color. How chic. One look at me now and one would never know I've lived underground for the past almost four decades."

Lisette gripped the phone in her hand and ground her teeth. "Get to the point."

"Congratulations."

"What are you talking about?"

"What a marvelous scheme you orchestrated. You would have pulled it off had it not been for our shared sight."

Lisette closed her eyes, feeling nauseous. Beatriz's words stopped registering and making sense, as if lifeless inanimate objects bounced around her head.

"Did you forget, Lis? Did you think that because I rested underground, was buried and forgotten, that my abilities were any less potent? You may have forgotten about me, but I've seen you the entire time. I've learned that you're lazy, and that you've also forgotten what you are, trying to fit in, doing good for other people, healing them with your potions and so-called psychic abilities. I am ashamed to call you my twin."

"Anything else you want to add?"

"Aren't you going to ask where she is?"

"What have you done?"

"I didn't kill her. I tried to. Gods, I wanted to and came very close to it at one point. Actually, looking back we weren't *that* hard on her, broke some ribs and broke her skull. You know, minor things. She might pull through. I don't know. She got stabbed pretty good. I'm positive she will lose her hand. It might have been her dominant hand. Well, never mind. Nasty wound. Couldn't be prevented, and my poor disappointed boys." Beatriz ticked her tongue. "They had fun with her. She really is sweet, Lis, and such a firebrand and stubborn. I never would have suspected that, living with you, for so long. She's just like her mother."

Lisette wiped tears from her eyes, steadied herself, swallowing her anger, sorry for the pain Peachy suffered. "You will pay—"

"Really. I'm going to pay? Pay for what exactly and what type of threat is that? I'm going to pay." She laughed. "Well, guess what? I have unlimited means, so sure, what's the damage? I'll add a shiny talent for ye as well. How is it that you have become less eloquent with your words? I'm the one who's been underground for thirty-seven-and-a-half years and twenty-two days!"

"Looks like my good fortune has finally—"

"Come *my* way. You see, if it weren't for a great storm several years ago that brought my cement tomb to the surface, and a great big pounding jackhammer thanks to economic development, I'd still be buried. But here I am." Beatriz took a dramatic breath in and out. "Want to know something else?"

"Do I have a choice?"

"I told the girl about us. About her mother." Beatriz laughed. "I told her that I killed her. Sorry, it sounded like I stole your thunder."

"What had you to gain by sharing that with her?"

"Doubt does wondrous things to a soul, twists it, contorts it, opens holes inside it for crawling into and exploiting. Tis basic conjuring, Lisette darling. Have you not been practicing? You should have seen her face when I told her she had the power of our kind. She went from frightened, to dumbstruck to angry, and then back to frightened all over again." Beatriz laughed.

Lisette covered her ears as Beatriz's laughter increased in volume. Soon it would shatter the inside of her head.

"The spectrum of emotions was painted over her pretty face, so visible, so animated like one of those silent movies. Remember when we used to see those pictures with our fancy clothes and fancy men, and we would walk with our gloved hands in theirs, just to fit in, even though we had the ability to crush them with our minds? Those old days and those old silly pictures, everything contingent on facial expressions, totally reliant on sight. So much could be read from the simplest of expressions. It was like that, all there, painted on her pathetic little face. I've never seen such anger, especially when she thought I was you the whole time." Beatriz laughed again.

"She would not believe that I am capable of—"

"Believe it or not. But you might be right. Though, she kept called me Lisette." Beatriz cleared her throat. "'Oh Lisette, how could you do this to me? You said it was to be mine. Why, why, why?' She begged like a puppy dog with big puppy dog tears." Beatriz cleared her throat again. "Child, this is for your own good. This mission was only a test. It must happen this way, blah, blah, blah."

Lisette cringed at the sound of Beatriz's spot-on impersonation of herself, but knew in her heart that Peachy would not have believed. "She only needed to take one look into your eyes to see you lacked a soul, to know that you were not me."

"Well I am the better-looking twin," Beatriz chuckled at herself. "Come to think of it, yes, one instance, when my beautiful boy cracked his pistol into her skull, I brought her back from the brink of death. She might have thought for a moment that you and I were not the same person, so hard to tell. Her eyes were bloodied and turned this way and that. How do they say? It was a sight for sore eyes. Oh, dear me, did I make a pun? I think I did! Look at me being so funny after so long. Yes…I still got it. It is so good to be back among the depraved." Lisette held the phone away from Beatriz's horrendous laughter.

"Peachy will not have believed. She is smarter than—"

"You think she is smart? One look inside her showed me that you hadn't done a thing with her. Why the girl chose you to show herself to you is beyond me. If she were under my care, she'd be more powerful than all of us combined, but you had her, and your inability to do anything with her probably means she has already bled out and hungry little animals have all but picked her bones clean." Beatriz smacked her lips. "So tasty."

"I'll ask you again and then I am hanging up. What do you want?"

"I want the girl. I want the amulet, both of which are missing."

Lisette sprang from her chair. She had not expected this.

"Your little saint took it and she has no business with it. She knew nothing, you dalt! Nothing at all! Who knows where she went with it? She could be anywhere. She sure as hell isn't anywhere here." She growled. "It was my turn, Lisette. It was mine to begin with! I earned it! I'm the one who should possess it."

Beatriz's voice reached through the airwaves and wrapped around Lisette's neck, choking life from her. Lisette closed her eyes, doing everything in her power to shut her sister out and barely succeeding.

"That little half-breed knew exactly what to do. Knew what to say, how to say it and when. Everything was orchestrated perfectly. You should have seen her! She glowed with the power of it when it rested against her heart."

Impossible. Lisette shook her head in disbelief. No one ever wore the amulet without years of training. Then again, it had belonged to Peachy's mother and so it favored her bloodline. Lisette knew it all along. Good, this was good.

"Are you surprised?" Beatriz laughed. "Did you not see this alternate ending when you planned your little swipe and swap? Goodness. She played you for a fool. I wonder for how long?"

"Have you ever entertained the possibility that I wanted her to have it? That perhaps I sent her away?"

"I do not believe you are *that* cunning, sister. Your attempt at fabricating confidence is unbecoming and ugly. Where is she?"

"How would I know?"

"I see that you have already started looking, or did you forget that as your twin, I see what you see. Where is she?"

"You will have to fight me every step of the way to get any information from me."

"You are willing to risk our existence?" she asked and then whispered, "are you willing to risk the girl's love for you? Once she finds out who you really are, that you share equal blame for her mother's death, do you think she will forgive you?"

"I think she will love me more."

"You are as lost in the heavens as Peachy, but that is beside the point. If Peachy is where I think she is, we are all as good as dead. It is only a matter of time before they come for us to finish out their sentence. But worry not, sister. *I* will help you. *I* will clean up your mess as *I* always have, but this time there will be consequences. People will die."

"People always die when you're around."

"Help me and you have my word that I will not harm her."

"Your words mean nothing."

"Okay, do not help me and when I find her, and I *will* find her, I will keep her at the edge of death for eternity. Being buried in a cement block for thirty-seven years will seem like a welcomed respite. Whatever you decide makes no difference to me. With or without you, I will not rest, will not close my eyes, won't even blink until I find her."

"If you are so sure in your ability to find her, why waste my time?" Lisette didn't let Beatriz respond. "You need me."

"I don't deny it. I do need you, but I don't need your consent to use you. It might take me longer, but I have the time." Lisette nearly dropped the phone. Her head burned in agony. "Do you feel that? Do you feel me crawling inside your head, searching your thoughts, building walls to entrap you to get what I need? I've already found Peachy's soul and have begun working."

"So pathetic and weak." Lisette gripped the phone so tightly she could've bent the metal in her hand.

"I suggest that you hide. Our sister will not be happy that you have given the only remaining amulet to your street rat. Alone I may not be able to take you, but with Adèle, you are as good as dead."

"She will not believe you."

"She needn't believe *my* words," said Beatriz. Lisette's phone chimed with an incoming text message. "Goodness, did I send all? I'm all thumbs, I'm afraid. Call me if you have a change of heart. Ta." And the phone went dead. Lisette thumbed through photos of the incoming text message. Peachy running for the carriage house, inside the big house itself, on the ground, scared, bloodied and finally with the amulet around her neck!

Lisette took her SIM chip out of her phone, bent it in half before obliterating it in the garbage disposal. She threw only what she would need into a bag and rummaged through her workroom for essential supplies. She needed a safe place where she could work to ensure that no one would be able to get to Peachy. But first, she needed to find the other person that had been with Peachy that day.

CHAPTER NINE

"Come on, pick up." Minette tried Peachy's cell phone for the thirtieth time. It went straight to voice mail again. She didn't worry about someone trying to trace the call; she used a burner. Her fear that something major had gone wrong was confirmed when Peachy didn't meet at the agreed-upon location and a week had passed with no word. But the worse thing was that Minette had no one to call. Their mission only involved the two of them. Peachy never mentioned anyone else. As far as she knew, Peachy was as alone as Minette.

She swallowed the last of her bourbon even though she didn't need it. It had already done its job of numbing her. She threw the empty bottle across the room of her tiny dwelling, a shack on stilts, a few feet of air between the floor and the Mississippi River and all its hissing, jaw-crushing inhabitants. The bottle didn't even shatter as she hoped it would. Funny thing was, now with a mind full of alcohol, she finally saw how dangerous the job had been.

Everyone knew of Adèle Blanque's reputation and the type of person she was—a known murderer for hire, untouchable, with unlimited means. What if she had found the USB safe hacking drive and had the means to trace it? Minette took the SIM out of her replacement phone and chucked it out the window into the Mississippi. She ran her hand through her short black hair; it was greasy and hadn't been washed for days. She smelled too, but who was going to say something to her? She opened her fridge and pawed around for a beer, found one, twisted the lid and tossed that out the window too.

Until the alcohol-induced state of mind, it never occurred to her that perhaps Peachy had been successful in her quest to get the goods and maybe she'd decided to keep it to herself. Peachy had gone on about how expensive it was, and she had speculated about how much they could get for it on the black market. Peachy had never double-crossed Minette before, but she was human and apt to change her mind when it suited her. Maybe she took one look at the jewel and said fuck it, she'd try a new life on her own. The thought crossed Minette's mind from time to time when she went on jobs with insanely high rewards. She didn't want to think that Peachy would do that to her. They were in love—well, Minette was the one in love.

Minette didn't know if her tears were because she was angry that perhaps Peachy had ghosted her and left with their share of the money, or because she might have been caught, tortured, and killed. In either case, Minette felt incredibly devastated and lonelier than she had ever felt before.

Minette was startled by the sound of pounding on her door. She pulled herself to her feet from where she had passed out on the floor. Someone was about to get their ass handed to them for bothering her at this god-awful hour. "Whoever the hell you are, you better have a good fucking excuse! It's three in the goddamn morning." Minette opened the door, leaving one chain locked, but with enough visibility that the person on her doorstep could see her Louisville Slugger resting at her shoulder. "Who are you and what do you want?" It was an older woman. The only other detail she could see was that she carried a large travel bag.

"I am looking for a mutual friend."

"Sorry, wrong house." She slammed the door, sliding bolts, fastening locks. She knew this day might come—the day Adèle's people would track her down. She should have thought through an escape plan instead of drinking and feeling sorry for herself for five days straight. But what did it matter? What did any of it matter now? She hadn't any more energy to devote to it.

"I am looking for Peachy."

It was as if someone reached inside her and put a chokehold on her heart. "Sorry." Minette knew her voice quivered. "No one by *that* name lives here."

"Listen to me. I know about the job. I know it wasn't successful. I am here to help."

Minette rested her head against the door, speculating whether she should trust this stranger.

"Please, Peachy is in grave danger. She's alive, but she needs help. Let me in and I'll explain as much as I can."

Against her better judgment, Minette opened the door. If she were to find her friend and know the truth, she'd need to take the risk. More sliding of locks and metal on metal, Minette peered around the tall woman before hurrying her inside. Minette's grip on the baseball bat was still white-knuckled. She flipped on a small lamp and got a better look at her visitor. She was a black woman in her sixties or seventies, dressed in a long gold and teal dress with a tignon, more befitting of going to the opera—rather performing at the opera given the way she stood—tall and regal, than standing in her shitty one-bedroom shack.

"Thank you, child." Minette joined the woman in surveying her tiny home, noticing for the first time how much of a sty it was. Every surface was littered with beer bottles, empty cups, and dirty plates. She suddenly noticed a smell and realized she needed to take her trash out, like last week.

"Look lady, I got like two hours before I need to get up. Maybe we can start with who you are and how you know our mutual acquaintance."

"My name is Lisette. Peachy is like a daughter to me. I am the one who sent her on the job to the *Spanish Rose*."

"You sent her on the job?" Minette reaffirmed her grip on her baseball bat. "Look, lady, if you're here for your cut, I didn't get shit, so you're wasting your time."

"That is the furthest thing from my mind."

"Mine too." Minette slumped into a chair as the baseball bat clunked to the ground. "Is she okay?"

"I've reason to believe that she is okay. Hurt, but alive. How are you child?"

"How did you find me?" Minette took measures to ensure no one knew where she lived. She didn't get mail and siphoned utilities. Her place was only accessible via boat. Not even Peachy had stepped foot into her home.

"It wasn't easy. I'll give you that, but I have my ways."

"You talk like her." Minette snuffled.

"Like how, child?"

"Cryptic. Evasive. Like she didn't want me to really know her."

"I see." The woman eyed the chair. "May I?"

"Sorry, I'm not usually *this* rude." Minette stood to clear items off her only other kitchen chair. "Have a seat..."

"Lisette."

"Right. Sorry. Have a seat, Lisette."

"Thank you, Minette."

"So."

"Listen to me, child. I am not here to hurt you or to find fault. I am here because I love Peachy and will do anything in my power to find her. It was my fault for sending her on the job and taking her away from you. I can tell that you love her very much."

Minette thought she was done with the waterworks, but they came back as plentiful as ever. "I love her, but I don't think the feeling is mutual, and I'm okay with that, for now." She laughed at the absurdity of her statement and how pathetic it was that she was in love with someone who didn't feel the same way. Peachy wasn't available, never had been. She kept her secrets inside her, never divulged anything private, even when they were intimate. Minette had spilled her heart, but Peachy never shared so much as a story or memory of herself, let alone the fact that she lived with a woman who looked like she was Marie Laveau's twin sister.

"Peachy expresses love in her own unique way. Do not take it personally. She has always been that way since she was a child."

"A child? How long have you known her?"

"I raised her from the age of twelve."

"Raised her?" Minette failed at holding back tears because she didn't know a thing about her supposed lover, tears because her supposed lover had family that she never mentioned, and tears because she missed her supposed lover more than anything in the world.

"The fact that she trusted you on the most important job of her life tells me you are very important to her."

Lisette's words didn't help soothe the ache she felt inside. She wiped her tears with her hand. "So what do you need from me? I can run through the job if you want, tell you where I think it went south."

"I know as much as I need to. That's not why I am here."

"Why are you here?"

Lisette looked around the house. "I need a place to stay."

Minette only had one bedroom, one bathroom, two TV tables, a couple of chairs and a crappy couch. "You want to stay here? What you see is what I have. This place isn't even mine. I found it abandoned about a year ago. Electricity is spotty at best."

"And who else knows about it?"

"No one."

"It's perfect. Before I say anything further, there are things you must know."

"Like?"

"Peachy was successful in retrieving the amulet."

"She was!" Minette sat up straight. "Holy shit. So where is it? Where is she?"

"That is complicated."

"Do you think she pawned it?"

"No. That I know for certain."

"So what then?"

"It is complicated."

"So it's going to be like this? Everything's *too* complicated to explain to me and I won't understand?"

"That is not what I mean, child. I am sorry I gave that impression. There are things I want you to know that will impact your decision to be further involved."

"What the hell does that mean?"

"I am in danger."

"What kind of danger?"

"Adèle is my sister—"

"Oh shit." Minette wondered how fast she could make it out the open window, thinking she would fare better treading water in the Mississippi rapids than tangling with Adèle.

"Please child, do not fear me. I do not share the same beliefs as my sister. She has gone one way with her practice of voodoo, and I've gone another. We couldn't be more different. There was a time when we were close, but those days are long over. She's grown evil in her heart and to complicate matters even more, another one of my sisters has shown up. I've reason to believe that Peachy encountered this particular sister on the job and that is where things went sideways."

"Damn." Minette stood, feeling both elation that her friend hadn't abandoned her and also anguish knowing that she was missing. "So this sister, where is she? What do we need to do to find Peachy?"

"Again, complicated. Going about finding her won't be easy, for this sister is more powerful than Adèle and I combined."

"When you say powerful, you mean like voodoo? Like you're a voodoo*er*, or practitioner queen or whatever?"

"Something like that."

"Wow." The way Lisette dressed and spoke suddenly made a world of sense. A living breathing voodoo queen sat in her midst. Minette's furnishings seemed entirely inadequate. She sat back down but mimicked Lisette, sitting up straight and crossing her legs, as if befitting herself with a little bit of elegance would make up for her lack of decorum. "So what do they know?"

"They both know of my involvement, but I am confident they do not know about yours. That likelihood will increase if I were to stay here. You have my word that I will take protective measures to prevent our discovery. So I'll ask you again, knowing what you know now, am I welcome here?"

"If it means finding Peachy, you can live here forever. You can have my bed."

"That's not necessary. The couch will suit me just fine."

Minette eyed the couch and chose not to reveal that she'd found six cats living in it before claiming it as her own.

"I will not forget your hospitality."

"Unfortunately, that is all I have to give."

"Certainly there is more, child. Tell me, what is your specialty?"

"Tech. Hacking. Invisibility. I can get inside, blend in plain sight and get upward of twenty cameras wired in under an hour."

"And on the up-and-up?"

"Freelance swamp boat tour guide."

"Good. Good. I will also have you know that going about finding Peachy requires that I search in ways that are untraditional."

"What do you mean?" Minette eyed Lisette's bag. "Oh. Got it. Voodoo queen, big, big bag of voodoo things."

"And there are items that I might need from town from time to time, odd items that do not mean much by themselves, but when they are brought together, they are important. If you are willing, there is an opportunity to be more involved, but I do not want to further risk your safety until you are ready."

"I'll do anything, anything I can, if it means finding her. I'm ready right now."

"At three in the morning, child?"

"Right." Minette stifled a yawn, reminding her that Lisette was probably right. "I'll get you blankets. What's mine is yours. The bathroom is right over there." Minette stood and paused.

"She might show up, right? We've had to lay low before. Do you think it's just that?"

"I believe that anything is possible."

"Do you think she is hurt?"

"I pray that her spirit isn't broken."

CHAPTER TEN

Peachy jolted awake. Someone screamed bloody murder! They were crying, sobbing more like. It annoyed the hell out of her. They needed to stop. She needed to rest. She felt tears on her face. *She* had been crying and that annoyed her even more. The goddamn dream felt so real this time. Her heart pumped as if she had been physically running through the marble maze of the *Spanish Rose*. She still heard the laughter of that disembodied voice reverberating in her head, the taunts and the screams bouncing around and knocking her down. This time, though, that guiding voice that had shown her how to escape last time almost didn't show up.

Peachy barely escaped a bullet to the brain. She still felt the cold steel upon her temple, still felt the vibration of the cocking of the hammer. She tried to move, wanted to get up, but her efforts were futile. She was too weak, and she would pay too painful a price to even try. She couldn't stop hyperventilating. Tears overwhelmed her. The pain of her injuries was more than she could bear. The pulsating feeling against her chest, the radiating energy of the amulet, were constant reminders of the price she'd paid for taking it.

She squeezed her eyes shut, hoping against all odds that when she opened them, she would be at home, in her own bed and Lisette would be down the hall. They'd share a pot of coffee.

"Druem," Peachy heard. "Druem."

The soothing voice of her captor. The voice of the woman who whispered tranquilizing words—words that Peachy didn't understand but felt like a familiar memory, bathing her with comfort, warmth, and light. Why did her captor care if she lived or died? Who was this woman that held her when she awoke in agony? Peachy wasn't frightened of her anymore, couldn't be, for she felt peace when the woman held her body against her own when she awoke from a nightmare and couldn't catch her breath. Peachy inhaled her scent, an intoxicating mix of flowers, pages of books, fire, smoke, and something else…paint.

The woman's home was a refuge and the woman her haven. Peachy felt it when she grazed the woman's soft skin with the very tips of her fingers and when she gazed into her expressive gold and yellow eyes, the last image she saw before falling asleep. The woman caused her no harm. The horror existed in Peachy's own mind. As long as she stayed awake, she was free from it. That was harder than it seemed and always a battle. Her routine became predictable: she'd awaken from horror and in pain, fall back to sleep, awaken again, more horror and more pain, and again and again and again. She lost track of how many times the cycle occurred. One thing remained constant: the woman was there to hold her throughout.

Just because Peachy felt safe didn't mean she didn't want to get the hell home. When she could stay awake for extended periods, she looked for that opportunity and kept a watchful eye, observing her surroundings and the woman. She mentally recorded everything about the woman in order to use it against her when the time was right. That goal proved difficult because this woman with catlike eyes and reflexes did everything with fastidious precision. The way she cleaned, how she arranged jars on a shelf—according to height—how she cooked, and how she cared for her home seemed measured and exact. Peachy looked for hints or cracks, noting what to touch and not touch, what to move and not to move, for when she exited, if there ever came the right time.

One major two-hundred-pound obstacle stood in her way, the beast. It always eyed her every movement. She would lift her arm and the cat would look. She wiggled a toe and the cat would look. In addition to the cat, there were also the rodents, one black the other white, who appeared from time to time, who always seemed to alert the woman when Peachy tried to get up or slip out the back door. They were little fucking tattletales as far as she was concerned. At this rate, she worried she'd never find her moment to escape.

When she tired of looking for ways to breakout, her observations turned to studying the woman. They were the same build, height, and same weight. The woman had more muscle tone and she also appeared a few years older than Peachy. She had lustrous, wavy black hair with copper, gold, and red tones that cascaded down her back. She tied it with a bit of string or wove it in a braid when she cooked, cleaned, or tended to Peachy. Peachy wondered how long it took her to braid it since the woman had so much of it. Her olive skin shone gold at times, especially in the light of the fire or when sunlight filtered through the diamond-shaped windows, some of which had bits of colored glass that cast rainbows throughout the house.

Peachy swore that one time she had noticed copper spots on the woman's skin, but she couldn't be sure because the woman usually wore several layers of clothing. When she returned from the outdoors, her cheeks were flushed, her lips were pink and her hair sometimes stood on end from the static. Peachy's favorite thing about her were her intense, mesmerizing cat-like eyes that constantly transformed depending on her mood. At times they were slivers of black within rich golds, yellows, and greens. At other times, they were dark and accepting, especially when Peachy caught hold of her gaze and held it. It felt like the woman was reading her soul, and it stole Peachy's breath every time. The woman would tell her to breathe, though not through words, but in a way that Peachy could not describe, as if it originated inside her mind. The sensation felt familiar.

"I am Peachy," she told the woman one night after a horrible dream.

"Peachy?" The woman pointed to Peachy's chest and then to her own. "Noomi. Ti. Noomi," she said.

"Noomi." Peach placed her hand upon Noomi's chest, where it rested until they woke up the next day.

Peachy had finally found her opportunity. She made it out the door and beyond the tree line—almost. She even managed to get her shoes on, though tying them was impossible with one bandaged hand and the other still braced against her chest. Her energy grew, though, every day, making her somewhat faster and able to trudge through the knee-high drifts of snow, but she needed better shoes and proper clothing. She had a knife in her hand this time too. One she'd swiped the day before. Out of the corner of her eye, she felt the cat. It slinked toward her followed by Noomi. She felt a twinge of regret that leaving might have been a bad idea.

"Oh, hey. Hi. Yeah, so I'm leaving now. Thank you for everything. Seriously. Thank you. You saved my life and I'll forever be grateful." Peachy grabbed her side that ached from her effort and everything tender and sore. "I mean that."

"Kudo," said Noomi. "Hurt."

Holy shit. Noomi had spoken English. Her tone and enunciation were all wrong, as if she had moments ago learned that one single word. Peachy hadn't the time to interpret how, but her curiosity won her over. "What did you say?"

"Are hurt."

"Wow. Um, yes, I *was* hurt. I'm feeling *much* better, thanks to you. I hope you don't mind, but I needed the coat, the one I came with isn't quite vogue, if you know what I mean. I'd stick out like a sore thumb." Peachy attempted to laugh at her joke, but her world faded and she stumbled backward, thankfully against a tree. Her heart raced at an ungodly speed, and the blood in her head swirled about. "So," she played it off, "which way to… town?" She swallowed the lump in her throat.

"Nokita tu." Noomi held her hands in front of her, shaking her head.

"I've taken up too much of your fffloor." Peachy patted her broken arm. "It feels mmuch betterrr…" She began to shiver uncontrollably. "Thanks ffffor eve…" She dropped the knife. Her eyes widened, wondering what Noomi would do about that, but she didn't do anything, didn't even eye it. Rather, she approached Peachy, opened her coat, pulled the oversize shirt from Peachy's jeans, and placed her hands on her skin. Peachy nearly lost her breath at the sensation. A liquid warmth overtook her and filled her from the inside out. She moaned and closed her eyes and fell into Noomi's arms. When she opened her eyes, Noomi nodded, as if she understood her wish to leave. She led Peachy back inside.

"Um, can I take some food, maybe some of that?" Peachy pointed to a cut of bread and wedge of cheese.

The woman nodded and gathered the items along with fruit and a small jar of something, probably jam.

"Thank you."

Noomi eyed the canvas shoes at Peachy's feet and fetched her own fur-lined boots.

"No, those are yours. I can't take them."

"Take."

"Thank you." Peachy's growling stomach filled the silence and suddenly her eyes became much too heavy to keep open. "I need…" She felt light-headed and fell into the chair, doubting the entire day. "Can I have…" Her mouth felt dry and she felt ravenous. Maybe a light snack would help. Noomi placed a steaming bowl of soup and a thick crust of bread before her. Peachy devoured everything, closed her eyes and leaned back in the chair. She thought about where she would go, but she must have fallen asleep, for when she awoke, she wore another soft, oversize nightshirt and was inside her bed of pelts and blankets. She felt the warmth of the crackling great fire. She inhaled Noomi's scent deeply and held on to her tightly. She stopped thinking about trying to escape. It was a dumb idea.

Another evening turned into another day and several days went by, and Noomi continued to help Peachy with everything, nourishing her body with soups, crisp water, and herbed teas. She bathed her, changed her clothes, and soothed her healing body with salves that she had blended herself. She changed her bloodied wraps from her hand and her head that hurt nonstop. She made Peachy get up and walk, even when she didn't want to because it hurt, but Peachy was glad because she felt stronger every day because of it.

When Peachy wandered about Noomi's home by herself, she learned more and more about her savior. Her gray stone walls were covered with fabrics of rich colors—golds, reds, oranges, and colors that Peachy couldn't describe because she hadn't seen such beautiful colors before. Down another corridor were Noomi's pools where she had started taking Peachy for baths. It was Peachy's favorite room that had both cold and hot bodies of water that filled with runoff and heated from underground springs. Whenever Noomi was outside for extended periods of time, sometimes she reentered the home from that room, with her hair wet, freshly bathed, which led Peachy to assume that it was also accessible from the outside too.

There was also a great room separated by a thick pelt that held empty shelves, cuts of boards and tools, stacks upon stacks of books, loose papers, art supplies, brushes and jars of paint. The room looked under construction, as if the builder stopped one day and never came back. Peachy surmised she was the reason the room had been abandoned. She required almost nonstop care, though not as much as before. She spent more and more time upright in a chair. She still fell asleep at times, but she tried not to, for she still had the nightmares. She spent her days gazing out the window. She hoped for sun or to see the stars at night, but a great storm blanketed them and shrouded them in white.

Every day Peachy listened to the way Noomi spoke, hoping she would recognize a pattern within the woman's strange dialect. She listened for clues of her whereabouts, and whenever possible, they shared their language with each other. Noomi showed her an item like a spoon, or a bowl or pot, or piece of food. Peachy would repeat the name in her own language, and they learned much from each other and shared several smiles.

Always at night, Noomi held her when she broke free from her nightmares and soothed her with whispered words and touches, which was the only thing that helped Peachy remember she wasn't playing Russian Roulette and losing.

CHAPTER ELEVEN

"*She is scared of you. Why do you think she wants the amulet? Anything you want can be so. Be here, be there, be anywhere. The power is already yours!*"

"*Child, listen to me, tis Lisette—*"

"*Don't listen to her. Listen to me, child. Tis Lisette's better half. The one who did not lie to you. Oh my, how you've grown. You're still a weak and pathetic image of your mother. You can run, but sooner or later you'll tire and when that happens—*"

"*Imagine that you are a bird; imagine you can fly. Go there now...*"

"*No. No. No! I have clipped her wings. Let's play a game instead!*"

Noomi pulled her hands away from Peachy. There were two spirits this time. One providing aid, fending off the evil entity, attempting to neutralize it and steer it awry. The other presence pulled her to that dark place and made every attempt to cripple her spirit. Noomi had long ago made peace with the fact that Peachy had not given her consent to see inside her. Noomi had no choice. Aside from Peachy's body, which healed at a remarkable rate, her mind seemed to decline. There was no doubt she battled constant torment. As a result, she would avoid sleep if she could, pacing the halls, looking at books, drawing—anything but closing her eyes and resting. When she did succumb to slumber, she would hold on to Noomi as if clinging to her meant life or death. She began following Peachy into her dreams, helping her navigate the misery that crawled inside.

Noomi became further involved, delved deeper, and ached for Peachy, especially when she saw images of two giant beasts of men beating her senseless. Noomi felt her pain and began sharing it with her. She helped Peachy conjure dreams about better times. She helped her replace the horror with calming memories. Lately, Peachy had dreamt about another woman with whom she was intimate. Noomi took refuge in knowing that Peachy had lovely memories to hold. It was no wonder Peachy avoided sleep, a time of chaos, in favor of the serenity she found when she was awake.

For now, while the spirits battled in her mind, she appeared to be getting some rest in her favored spot, a great plush, green felt chair that sat near the warmth of the fire and faced a great window displaying the majesty of the Blue Mountains shrouded in snow. Peachy's legs were stretched on the stone ledge, a pillow propping them up, one arm resting at her side, the other still bound against her chest. Save for the casting of her arm, she was nearly healed. Without the covering of bruises, Noomi could see that Peachy was young and beautiful—high cheekbones and thick eyebrows that nearly connected in the middle of her forehead. Her copper-colored eyes took in every detail of her surroundings. When she locked her gaze with Noomi, she pulled everything that she could from her, like tranquility and assurance.

Her voice was soft, with a provoking and playful tone. She smiled whenever Noomi tumbled over the pronunciation of her language, which was getting better every day. As a Seer, Noomi possessed the gift of language arts. Coupled with seeing into Peachy's soul, she nearly understood Peachy's dialect, although pronouncing the words was a different story.

Nothing spoke more to her than the delicacy of Peachy's laughter. Her mere smile filled Noomi with light and made her feel shy at times, especially when Peachy lingered a look. Despite Peachy's outward display of strength and confidence, she struggled with anger every day, more exhausted from lack of sleep.

One thing was for sure: Peachy's body, which Noomi had come to know from bathing, dressing, and sleeping with her, made Noomi ache with desire. Peachy always wanted to be touched, as if she hadn't been held a day in her life. Another certainty was that her body lacked the identifying and unique markings of her kind, which let Noomi know that she may not be a Heather after all. However, the fact remained: Peachy possessed an amulet with script from their realm. To complicate the matter, the spirits inside her demonstrated traits of Noomi's kind, but a different combination, one more archaic than which Noomi was familiar. There was no doubt that these entities wanted the amulet and would kill her for it. The only peace Noomi held inside her own heart was that these entities could not physically harm Peachy.

Noomi needed to consult her most trusted mentor, an ancient and enlightened Heather, Nefertari the Only, whose mastery of several gifts had earned her a long-held position as one of the five leaders in power over the Realm of the Heathers. Nefertari would have the answers to Noomi's questions and provide guidance and strategy for helping Peachy. *Peachy of the Sky*. That time would come soon, but for now, Peachy needed rest, and for now, she seemed to be doing so without much trouble.

Noomi covered her with a blanket and then made her way into her reading room with the intention of getting some work done. She found Sissy and Missy brushing Gabin's long tail while they chatted, played, and rested beside the fireplace, their new favorite spot, one that was away from the healing of their guest.

"*How is she?*" Gabin asked.

"*One would think that ye care about her the way you're talkin'.*"

"*I'm not completely heartless.*"

"*I know,*" Noomi said. "*Thanks for the space, for sleepin' in here. I know it's not your usual spots.*"

"*Sleepin' here is much better'n bein' roused by a terrible rage and her overly loud and dramatic dreams,*" Gabin replied. "*Her kind has a primitive way o' reactin'.*"

"*And ye and I are better?*"

"*Better'n that.*"

"*Would ye not be scared if ye were lost and hurt and totally reliant on strangers for kindness?*" Noomi emphasized that last part.

"*She is as strange and awkward to us as we are to her,*" Missy said.

"*Tell that to me dear sister, would ye?*"

Gabin stood, stretched and shifted away from Noomi, an action Noomi had seen too much of these past few weeks. Gabin pretended not to hear the wisdom in Noomi's words.

"*Tis sad that she fights while she sleeps,*" Sissy said, joining Missy as they crawled onto Noomi's hands and then her shoulder.

Noomi sighed deeply. "*I don't know how to help her.*"

"*Nefertari will know,*" Gabin said. "*When will ye journey?*"

"*When I can afford to step away. I worry that she will spiral while I am gone.*"

"*We will take care o' her,*" Missy and Sissy said.

"*I wish I could help,*" Gabin added. "*I need to hunt.*"

"*Gab, please. I'll need your help if I am to journey with haste.*"

"*Gawf. So much haste and unpredictability. Tis almost too much to bear.*"

"*Gawf yourself, while ye lay there, preenin' about as if ye hadn't a care in the land.*"

"*If ye would have listened to me, ye would also not have a care in the land. Look 'round. Tis in utter disarray with a quite unstable woman with an amulet 'round her neck that causes her pain. I told ye.*"

"*I made me decision. The least ye can do is support me with it!*" Noomi said and held her head in her hands. "*Sorry, I didn't mean to lose me temper. Again.*"

"*Have ye eaten?*" Noomi's mice friends asked her.

"I am not hungry."

Noomi had put her life—all of their lives—on hold to help Peachy. When she had begun her journey from Heatherton all that time ago, an almost full passing of their moons, she had been eager to resume work on her reading room—set the stone tiles, stain the shelves, arrange her books according to numbering scheme, and display the maps she had created on her walls. Peachy took all her time and mental energy. Gone were her carefully planned hours and days, her regimented routine, her once-upon-a-time list of projects that she'd complete, one precisely before the next and in an order that made sense and relied on efficiency.

Now her array of tasks presented themselves in no particular order because they needed tending to all at once. It mattered not which order she approached the mountain of dishes or the scrubbing of her tabletops, or the sweeping and washing of other surfaces and floors. Likely her fireplaces, pits, and hearths should be tended to first, for soon they would suffer needlessly in the cold, and meals would also be cold if she didn't make a trip to her outbuilding for more wood the priority.

"Let us make ye a soothin' tea? Even Gab will help won't ye?"

"'Tis okay. I'd rather have grass leaf. I am utterly spent."

Noomi ventured to her bookshelf to retrieve a wooden box. She slumped to the ground, joining the rest of her family nestled in a pile of pillows and pelts. She wrapped a blanket around her shoulders. She stuffed the special grass leaf, which she handpicked and cured over the past harvest, into her pipe, lit a splinter of wood and ignited a whole new world. She closed her eyes, inhaled, and blew out white sweet smoke that instantly calmed her nerves, her frustration, and confusion.

Sissy and Missy joined her on her lap. Noomi didn't mean to fall so deeply into sleep, but the warmth of the fire and being nestled against Gabin and the glow of the setting sun, meant she had no say in the matter.

A terrible sound woke them. It was Peachy, again, though this time it sounded as if she was in physical pain. "Her lands!" Noomi exclaimed. She met the concerned gazes of her friends and her sister. The four of them raced from the room to find out what happened.

"Peachy!"

She lay on the floor.

"Wake up, please." Noomi shook her, but she wouldn't rouse. Noomi gasped upon seeing a trickle of blood from her ear. She placed her hands on the woman, shut her eyes and felt the iron grip of the evil entity choking the life from her. "Out!" she yelled and cast the thing onto its back. The images in her mind showed the evil being wrenching in pain and sniveling in defeat. Gone for now. "Peachy, please wake up," she said, smoothing her hair from her face.

Peachy groaned and shook her head.

"I am sorry I wasn't here to help. Please forgive me."

Peachy couldn't catch her breath, and she winced as Noomi pulled her to a sitting position. "Are ye okay?"

"Heni," Peachy said. The word that meant help.

Noomi nodded and closed her eyes, giving her the strength to mask the pain until Peachy's breathing came easier. Noomi realized she was drenched in sweat. *"She's hot with fever,"* Noomi said to her friends. *"Why does this keep happenin'? I will kill whoever keeps hurtin' her. What do I do?"*

"Get her in the pool," Gabin said. *"We'll figure it out later. Go!"*

"Let's go." Noomi carried her to the pool and set her down on the wooden bench. She unbuttoned her sweat-drenched nightshirt and tossed it aside. "This will feel better." Noomi smiled and smoothed Peachy's hair from her face. She began unraveling the strips of cloth that had bound her ribs and her arm since the beginning.

Peachy took a deep breath. Noomi held her chin and made her look into her eyes. "Be careful." Noomi rested her own hand on Peachy's broken arm, no longer braced or stabilized within the wrapping.

Noomi unraveled the rest of the brace, and when she saw the amulet, Peachy's eyes widened and she looked around as if she was expecting to be discovered. She began talking so quickly that Noomi couldn't make anything out. She took hold of Peachy's hands and closed her eyes.

"They want this. They will kill me for this. Please, you can't tell anyone that I have this."

Noomi opened her eyes and touched the amulet, fixing it jewel-side out. She placed her hand over it. "Ye are safe here."

"Sabi Tu," Peachy repeated.

"Yes. Safe with me and very good pronunciation." Noomi helped Peachy out of the rest of her clothing until she stood naked, free of bandages and wrap. Peachy displayed no unease or nervousness at her nakedness, even when Noomi studied her body. Noomi took her hand and helped her into the springs.

"Pa," Peachy said.

"Don't be scared."

Peachy shook her head. "Pesi." She placed her hand upon Noomi's chest and unbuttoned the top button and then the next, shaking all the while. Noomi understood what she needed. She took over and removed her own clothing until she stood naked with Peachy. She tensed when Peachy gazed at her, as if Peachy possessed the gift of sight and knew of Noomi's desire.

Noomi took her hand and led them into the steaming hot pool. She sat first and guided Peachy between her legs. Peachy rested against her and Noomi wrapped her arms around her. Peachy relaxed and Noomi knew what she wanted. So she gave it to her—the strength from her own body, her healing touch that Peachy craved. Noomi closed her eyes, but she didn't need to see inside Peachy to know that Peachy desired her. She felt Peachy's need in her soft whispers, in the way that she looked into her eyes, the way she wove their fingers together, the way she squirmed between her legs and grazed her fingers down Noomi's forearms. The sensation sent Noomi over an edge, fueling her inner animal. She nearly growled her desire, but she kept it from her lips so as not to scare Peachy.

Noomi whispered into her ear that it was time to get out. She helped Peachy from the pool and into a dry nightshirt.

She felt Peachy's tentative touch upon her hand. "Pesi. Alar ti."

Peachy had asked Noomi to see into her and had given her consent. Noomi closed her eyes to retrieve her message.

"Help me, please. I don't want to die for this thing around my neck. I'm so tired of fighting on my own. I know you are with me. I feel you inside. I can't do this by myself."

Noomi felt Peachy's lips upon her own before she opened her eyes. Peachy's kisses were tender at first and so were hers, both content to share the air between them before they deepened their connection. Peachy pressed against her. Noomi couldn't hold her any closer, so instead, she held her tighter. She gasped when Peachy's tongue grazed her lips, offering gentle licks that searched for more. Noomi claimed Peachy's mouth and moaned as she tasted her for the first time. Noomi was the first to pull away for fear she'd tumble off a ledge into an abyss she couldn't climb out of.

She rested her forehead against Peachy's, took her hands and closed her eyes. *"I will help ye to the best o' me ability. It will not be easy. I will need to seek guidance, but ye can trust me. I will not hurt ye. I need to know more, about ye, about the amulet. Can you do that?"*

Peachy nodded. "Beauaki kmai."

"Ye have a beautiful heart too, Peachy o' the Sky." She took Peachy's hand in hers and led them to her room. They would no longer sleep together on the floor. They would sleep in Noomi's bed. Together. Noomi knew that Peachy was sent here for a reason. She needed help, protection, and love.

CHAPTER TWELVE

Lisette awoke with a start. Her heart pounded and the veins in her head throbbed. Her twin! Crawling, creeping, digging for secrets in the recesses of her mind. Turning over memories. Latching on to certain ones like a laser lobotomy to her left temple. Looking for the amulet. Peachy and revenge. "Out!" she yelled. Her twin, cast upon her back, twitching and grabbing hold of her head and muttering rabid and rage-filled rancid words. Lisette flipped on the table lamp, reached for her glass of water and found it empty. More coughing and searching for her next breath. There was a rustling in the background. She had awoken Minette again.

"Lisette?"

"I am fine, child, just a bit of a scratch in my throat. I am sorry to keep you from your slumber."

"I was up," Minette said, but the shock and awe on her face when she opened the refrigerator for a pitcher of water told otherwise. She refilled another glass and handed it to her. Under the cast of light from the table lamp, Lisette realized how beautiful the girl's tattoos were: colorful and intricate designs and patterns that looked like a spider's web with fantastical creatures crawling about. The colors were vivid against her ivory skin and her shock of short black hair and green eyes.

"Thank you," she said after a cleansing drink. "Word to the wise, don't get old."

"It sounded more than a symptom of being old."

"I am an old lady, but a hearty one at that."

"Is there anything I can do? Another pillow, a fan? An exorcist?" Minette let out a nervous laugh and ran her hand through her hair. Her bangs were usually in her line of sight.

"No, no, child. All is okay." Lisette got up and joined Minette at the kitchen table.

They sat in silence until Minette exploded. "What are you even doing in here that helps you find her? I mean I get Voodoo, kind of, but you haven't left since you got here. I don't understand what you're doing. Who the hell are you yelling at? I might be able to help if you told me something. Anything. Have you thought of that?"

"Sit down, child. Let's talk. It is time."

"So talk," she said. She eyed Lisette's bronze basin she used to contact Peachy. "Maybe start there."

"This is not easy to explain."

"Yes, I know. None of this is easy to explain, but can you try? You're in my house for a reason. I refuse to believe it's simply because I'm off the grid. All I've been doing is running errands, retrieving black candles this week, loaves of blessed bread the week before. I hate being in the dark. You need to tell me what this is all about, give me something to go on. I can't sleep. All I think about is her. I wonder if she's hurt, if she's cut and run. I wake up every time I hear the slightest noise outside, thinking that it's her, and it isn't."

"I know, child." Lisette had kept Minette in the dark since taking up residence over a week ago. She had sent her on menial tasks, if only to get a sense of her work style and dedication. Though Minette's love for Peachy had already proven both of those things, Lisette wanted to be certain. She wanted Minette to ask for more responsibility, but it needed to be at Minette's explicit request. "When I explain there is a risk, you'll not believe me."

"Maybe I will, maybe I won't."

"And at any time, you can ask me to leave and I will."

"I can't decide until you tell me."

"The amulet I sent Peachy to retrieve wasn't simply jewelry. It was a priceless family heirloom. The amulet belonged to Peachy's mother. Her name was Rahimah. She was more powerful a practitioner than I will ever be. She would have given the amulet to Peachy herself, but she died before they got a chance to meet."

"That's sad." Minette cast her eyes downward.

"Tell me about your family, child?"

"There's nothing to tell. I didn't know them. My grandmother raised me until she died when I was twelve. I went into foster care but only lasted a month before I left. I've been on my own ever since. Put myself through high school and a little bit of technical school too."

"I can tell that your spirit is big and strong, Minette, albeit in a small frame." Lisette admired the girl's determination, tenacity, and strength packed into her petite body. "I am forever indebted and grateful for your generosity. I am glad we met, though I wish the circumstances were different."

"Me too," Minette said with a faint smile. "So how did you know Peachy's mother?"

"She was my sister."

"So you're Peachy's aunt and she didn't know that?"

"There are many things that I regret not telling her, but I proceeded in a way that I felt fit the situation. All would have been in the open once Peachy had returned from the job."

Minette rubbed her face in her hands. "So the amulet was her mother's, and something tells me it wasn't just worth a ton a money."

"Within it exists a form of energy with the ability to cause a chain of events to occur through written accounting."

Minette shook her head. "Like whoever wears it can tell the future?"

"Whoever wears it can *create* the future."

Minette leaned back, crossed her arms and knitted her eyebrows. "Go on."

"The rest might sound ludicrous, irrational, illogical, and by telling you, I am placing my entire trust in you."

"Have I not proven myself?"

"You have."

"Well then, out with it. Whatever you have to say I can handle."

"Voodoo is a disguise."

"Wait. What?"

"We, my sisters and I, are not Voodoo queens, far from it. Tis a total scam. The true queens of old died long ago and are no longer able to protest our methods. No one alive today would dare challenge our authority, especially because of the reputation that we've built and the fear that my sister perpetuates."

"Why a Voodoo disguise? That's very specific."

"Voodoo was an easy cover that allowed us to prey upon people's misunderstanding of the religion as well as their greed. In the end, when someone gets what they want, they really don't care what it's called. The story that the tour guides tell about the *Spanish Rose* isn't that far from the truth."

"You're talking about the slave revolt? My friend Jean runs that tour. That was your great, great, whatever ancestors, right?"

"It wasn't my ancestors who took the *Spanish Rose*. It was me and my sisters."

"Oh geez." Minette stood and looked out the window and then turned back around. "So you're a little older than I thought. No big deal. Go on. Go on." She let out a nervous laugh and blew her bangs out of her eyes.

"I led our home's participation in the slave rebellion, while my sisters Adèle and Beatriz, my twin, stayed behind to secure the home. However, their way of securing the home included murdering the family's children. They did not consult me in their plan of attack. They knew that I would not agree to their methods, and I knew that they would not listen to reason. When I returned home, it was too late. The children were dead. The heartbroken family promised us whatever we wanted if we would bring them back. We cannot raise the dead, but we could conjure images in their minds that their children were alive. Shortly thereafter, the family went insane, but only after giving us everything—the house, land, money, status. Word got out about our mastery of Voodoo. People sought our counsel and paid us exorbitant amounts of money to give them what they wanted. From then on, we assimilated, and we've done so ever since.

"Deep inside I wanted nothing to do with it, but for the love of my sisters, my twin especially, I went along willingly. I've lost count of the numbers of lives I destroyed for my own greed. There came a day when I couldn't do it anymore. I moved out of the *Spanish Rose*, distanced myself from my sisters and took no more from the fortune that we had created through our destructive ways. The day I found Peachy, the moment I saw her hiding in the alley behind my store, I knew I was right to change. My heart would have been too full of corruption to give her the love she required."

"So Peachy is, is…"

"She is of my blood as well."

"What does that mean? I mean, what are you exactly? You don't look any different than me. I've seen Peachy." Minette's cheeks blushed. "I didn't see…I mean, she looks like me."

"You are right. She looks similar to your kind, which is why we chose this world. We are similar in our physical makeup, save for a few key differences. The biggest is our skin, which bears markings similar to a zebra or a cheetah, but not as pronounced. Mine have faded significantly over the years."

Minette gave her a once-over, understanding. "But what about Peachy? She doesn't have markings."

"My assumption was that she was born more of this world than mine. There are still questions that I can't answer despite my long years."

"How old are you exactly?"

"Six hundred and seventy-three years old."

"Damn. And where are you from?"

"I am from the Realm of the Heathers. I am of the Fae race of Heathers. We are born with unique gifts. Some are born with the ability to shift into creatures. We can read minds and provide counsel. We possess a mastery of plants and minerals in order to heal, and we are gifted strategists with the ability to ensure a favorable outcome in times of war. My sisters and I were born with the ability to ensure the future. We are Tellers and can conjure any gift we want, anything we want, and we abused it. We became so powerful, shifting the balance among our kind to grossly unstable and in our own favor. No one dared challenge us. Anyone who tried regretted the day, and we began our murderous reign.

"Before we arrived here, we were moments away from our death. Before you ask, we deserved our sentence. We were eviler there than we were here, for we didn't need to hide our abilities among our kind."

"So the amulet is your kind's power source?"

"Not entirely, though it's because of that amulet that we've been able to exist for so long in this world."

Minette shook her head. "How did you manage to share it in your old world?"

"My sisters and I possessed our own amulets that were forged specifically for us. They were destroyed."

"But you can use Peachy's?"

"Not to the extent as if it were our own."

"So what happened? It kind of sounds like you lost."

"We were betrayed."

"By who?"

"Peachy's mother."

"Jesus."

"Our amulets were stolen from us one by one. Fate again became wild and free, and our time had run out. Moments before our sentence, my sisters and I had lost hope. Rahimah had convinced the elders to let us speak one last time. She had a plan. She had forged another amulet."

"Peachy's amulet?"

Lisette nodded. "Rahimah had learned she was pregnant and wanted to live, to ensure that she and her unborn child would be free and redeem our kind. She intended to save us, but my twin had her own ideas. Once she saw the new amulet, she had to have it. To this day, I can still hear Rahimah's cries, her pain, and agony for what she had lost. I wish I could tell her that she didn't die in vain, that her daughter is alive, beautiful, and gifted."

"You forgave your sister?"

"It only took a couple hundred years."

"Where was Peachy this whole time?"

"Another question that I do not know the answer to. I only knew that when the child showed up in the street behind my shop, there was no doubt that she was of my world and of my sister."

"Do you think Peachy could have cut and run? I mean, damn! With a weapon like that, you can give yourself anything you want, do anything you want." Minette nibbled on the tip of her thumbnail.

"Highly doubtful. She was unaware of its power, unaware of the gifts she possessed, and it isn't as easy to wield as you would think. It takes years of training. I regret sending her in there with no information whatsoever and now..." Lisette shook her head. She felt the tears building.

"What is it?"

"I do not want to tell you the rest of the story for it is the most difficult part."

"What else could compete with the story you just told me?"

"Peachy is hurt, badly. I am ashamed that I brought it upon her. I am doing everything that I can to help her."

"Hurt how? Tell me please?" Minette got up and knelt before Lisette. "Tell me what happened!"

"My sisters will stop at nothing to get the amulet back, and they search day and night for her. If they find her before me, they will kill her. I do what I can to impede their progress. I don't know how much longer I will be able to do so. I can't keep them from her without knowing more of what they're planning."

"Know more *how*?"

"I do not wish to risk your life along with hers."

"My life isn't anything without her! Please."

"The forces against us are brutal, Minette. You need to see what you are up against before you agree to go all in."

Minette nodded and wiped her eyes with the cuff of her sleeve.

"It pains my heart that you must see this, but you must know." Lisette handed her the cell phone. "Press play."

Minette ripped the phone from her hands. Lisette closed her eyes when she heard Peachy's screams at the hands of her twin.

Minette placed her hand to her mouth and shut her eyes. She turned off the recording and handed it back. "I'll kill them."

"They will not stop until Peachy is dead and that amulet is in their possession."

"Then what?" When Lisette said nothing, Minette shouted, "Then what? I still don't know what the hell you're doing!"

"I am doing everything I can to slow my twin's search, steer her away and provide counsel to Peachy. The basin is how I conjure a connection to her spirit, which exists in the Realm of the Heathers. I can communicate with my twin because we share a familial bond. I can see into her mind and she can see into mine. It is becoming increasingly difficult to protect Peachy. I have reason to believe that my twin will join with Adèle, and the two will work against me. I can only get the upper hand if I can see and hear their planning. I need eyes on them, Minette. I need eyes in the *Spanish Rose*."

"Tell me what to do."

CHAPTER THIRTEEN

"Ka?" Noomi asked. "Is yes?"

"Yes," Peachy nodded. She held up her newly casted arm, inspecting Noomi's work. She avoided eye contact. They both did for much of the morning. The blistering kisses they'd shared the night before propelled their relationship into tumultuous territory where they'd need to exercise caution. Peachy didn't trust herself to keep a safe distance from Noomi. "It's perfect." She wiggled her fingers, the only part of her forearm not wrapped in the cast. "Thank you."

"Is certain?" Noomi got up and gathered her supplies. The assortment of tools and bottles didn't fit in her hands, and a bottle fell off the table. "Gawf." She blew a few strands of hair from her eyes.

To make matters worse, Noomi's mice friends, who had long ago given up helping, now sat with Gabin playing with a pinecone, squeaking with childlike glee. Peachy wondered if they were having fun or making fun, or if they were simply animals making noises. The looks they gave Noomi caused her to flush and clench her jaw. Of all of the animals that Peachy knew, none of them elicited that type of reaction from people. Peachy still wrestled with the fact that they might be intelligent beings that could communicate with Noomi. The woman had several one-sided conversations quite often. Peachy learned their names were Missy, Sissy and the great cat's name was Gabin, who Noomi referred to as sister.

"Noomi? Can we talk?" Peachy needed to put to rest her uncertainty. She sucked at interpreting body language and decoding nonverbal cues. She wondered what Noomi's raised eyebrows meant, or the nibbling of her lip, or a glance upward. She already struggled with Noomi's language. More complications accomplished nothing.

"Time is healin' salve," Noomi said as she faced her bottles forward, organizing them according to height, taking longer than she normally did according to Peachy's past observations. Noomi gathered another set of bottles and dried herbs from a higher shelf. She looked at them before rummaging through a basket filled with strips of fabric. Peachy had never seen her rummage for anything.

"Please." If Peachy had the energy, she would have walked to Noomi and forced her to do as she said, but she still felt weak and needed help doing the simplest of tasks, one of which was standing on her own two feet and strong-arming the woman to look her in the eyes. "The salve can wait."

"Is risk to infect," Noomi said and glared at the cat. She muttered an acidic sounding word to her.

"Noomi, please, I—I already feel…never mind," she whispered. She looked at her cast that had already hardened. "Thank you so much for this."

Noomi sat opposite Peachy, finally making eye contact. "Is happy ye didn't have lastin' damage."

The way Noomi stumbled over pronouncing the words caused Peachy to want to kiss them right off her lips.

"Are sad?"

"No. Not at all. I feel great. Last night was the first time I slept, really slept in I don't know how long."

Noomi nodded. "Is relief to all." She motioned to her animal friends.

Peachy focused on her cast. "I just wondered if I made you feel uncomfortable. If I did, I'm sorry. Pesi, pesi." She hoped she pronounced the apology the right way. "So you can stop walking on eggshells." Noomi looked down and rubbed her temple. "Not literal eggshells. You don't have to tiptoe."

But that didn't help either because then Noomi looked at her feet, alternating between her toes and Gabin. "Oh, ye ask to me, last night we..." Noomi touched her lips and her cheeks flushed. A faint smile spread upon her lips.

Peachy made eye contact with Gabin who blinked at her slowly, got up and stretched before settling in her favored way, with her backside toward them. Peachy leaned back and cursed at herself. So stupid. Such a pathetic, injured and broken shell of her former self. Lost and at this woman's mercy. "Forget it."

"Forget it?" Noomi mimicked the words.

"Forget it."

She doubted Noomi understood a word of what she had said, but then Noomi stood and rounded the table. She knelt between Peachy's legs and took her hands into her own. She looked at her and made her feel like she was the only person on the planet. Noomi leaned toward her, hesitated, and then grazed her lips across Peachy's. The kiss's power ignited an inferno, robbing all the oxygen in order to do so. Peachy felt as though she'd combust and set the entire house aflame with the awe-inspiring magic within that kiss. Noomi's lips felt better than anything she'd ever felt, tasted better than any woman's she'd ever tasted. With that kiss came a renewed sense of wonder and hope all wrapped within the message.

Peachy took Noomi's face into her hands. It was her turn to pull everything she could from Noomi—her spirit, her longing, her arousal. She took and she took, and with it she hoped for her heart. Peachy pulled back. Both were breathless. "Fuck," she said. She felt her face flush. Now *she* avoided eye contact when she realized Gabin and the mice were staring at them.

"Does not need eggshells," Noomi said. "No to forget." She placed a gentle peck on Peachy's lips, as if that was the last word on the topic. Peachy laughed and met Noomi's eyes. They exuded warmth and tenderness and flickered a color she hadn't observed before. "Is good?" Noomi asked as she stood, motioning to the cast.

"Pa."

Noomi wore a confused look. "No?"

"Where I come from, people write stuff on it. Usually people sign their names or draw something."

Noomi shook her head. Peachy reached for one of Noomi's brushes and mimicked drawing on her cast. Then she handed the brush to Noomi.

"Aye." Noomi's eyes sparkled and she gathered three small jars of what looked like paint and dipped a brush into the well and started.

"How long do you think I'll have to keep this thing on?"

Noomi shook her head. "Nokita tu."

"Um, when can…" Peachy pointed to a knife and mimicked cutting the cast. "Off?"

Noomi pointed out the window. "When is green about, not white."

"Springtime?"

Noomi rose to retrieve a book and opened it. "Springtime?" She pointed to flowers, green grass, trees with leaves, creatures that were part animal and part whatever Noomi was—bronze beings with markings on their skin, morphing into birds or large cats. Peachy's heart thumped again. She tensed and shut the book.

"Is safe," Noomi said and opened it again. She turned each page, pointing to images and saying words in her language. Peachy repeated them until breathing came easier. She focused on Noomi's work. It looked like the beginnings of a map coming to life.

"What is fuck?" Noomi asked.

"What?" Peachy cleared her throat and sat up straight.

"Is fuck? Fuck, fuck fuck…when hurt, when happy, when kissed me."

Peachy couldn't help but laugh at this.

"Is important?"

Peachy laughed again, this time louder. "It means a lot of things."

"Fuck," Noomi said as she gestured to Peachy's cast presenting her work of art. "Fuck?"

"Sure. That works. It is fucking beautiful."

"Fuckin' is good?"

"Very!" Peachy laughed.

"Peachy likes fuck?"

Peachy smiled and nodded, feeling heat climb up her neck and settle on her cheeks.

"Me too." Noomi dipped her brush into her inkwell and resumed her art on Peachy's cast.

A few days later, after the dinner dishes had been cleared and put away, Peachy looked at books and watched Noomi mix a new batch of her healing salve. The hand that Beatriz had stabbed was the last to heal and still tender and stiff. It hurt more at night after a long day. Noomi must have sensed her pain, for she massaged it and it instantly felt better.

"How do you do that?" Peachy asked. "How do you heal me with your touch?"

"I give ye what is here." Noomi flexed her own arm and smiled.

"You give me your strength?"

Noomi nodded.

"You don't even need the salve?"

"Herbs for infection. Not Healer kind, from…" Noomi motioned upward, their mutual gesture to indicate where Peachy came from, the sky.

"The closest thing I can think of is a hundred-dollar-a-minute Swedish massage with a happy ending." Peachy doubted Noomi understood, so she rephrased. "No, our healers aren't quite like this." She closed her eyes, letting Noomi's touch take her to that happy ending.

She nearly fell asleep but for a sharp stabbing into her brain. She jolted and her heart beat uncontrollably, thudding and thumping, tearing her down. Then a heat upon her body. Noomi tightened her grip. Peachy felt her inside her mind, helping her regain control of herself.

"Peachy?" Noomi's voice called her back.

"Just when I think I am free from the images, they come back." She closed her eyes, shutting everything out, rubbing her temples.

"Bed for us?"

"No. Pa. No. Not yet. Talk to me. Tell me about you, about her?" Peachy pointed to Gabin in time to see her retreat from the room with the mice atop her back.

"Aye." Noomi took the book from Peachy and flipped through a few pages. "Here to start." She pointed at an image of a woman under a massive tree heavy with bloom, with a vivid orange sun rising. Countless children were seated around her.

"Beautiful, uh, beauaki." Peachy tried in Noomi's language. She didn't really need to try. Noomi understood her better and spoke her language better than Peachy's mastery of hers. Noomi's language was full of vowels and spoken using a part of her tongue Peachy didn't normally use in verbal communication. "Who are all these people, these children sitting with this old woman?"

"Is elder. Gifted Heather."

"Heather?"

Noomi pointed to her own chest. "Heather. Noomi. You?"

"Human."

"Human?"

Peachy nodded. "What is she doing?"

"The Bestowin'." She leaned in. "Every Heather child hears." Noomi tapped on her own ear to reinforce. "Is how Heathers receive gifts. Tis how I received me own. Is celebration."

"Will you tell me the story?"

Noomi shook her head as if the idea was preposterous.

"No? Why?"

"The Bestowin' is told by elders who have seen, have known. Tis a time and place."

"When?"

"Trees pink, eh the water isn't a freeze. Moons are one. Springtimes!" Noomi shouted her newly learned word.

"Wait. Moons? Did you say moons?"

"Come." Noomi held out her hand.

Peachy took hold and rose to her feet. She followed Noomi through the cloth drape that separated the main room from her under construction reading room. There were wooden boxes and baskets, jars, tools, and books—many, many books of all shapes and sizes. Peachy felt surrounded by them because they sat in tall piles, some of them so high they threatened to topple over and bury her in information about Noomi's world.

Peachy shivered despite the warm glow and heat that emanated from the center of the room. The walls lacked the fabric hangings that the rest of the house had, which made it colder. Gabin and the mice slept in a bed of pelts and pillows close to the stone fire pit.

Noomi led them through the room, picked up a wooden box along the way, and then pointed up a ladder. It led them to a loft area that felt wonderfully warm, heated by the stone chimney of her fireplace. There were pelts on the ground and books everywhere. After taking in her surroundings, and after her eyes adjusted to the dim, Noomi pointed to a glass dome. Peachy gasped and let out a cry for the glorious night sky, full of countless stars and several moons hanging low on the horizon. "My God. There are three of them."

"Muri, Myla, and Maree," Noomi said and she knelt, still with Peachy's hand in hers. She tugged gently. Peachy joined her, her eyes still fixed, her face aglow in amazement, at the celestial wonder. Noomi pointed. "Peachy o' the Sky."

"They're beautiful." She rested against the warmth of the chimney and kissed Noomi's hand, her wonderful hands with her slender, tapered fingers that elicited magic and mayhem from inside her spirit. "Tell me more about The Bestowing. What exactly is bestowed?"

"Five gifts. One is Shifter. Can go between Heather and animal kind. Like me, like Gabin, is Shifter."

"You're also a Shifter?"

"Ka."

"What do you transform into?"

"Like Gabin."

"Wow."

"I prefer me." Noomi pointed at her own chest.

"Why?"

"Is painful for me to shift, and so I can do this." She leaned over, startling Peachy when she kissed her.

"You taste amazing."

"Taste?"

"Taste." Peachy leaned toward her and licked Noomi's lips with her tongue. "Taste." She nibbled and bit gently. "Yummy."

Noomi laughed softly and Peachy thought she heard a quiet purr deep inside the woman's chest.

"Am I crazy or can you and Gabin talk to each other?"

Noomi nodded. "Yes, like most Shifters, can do."

Peachy peered over the edge of their loft, spotting Gabin with an eye open. "What is she saying?"

"Hush voices so she can to sleepin'." They laughed at the request.

"What else?"

"Tellers."

"What do they do?"

"Are no longer here."

"Why?"

"Long ago, before Noomi, they carried evil here." Noomi pointed to her heart. "Sentenced to death. Are no more."

"That's sad."

"'Tis."

"But—"

"Heathers do not talk."

Peachy nodded. "I understand." Peachy placed her hand over her amulet. "What other gifts are there?"

"Next is Protectors. Use strategy, enchant and bless weapons. When is harm, they absorb it."

"Like fuel?"

"Yes." Noomi nodded. "Tis peaceful times. Most now teach others."

"And how is it that you can talk to me without words?" Peachy whispered.

"Tis me gift as Seer. I am Shifter and Seer."

Peachy wondered what all Noomi saw. Did she see Peachy's hurts and worries? Her confusion and sometimes fear of her new world? Did she see Peachy's desire for her? "Can you control me?"

"No. Only aid ye. Is how I help in dreams. I don't see all o' ye."

"I was wondering about that."

"Is okay?"

Peachy nodded.

"Tell me how it makes ye feel."

Peachy couldn't describe the sensation she got when Noomi touched her and pulled her thoughts from her mind, as if she merely reached for a book upon a shelf, opened it and read it. Read *her*. "When I tell you about me, it's like I can't hear myself talking. I know what I'm saying, but I can't hear the words."

"Does it scare ye?"

"Nothing you do scares me."

"I am sorry to see inside ye without askin'."

"I would've done the same if it were me. You needed to know who I was. If I presented danger. I wish I could learn how to hear you better. I wish I could touch you too and know what you're thinking. Sometimes it's difficult to understand. Mostly I wish I could fight my own battles inside my head."

"Ways to Peachy can escape false dreams. I know to show."

"You do?"

"Will take time. Need to learn. For now, use me."

Peachy nodded. "Tell me more. What other gifts are there?"

"Healer is gifted to aid sickness."

"Like when you help me heal? That feeling I get when you touch me?"

"True Healer do more. With more pace. I take from me to ye." Noomi demonstrated by wagging her finger in between the two of them.

"Does it hurt you?" Peachy ran her hand the length of Noomi's arm, seeing that she left goose bumps in her wake.

Noomi's gaze followed the movement of Peachy's hand. "I am strong."

"You feel amazing. I can't get enough." Peachy wondered what Noomi felt when she touched her. Did Noomi tremble and ache when Peachy grazed her body with her fingers? Did she feel aroused? Did desire's smoldering ember push her over a ledge if she were to trace her tongue upon the sensitive skin of her neck? Would it coax her liquid essence from her body?

Noomi closed her eyes and cleared her throat. "Healers best use land." She pointed outside. "Plants, rocks, sun, herbs."

Healers reminded Peachy of Lisette and her countless jars of herbs and her ingredients for gris-gris, and all her books and odd things that she kept and used for Voodoo. Images of Peachy's once-upon-a-time life flashed before her—New Orleans and the beautiful way Lisette was with her own type of magic that drew people in. Images of Lisette in her beautiful long dresses that made all sorts of rustling sounds when she moved about. How she would dress up even for something as simple like a stroll in the evening, as if she was a debutant from the past sent down to earth to remind people how it used to be. Lisette's beautiful tignon head wraps, large hoop earrings, and her funny, archaic sayings. Within Peachy also existed anger and confusion. She wished that Lisette had been more honest with her, told her more about the amulet and why they needed it.

Then the images of Minette, her sometimes lover, who Peachy knew was more in love with her than she was. Minette was okay with that, at least Peachy thought she was. Minette knew Peachy was complicated and never questioned, only loved her. She imagined that Minette was also confused, worried, and angry that Peachy had disappeared.

Everything from her old life engulfed her mind, as if life was paused and now played in fast forward. It felt like a lifetime ago. She wondered if her friends were still looking for her. Were they worried? Why had Lisette sent Peachy for the amulet to begin with? What did the amulet do? Why couldn't she bear to remove it? Why did it make her feel like a hostage? She dare not try. She didn't want to go back. She didn't have it in her to face Beatriz and Adèle. She couldn't bear to know if they had found her friends and tortured and killed them. She didn't want to go home and find out. Not yet. Not now.

"Ye wish to go?" Noomi pointed upward.

"Sometimes I wish more than anything to get home. Other times…" She wished to stay and leave her old world behind and be with Noomi and explore her new universe where the wind howled and the snow fell, where the heavens had several moons, and a fireplace where a huge beast of a cat and two tiny mice warmed themselves and bickered at times. She wanted more of the woman and her undeniable healing touch, golden eyes, and skin that appeared gold with faint spots, more pronounced at times, especially in the firelight. "I've caused you pain. I've interrupted your life, your sister's, your friends'. No one asked for this."

"Tis true. Have turned me life upside down. Is now right side up."

Peachy smiled. Noomi understood her conflicted heart.

"All because of this." Peachy reached into her shirt and held the amulet. "This is the reason why I'm here, and why I fear sleeping. And I've brought this inside your home. If I can get back to where I belong, all this will go away." Peachy made a fist.

Noomi looked skyward. "Death is there, not here." Noomi worked apart Peachy's fist and placed Peachy's hand on her own cheek. "Safe with us."

"I've never felt safer than with you," she said. "I've lived a fast life, stealing from others, running jobs, taking advantage of people, wondering what's next, *if* there's a next."

"Perhaps here is next?"

"I think you're right," Peachy said and met Noomi's eyes. The orange cast of the firelight reflected in them. "Would it be a bad thing if I wanted to stay?"

"No."

"Good. Because I happen to find you attractive." She smiled.

"Attractive?"

"Beauaki, beautiful, your lips, your eyes, your hands, your body, your spirit."

"I find ye beautiful beyond me words, for I lack them both in me language and yours."

Peachy had no adequate words to follow. She took Noomi's face into her hand. She studied her intense eyes that beheld a thousand stories filled with kindness, compassion, and desire—smoldering desire that Peachy ached to feel. She settled her gaze upon Noomi's lips and kissed them. She kissed her chin and caressed her tongue along the soft skin of her neck. Noomi's gentle moans and her whispered words told her everything she needed to know about the power of her own touch. "What is…" Peachy leaned back and rubbed a pain in her side.

"Me box o' smota."

"What?"

Noomi smiled and then focused on the box in between her legs. "Is smota."

Peachy shook her head.

"Look." Noomi opened and pulled out what looked like a pipe and a pouch.

"Is that what I think it is?" Peachy had never felt so excited. She followed Noomi's every movement and nearly salivated when she filled the bowl of her pipe with fragrant leaf. She struck a rock onto the side of the chimney, which lit the end. She set the flame into the bowl and began stoking her pipe, inhaling and exhaling, sending sweet smoke into the air.

Noomi laughed. "Peachy like?" She handed it to her.

"Yes." Peachy licked her lips.

"Treat."

"You have no idea."

"Easy…" Noomi placed her fingers on Peachy's ribs. "Healin' here…"

Peachy assured her that she would.

Noomi kept hold of the pipe, raising it to Peachy's lips, but hesitated at the last moment. "Ye like smota better'n kissin' me?"

"Can't we do both?"

Noomi laughed. "Easy. Is strong."

Peachy closed her eyes and took a giant puff. She popped open her eyes and coughed. She sputtered, grabbing hold of Noomi's arms.

Noomi laughed at her. "Peachy does not listen."

"Wow."

"Yes, wow. Warned ye."

"That was..." Peachy leaned against the warmth of the chimney. "That's good shit."

Noomi mirrored Peachy, leaning against the chimney, as relaxed as Peachy had ever seen her. Noomi's soothing, soft, sultry, and playful laugh punctuated the euphoric feeling.

"Tell me more," Peachy said.

Noomi talked of her world. Peachy didn't remember closing her eyes, but she must have, for the next thing she knew, she was in the marble maze of the *Spanish Rose*. This time, though, everything was quiet.

She heard only the sound of her feet meeting the floor and her own breathing. She walked down one of the corridors. She froze when she spotted objects littering the floor—her lighter, the USB drive, her pack of smokes. She looked over her shoulder. Nothing. No one. She kept walking, feeling a slight breeze in her hair. She looked behind her, a door. A soft glow of pale light emanated from underneath it. She reached for the doorknob. She couldn't stop herself. She opened the door. It was Lisette.

"Lisette!" She was sitting in a tiny, strange old room with wooden floors, one window, and a wooden table. She looked into a large dish filled with liquid. "Lisette!" She couldn't hear her. Lisette kept stirring the water in the dish and talking. The slamming of a door behind her caused her to jump. It was Minette. "Minette!" Again, nothing. They couldn't see or hear her. She kept watching. Minette carried a box of wires, laptops, electronics. Minette was getting ready for a job of some sort.

A light flickered down the hall of the tiny space. Peachy followed it. Another door. She opened it. Peachy couldn't see much of anything—green walls, rust, concrete, standing water on the floor, she lifted her foot, the floor was sticky. Then a shock of bright light. Beatriz! "No...no..." Peachy turned to leave but ran smack into a wall. The door was gone. She closed her eyes, realizing no one could see her. She watched Beatriz walk to a metal table. A large man lay strapped upon it, full of muscle, huge. He was crying, naked, and scared. Beatriz held a rusty knife in her hand. "No!" Peachy cried. She closed her eyes, but what she heard sounded more vivid than witnessing it. Screaming, gurgling, chopping sounds, the smell of blood, then silence. When she opened her eyes, the man was standing before her. Blood poured from his eyes and mouth. She screamed and again everything went black.

She was back in the *Spanish Rose*. Inside Adèle's workroom. Adèle sat in a chair and was crying, looking into a handheld mirror. She was touching her face, muttering expletives. Peachy backed up, though this time was different. Adèle looked at her, walked up to her, and gnarled her teeth. She screamed and pushed her finger in Peachy's chest, sending her backward. "You!"

Peachy jolted awake, feeling everything around her, wondering where she was *this* time.

"Is safe. Peachy," Noomi said.

The heat was too much. Her chest burned. She ripped open her shirt. A bruise started forming on her chest. "Touch me, please. It hurts."

Noomi covered the bruise with her hand.

"Did you see that? Did you see…" Peachy's entire body shook.

"I saw everythin' with ye."

"What does it mean?"

"Are lookin' for ye."

"How? How could I have seen that?"

Noomi shook her head.

"Before I fell into your world, moments before I thought I was going to die, Beatriz told me I was one of them. What *are* they? Who are they? Am I like them, like her? I feel no evil in my heart, and I couldn't do to another person what she did to me." She closed her eyes. "Never."

"Your heart is pure."

"What if it isn't?"

"I'll help ye. I need to learn more from Peachy. Who is? Where from? The womans in dreams."

"I'll tell you everything."

"Then I must journey to answers."

"Then go. Please. I need to know." Peachy sat up and drew her knees against her chest. She wrapped her arms around her legs. Noomi leaned next to her, and Peachy rested her head on Noomi's shoulder, trying not to lose her mind.

CHAPTER FOURTEEN

Neither of them slept after Peachy's disturbing dream. Noomi felt useless, unable to alleviate Peachy's confusion and lessen her worry. She needed to learn more, a lot more. She needed Peachy to tell her more, but the woman was clever, avoiding things she didn't want to do. Noomi worried about leaving her, but knew that she had to. Peachy insisted Noomi go, insisted that she would be fine and that it would only be two days.

Noomi would leave before first light for the Realm of the Keepers in search of guidance from her mentor Nefertari. She did not like that she would have to leave before the dawn and forgo their normal routine of waking up slowly, Peachy stirring in her arms and tickling her skin with her fingers, tracing her markings and rousing her with kisses as they came alive with the sun. The glimpse into Peachy's dreams that night frightened them both beyond anything before and left Noomi with more questions. At the top of that list was how Peachy navigated her dreams, similar to how a gifted Seer would do so. If Peachy wanted to get home, she should have that option. Her leaving, though, would cleave Noomi's own heart in two irreparable halves, but if that's what Peachy needed, then Noomi would do anything to help.

She begged Gabin to stay behind to help Peachy make fires or cook, or be there for her in the event she fell into a horror-filled nightmare. Gabin put up a little fight, but Noomi knew Peachy was growing on her. Gabin no longer spent *all* her time in the library. She found excuses to be in the great room. The beam of sunlight that shone there was the warmest against the stone. The library was too cold and tightened her muscles. She wanted to warm them by the great fire before she went hunting.

Noomi would often catch her sister deep in curiosity, watching Peachy with amusement, especially when Peachy told Noomi about her strange world or Peachy would say her funny words or stumble over the pronunciation of their language. Gabin would help if Peachy needed it. Her sister's heart was much bigger than her great size and outward ferocity, and her love for their family was the biggest part of her.

After a silent dinner, after the mice and Gabin had long retired, Noomi could wait no longer.

"I have to leave at first light."

"I know," Peachy said.

"We need to talk."

"I don't know where to begin."

"Where did ye get the amulet. Who are the women in your dreams?"

"You just jumped right in. No foreplay even."

"Foreplay?"

"Sorry. Bad joke."

"Ye joke to when is difficult to talk."

"Do I?"

"And ye answer me questions with more questions."

Peachy blew out a short puff of air.

"I know that me world is strange to ye, that Gabin, the girls, our ways are odd."

"It *is* odd. All of it. One day I'm there and next I'm here. I'm not going to pretend this whole thing is a total mind fuck."

"Tell me o' the women first, the one in the small room with the younger, the girl."

"Lisette and Minette. I know both of them well."

Peachy placed her injured hand over her chest where the amulet lay. "Lisette was like a mother to me."

"*Like* a mother?"

"I didn't know my mother. Aside from Lisette, I had no one else."

"Peachy has no family?"

She shook her head. "I grew up in foster care. It's a place for kids with no families. I didn't live there long. I hated it. I hated the rules and I left. I had a sweet little setup in this alley where people sold art. There were so many unsuspecting tourists to pickpocket. I wasn't very good at it, though. I got caught a lot. One time I was moments away from getting my ass handed to me and Lisette shows up. It looked like she walked right out of a movie or something, dressed like she's going to a party. She wore this huge chiffon dress, bright colors, lots of fabric and a tignon, a head wrap that made her seven feet tall."

She told the guy she'd turn him into a snake and he ran away. I think he was more scared of her then her threats." Peachy laughed. "And so was I. I did whatever she told me. She took me in, let me stay with her, and threatened to turn me into a snake if I didn't go to school. She gave me these strange odd jobs, interesting jobs to a kid, thrilling. I never left. Lisette became my whole world, my most trusted friend. My family. I would do anything for her and she always put me first."

"'Tis no wonder that she aims to find ye."

"I don't know how she will know where to look. I don't even know where I am."

Noomi remembered the saucer that the woman had at her side. "In your dream, she had a dish with water. Do ye know about that?"

"Never seen that before."

"Here, tis an archaic form o' way to communicate across time and space."

"Does it work?"

"Yes, but I don't know how. I hope me journey can guide me to the answers. How would Lisette know to communicate in this way?"

"She did a lot of weird stuff that I didn't understand. She practiced Voodoo, like a real Voodoo queen."

"Is Voodoo a gift?"

"It's more like her religion. She described it to me as a blending of intertwined worlds, like between the worlds of the living and the dead. Sometimes she would pull inspiration or guidance from someone who had died to get into a particular mindset. She and her sister, the one in my dream with the mirror, are both known for it. Their entire family, her ancestors, practiced it, going back hundreds of years."

"They've seen a hundred years?" Noomi wondered if these women might be Fae. That would explain their way of searching and their access to Peachy.

"No. No. Their family over generations have practiced it for hundreds of years, handed it down."

"Ye say she is queen? Does she preside over a grand kingdom?"

"No." Peachy let out a soft laugh. "Nothing like that."

"And what do they do with their power. How do they contribute to your realm?"

"I wouldn't say they contribute. Their power, more like their mastery of the Voodoo religion, gives them an advantage over people. Usually, when people want something bad enough, they look to Voodoo and when people hear Voodoo, they go to one of two places. Lisette or Adèle."

"What do your people search for?"

"You name it. A job. Power. Stuff. Someone's love."

"How can one get a person's love? Tis unthinkable."

"With an exorbitant amount of money, that's how."

"Lisette would give love?"

"No. Her Voodoo was different than Adèle's. Lisette helped people, sick people or people in search of wanting to know what their future held. She didn't charge them their entire life's savings or take advantage of them like Adèle did. She's a known murderer."

"She sounds a fright," Noomi said. "And there would be a great ceremony when this possession, job or person is presented?"

"No. Everything would be done in hiding."

"But how?"

"Prayers. Sometimes she would mix strange things together."

"I don't understand how these queens gave people the things they wanted."

"Lisette said their spells were designed to show these people what they wanted to see. Sometimes I don't think these things actually existed. Sometimes the stuff that I witnessed scared the shit out of me."

"Does ye know how to Voodoo?"

"No, but I learned about it. I wouldn't say I practice it. I preferred the behind the scenes sorts of stuff. Running jobs was way more interesting." Peachy pulled the amulet from her shirt. "This was a job. Lisette and I stole it from Adèle. Lisette wanted me to have it. She said it was a family heirloom and power lived in it. At the time I thought it was absurd."

"Does ye think its power sent ye here?" Noomi eyed the amulet.

"I don't know what else to think."

"When I found ye, it had burned a horrible impression into your skin."

"Your healing salve has worked wonders." Peachy ran her hand over the smooth skin at her neck. "Thank you for saving my life, Noomi." Peachy reached for Noomi's hands. "I don't think I ever told you that. Thank you."

"The moment I saw ye, I know ye were special. I had to have ye."

"So you took me because you wanted me?"

Noomi smiled and nodded. "How many years do ye have?"

"I think I am twenty-five now."

"Ye don't know?"

"I do know, but I've lost track of time. I was about a month away from my birthday."

Noomi stood and went to a shelf and pulled out her journal. She showed Peachy one of the pages. "I've been keepin' record. The sun has risen forty-two times."

Peachy looked at the page. "Looks like I'm twenty-five."

"When I return from me journey, we celebrate."

"Sounds perfect." Peachy nodded. "How old are you?"

"I have seen seventy-two winters."

"What?"

"Ye do not believe me?"

"I wasn't expecting that. I guess I didn't know what to expect. We appear to be the same age, more or less."

"Heathers live long lives. I am young. Me mentor Nefertari has seen five hundred and seven winters."

"Jesus. I must say you look great for an old broad." Peachy laughed at her own joke.

"What means broad?" Peachy laughed even harder. "I see, tis another joke?"

"I'm sorry." Peachy smiled. "Can I ask you another question?"

"Please."

"Tell me about your family."

"Ye know me family. Tis Gabin, Sissy, Missy and I. Well, the wee girls aren't our blood. Gabin brought 'em home from a hunt one day insistin' that they live with us."

"Gabin is sweet."

"In her own way."

"What does she look like, when she's…not a cat?"

"She's taller'n me, lighter skin, more markin's, and her hair is gold."

"She sounds beautiful."

"She is."

"And your parents?"

"Parents have come and gone. They were old when we came along. Passed when I was fifty."

"Why do you live all the way out here?"

"Tis not forever. But for now, tis how I earn me livin'. I create maps for the realm and sell me art. I aim to map the north when it is green about."

"And you have no woman, no lover?"

"I've not found one to hold me heart for long periods o' time. One would think aft' seventy-two winters and springs, it would be different. Tis not uncommon. I am still young. And of this younger woman? I've seen her in your dreams before."

"Minette. She, she and I…We ran a lot of jobs together."

"She has your heart?"

Peachy shook her head and looked at her cast. "She wants it, but I… She's looking for me too. She loves me and I know her well. She will stop at nothing if it means being with me. I love that about her, and I know that she is broken inside, in pain." Peachy closed her eyes.

"The heart and the ways in which it speaks, tis not all the time clear."

"I'm glad you understand."

"I do. And Minette was on the job with ye?"

"She was my lookout, helped me get the amulet." Peachy patted her chest.

"And the woman with the man on the table? She is the voice that searches for ye. I know it."

Peachy closed her eyes. "She said she was Lisette's twin sister."

"This twin woman was a surprise to ye?"

"I had no clue Lisette had another sister that was still alive, and a twin at that. Her name is Beatriz. She did this to me, all of this." She held out her casted arm, felt her head, and placed her hand over her heart. "She wanted the amulet. I don't know why I didn't give it to her. I couldn't. I thought I could outsmart them, like I always do, run away, trick them. But she had these two huge men who were missing their tongues with hollow pits for eyes. I couldn't take them." She wiped the tears from her cheeks. "I should have handed the amulet over, but I couldn't. I tried. When I put it on, I couldn't take it off. I still can't bear to remove it. If I did, what would happen? Would I be able to go back there? Would I be right where I left off, moments away from death? The thought scares the shit out of me. I stabbed Beatriz and she didn't die. She should have, but she didn't. She just kept at me, saying that I was…"

"What?"

"One of them. I had power inside me. She said she killed my mother. She said she was her sister, and if that's true, then Lisette is my aunt. Adèle is my aunt, and... That was the last thing I knew before I woke up here." Peachy sniffled and dried her tears with the cuff of her shirt. "I have never cried this much. I feel like a fucking idiot."

"The tears ye shed are well deserved, Peachy o' the Sky. I saw your broken body and I felt your pain too." Noomi rounded the table and shifted Peachy's chair to let her in. She spread her legs, knelt in between and wrapped her arms around Peachy's waist, looking up at her. "And look at ye now."

"I may be strong on the outside, but not inside. Not even close. I'm afraid to be alone."

"I am leavin' Gabin with ye, and the wee girls love ye so much."

"They are not you."

The fright in Peachy's eyes would haunt Noomi until she returned. She smiled and wove her fingers through Peachy's hair before taking her face into her hands.

"Will you leave something else for me?" Peachy asked.

"Name it."

"Leave me a part of you that I can hold on to." Noomi closed her eyes when Peachy leaned into her and brushed her lips against hers. "Please."

With Peachy's hand in hers, Noomi led them toward their quarters and closed the door behind them. The soft cast of firelight reflected in Peachy's eyes and danced as if it had not a care. Noomi wondered if she had lost her mind for this woman. She pressed her lips against Peachy's and began nibbling, licking, coaxing Peachy's tongue from her mouth until their tongues danced like the fire. "Will this be enough?"

"No."

Noomi placed her hands on Peachy's waist and lifted Peachy's top, touching the swells of her hips, her ribs and her breasts. She left the comfort of Peachy's eyes to gaze upon her body, her heavy breasts and long neck meant for kissing. She twirled Peachy's locks of wavy hair through her fingers. She ran her hands down her back, and slid off Peachy's underwear. She held Peachy's bottom and pulled her against herself, nesting a leg in between Peachy's already wet center. "What about this."

"You know it isn't."

Noomi ran her tongue across Peachy's bare shoulder, tasting her, nibbling at her neck, sucking on her earlobe, kneading her backside while she urged Peachy back and forth on her leg, coaxing from her a harmony of whimpers and moans.

Peachy took Noomi's hands and placed them over her own breasts and Noomi trembled. She grazed her thumbs over Peachy's nipples, kneading them to tight peaks before taking them into her mouth, rounding each nipple with her tongue, encouraged by Peachy's hands in her hair. "And this?"

Peachy whispered her response that it wasn't enough, that she wanted—needed—more. Peachy lifted Noomi's shirt from her body and reached inside her underwear, dancing her fingers through Noomi's wetness. Her touch nearly brought her to her knees, and she almost came in her hand.

"I want this," Peachy said, coating her fingers in Noomi's essence. She trailed her wet fingers across Noomi's lips, and then Peachy kissed her, licked her lips clean.

Noomi guided them toward the bed. She topped Peachy, running her hands up and down her body. She spread Peachy's legs and took her into her mouth, creating a memory they both could find solace within while they were apart.

* * *

Noomi's familiarity with the land would help her make the best use of the winter's short daylight. As a skilled mapmaker, she knew the quickest and easiest routes to negotiate the terrain. Still using all her effort, the round trip to the Realm of the Keepers and to Nefertari the Only would take two days. She stopped only long enough to drink and remove one of her many layers, for she had built up a sweat at her eager pace. Noomi felt as though the Heathers were giving their blessing when the sun peeked over the mountaintop and began coloring her world. The howling of the wind had ceased as did the falling snow.

She prayed to the Heathers that her mentor would have the answers or know where to look. Much of Noomi's nervousness rested not in getting quickly back to Peachy, but how she would avoid discussing the amulet as Peachy had asked. It frightened Noomi at times, for it seemed to have a presence of its own. Noomi would often observe Peachy staring into it as if she were lost, her eyes wide, entranced by it, as if it spoke to her. Peachy looked always to be carrying the weight of an ox on her shoulders.

Now Noomi carried the weight of her secret. It felt hopeless, especially because Nefertari was one of the greatest Seers of her time. Noomi would have to rely on steering the conversation away from the amulet. She prayed Nefertari could not sense that she withheld information. She hoped that the Heathers before her understood her reasons why. If her mentor found out, Noomi would pay a price, and Nefertari had an everlasting memory with more than five hundred years to Noomi's seventy-two.

It was told that one of the original Heathers, the most gifted Seer, bestowed her gifts directly to Nefertari. Whether or not there was truth in that, Nefertari carried that esteem wherever she went and in all that she did. Nefertari was a fair and just ruler. She dedicated her life to the protection of their realm. She upheld the law and ensured peace, and their kind had not waged war in over four hundred years.

It was early afternoon when Noomi spotted the beacon of the Realm of the Keepers. A one-hundred-and-twenty-five-foot stone monument depicted the five founding Heathers. They stood back to back, their arms crossed, as if ensuring they would forever hold their people in their hearts. They looked in every direction. The Teller looked skyward. The collective, always ensured blessings and protections. Every time Noomi gazed upon the treasure of her people, she felt allegiance in her heart to use her gifts to help others, to benefit the realm and honor the existence of their spirit.

The Realm of the Keepers, their people's capitol, held other monuments, fountains, and sacred trees in tribute to legendary Heathers. The city housed everything that was precious—

their grand libraries, citadels, and the reliquary, which housed precious artifacts and scripts of their history. Keepers underwent rigorous training and dedicated their lives to their service. It wasn't uncommon for a generation of Keepers to be charged with caring for and protecting sacred relics. Like any other large city, the Realm of the Keepers also held stores, stables, pubs, and art. Like any glorious city, one had to walk sideways to navigate the crowds that were out in droves no matter the time of day or night.

Noomi was lucky to find an inn with a room to rent. She changed her sweat-soaked clothing, rinsed off in the communal pools, devoured a bowl of soup, and caught her breath before she went to the reliquary in search of Nefertari. Noomi spotted her at once. She was a graceful woman, worthy of all eyes and attention upon her. She wore the uniform of her order, a glorious indigo velvet robe that covered all of her six feet. She had deep bronze skin and silver hair that glistened in the light of the several fires that lit the building.

Nefertari sat in a cove, surrounded by her council, other Heathers dedicated to preserving peace and upholding their laws. Noomi caught her eye and found a quiet space, another cove with a fire inside, and a bench and table. She'd have to wait her turn and hope that Nefertari could make time for her. She didn't wait long. Nefertari approached with a few members of her council.

"Noomi, what a wonderful surprise." Nefertari handed a book that she carried to one of her council. "Ye appear with worry." She sat opposite Noomi on an empty chair.

"Can we talk?"

"O' course."

"In private?"

"Let us take this to me chambers," she said and excused herself from her council.

"With thanks."

She followed Nefertari down a corridor crowded with council people at work and in conversation. "Please come in."

Noomi had been there on numerous occasions in her training and mentorship. The mere presence of her mentor brought her comfort, as did her library with its walls of stained glass and glimmering wood. Shelves upon shelves held books, art, maps, herbs in jars, loose sheets of papers, pens, and brushes. A fire roared with life, illuminating her space and providing warmth. Noomi felt as though she could breathe again. Soon she hoped for clarity.

"Sit, please. Can I make us tea?"

"With thanks." Noomi sat in one of the comfortable chairs.

With tea in hand, Nefertari joined Noomi. "What can I do to ease the worry in your heart?"

"Tis under dire circumstances that I seek guidance. I found…I have taken in a woman—a traveler. She was injured. I could not risk leavin' her until now."

"Are ye safe?"

"Yes. I assure ye. Tis not why I come to ye with worry."

"Tell me everythin'." Nefertari leaned in while Noomi recounted the story of how Peachy appeared out of nowhere after a shock of electricity in the sky. How she arrived with strange clothing and was near death and with a broken body.

"She isn't a Heather as far as I can tell. Her body does not bear the markin's o' our kind. She speaks a language that I was not familiar with but have learned. T'was easy."

"Tell me a few words."

Noomi did as she was told.

"Interestin' dialect."

"Tis."

"Do ye know her heart?"

Noomi nodded. "Tis pure. Me concern is that when I see into her, she is with turmoil. Her people are lookin' for her, two in particular aim to harm her. They are reachin' across time and space for her. Tis in her mind that they look. She avoids sleep as to avoid confrontation. Tis too much for her. She is ever on the run. She's escaped death. I am sure of it. I do what I can to help her."

"Is she gifted?"

"Tis part o' me confusion. Tis why I risked leavin' her when I did. She was able to navigate a dream on her own as a Seer would, but she was unable to communicate, only observe. I know not what this means or how she was able to do it. Maybe tis through me?"

"Tis a possibility. Ye have grown close I presume?"

Noomi nodded. "I would do anythin' to help."

"Tell me more o' this dream. What did she see?"

"Three women, sisters, two are twins. The lot were plannin', lookin' for her, preparin'. I think they aim to get her back whether or not she gives her consent. What do ye think it means?"

"Tell me first o' the sisters."

"One was usin' a pool o' reflection as a means to contact her."

"Tis archaic."

"Their world sounds as such." Noomi took a deep breath in as if she hadn't done so upon arriving. "They mean to kill her."

"Have ye any thought as to why they aim to harm her?"

Noomi shook her head. "Can ye help me? Show me how to stop her dreams, help her contact her people, and if she wishes to return, offer her a path to do so?"

"What does she call herself?"

"Peachy."

"Peachy, just Peachy?"

"I call her Peachy o' the Sky."

"Tis fittin' for the way she came into your life." Nefertari rose, looked out her window, and turned around. "Is there more ye wish to tell me, Noomi?"

"Tis all I know. I aim to figure the rest o' her story out."

"What o' this object she arrived with?"

"Tis a mere trinket." Noomi closed her eyes. *Fuck.*

"Describe it to me."

"Tis a blue jewel. It hangs from a silver chain. Tis all know…" Noomi cast her eyes downward, ill in her heart for betraying Peachy. The one thing that she had asked her to keep within her heart.

A gentle knocking at Nefertati's chamber pulled her from her thoughts.

"Please enter."

"I am sorry to disturb your counsel. Tis an urgent matter to which your guidance is required."

"Give me a moment." Nefertari rose from her seat and consulted her bookshelves. She pulled several and placed a great stack before Noomi. "These references are precious to us. These are written documentation of Heathers who have left our world for another."

"Ye think she is from here."

"Or her people. Spend this aft'noon reviewin' 'em. They're not permitted to leave me chambers. Upon me return, I will identify more references and together we will outline a plan to help her. Carry no more worry this day. Await me return and we will pick up where we left off."

"With thanks." Noomi stood and watched Nefertari leave before sitting back down and staring at the stack, wondering where to start and what to look for that would help her identify who Peachy was.

The task seemed absurd. Her betrayal of Peachy's confidence filled her with self-doubt. She opened the top book, *Her People, Volumes 1-50.* She assessed the book in the stack that sat before her. The task would take a fortnight to sort through. She went page by page sorting through names, dates, gifts they possessed, and their reasons for leaving. She nearly fell asleep and shook herself to stay awake, thinking she needed to stretch her legs, get something to eat, and maybe spend a few talents on gifts for Peachy's birthday.

She selected a polished pipe, lots of fresh pipeweed, pages for writing, snow walkers and garments. Although she and Peachy wore the same sizes, she wanted Peachy to feel as though she had her own possessions. She could hardly wait to see the expression on Peachy's marvelous face when she saw her new gifts.

She hoped that Peachy had been successful in caring for herself, nourishing her body and staying warm by keeping the fires lit. More so, Noomi hoped for the sake of Peachy's health, that her dreams were free from menace. Noomi hadn't felt a word from her sister that anything was cause for concern. Instead, Noomi's thoughts were flooded with nonstop desire, thoughts of their growing connection and flashbacks to the night they spent together before her journey, touching Peachy's body, feeling Peachy's lips, feeling hope on her skin and feeling completely wrecked.

It was nearly nightfall when she went back to Nefertari's chambers to search through more references, feeling as though the task was a ridiculous waste of her time. She'd been there all day and only worked through one of the several volumes. It felt like busy work, as if Nefertari had wanted to keep her occupied with menial research. Noomi could have traveled home by now. She could have been with Peachy at this very moment. Noomi felt as though something wasn't right. She left Nefertari's chambers and spotted one of her council members.

"Will ye please relay word to Nefertari that I needed to journey and will seek her guidance soon again."

"I will upon her return."

"Her return?"

"She left this aft'noon with members o' her guard."

"Left? To where?"

"She did not tell me."

"With thanks," Noomi said. She felt a growing fear in her heart. Something wasn't right. She retrieved her possessions from the inn and made her way to one of the city's exits where she was stopped.

"Tis under the orders o' Nefertari the Only that ye are not permitted to leave."

"What are ye talkin' about?"

"I'm only relayin' me orders." He blocked her path out of the city.

She relented and turned away with a slight smile. As mapmaker and wayfinder, Noomi knew the quickest and easiest ways to negotiate terrain. She also knew all of the hidden underground entrances and exits from the city. She made her way to one of them. Nothing was going to stop her from getting home to Peachy.

CHAPTER FIFTEEN

Beatriz attempted to reacquaint herself with her beloved town, however nothing looked the same. Her old haunts were desolate shells of their former glory. She had learned that the tremendous storm that raised her cement coffin was named Katrina, and Katrina's destruction caused permanent changes to her city. Beatriz both thanked and cursed the Katrina. Similar to how her beloved home had changed, so had her powers. Rebuilding would take time, but soon all would remember who she was especially with amulet in hand. Until then, she remained weak from neglect and her neck still throbbed from taking the girl's blade to the hilt.

She dreamed of her revenge. She wrestled with what she would do first. Would she drive an enchanted blade into the girl's chest first? Would she twist it all sorts of directions, slicing her up, down, and sideways, spilling her blood and guts, and then take the amulet? Or would she make good on her promise to cut the amulet off her neck, hold it in her hand and drive the blade into her heart? Maybe she'd spread the pain over several years, hold her at the edge of death and enjoy her suffering. The order of what she did first seemed unimportant in the scheme of things, but fantasizing about it kept a smile on her face.

There was still the ever-watchful creature, the Seer and Shifter to contend with and eliminate. Maybe she'd gut the thing and stuff its body, but rather than remove its brain and set glass eyes into its skull, she'd keep everything intact. She'd hang it up on a mantel where it could watch her and always remember the consequences of getting in her way. Maybe she and the Shifter could witness Peachy's constant agony together. They'd watch it like they would a television show, and they'd laugh at all the right times and cry at the sad parts. *Yes!* The three of them would live in harmony with their eyes wide open. "Soon."

She only needed to find *where* the filth cowered and until then, she settled on the next best thing, terrorizing Peachy through her dreams, breaking her down, clawing through her brain, and tearing holes in her skull that would eventually be large enough for her to crawl out of.

She wondered if the Heathers would remember them. She wondered how their history reflected their kind. Were the ones who had sentenced them still alive? If so, would they forgive and forget? Would they demand their blood if ever she and her sisters were to set foot on their lands? If so, she would be ready. She'd wage a war so epic, that when she prevailed, the only thing left breathing would be her with the powerful treasure, her amulet, to satisfy and quench her never-ending thirst for blood. First, she needed the amulet and the help of her sister Adèle.

"You have some nerve, making me ring for you like a stranger asking permission to enter my own home," Beatriz relayed through the intercom of the *Spanish Rose*.

"You have some nerve showing up after the mess you left for me last time," Adèle said before buzzing her inside the property.

Beatriz approached the big house through a rush of memories. She climbed the few steps to meet her sister on the porch, who waited as if she awaited a package delivery instead of her flesh and blood.

"And which mess would you be referring to?"

Adèle crossed her arms and grimaced when she eyed Beatriz's slave men, as if they were simple hunks of meat and not the works of art and great warriors that they were. Her newly converted soldiers stood ready and able. Their tongues and eyes had been cut from their bodies mere days ago, having gone through their training, beaten and cracked, tempered and tamed, and now awaiting her command.

"What? Oh, that. Sad I know." Beatriz puckered her lips. "Unforeseen casualties of war. There was no way I could lift him, so I left him for you. I figured you had people to get rid of it." She turned and took her man's face in her hand and squeezed his cheeks. He grunted. "One would think for their size that they are fearless, but they aren't, not really. They whimper and whine when they get bored and restless. Such simple tools—men— with their muscular and powerful bodies but with malleable and empty made-to-order minds. The perfect combination, a beautiful show of force when needed, all created for my will. Aren't they a marvel?"

"Uh no."

Beatriz spotted a work van parked outside the old carriage house. "What's that?" Two people rummaged about the back with spools of wire and bags.

"Security measures."

"A little too late, wouldn't you say? Surveillance works much better when you *have* priceless objects in need of protecting."

"Better late than never."

"Not in this case."

"What was your excuse for failing to protect said priceless objects that night?"

"I did what I could."

"The fact that you let a child get the better of you leads me to believe that you are weak, and you know how much I loathe weak things."

"My extended hibernation has resulted in diminished capabilities," Beatriz said. "But only for so long. Similar to a ravenous Grizzly Bear upon waking, I too am searching for something to rip apart and eat, and when that happens, you'll be the weak one."

"And what would you have done had you been successful?"

"What exactly are you insinuating?" Beatriz asked, clutching imaginary pearls. "I tried to save you, save us, our way of life. You come off as most ungrateful."

"I believe that you intended to take the amulet for your own."

"And so what if I did? Does it matter which of us has it, so long as *we* have it? Really Adèle, if we're going to spend time assigning blame, then shouldn't you be the first to accept the responsibility that *you* failed? It was under *your* care that it simply walked out of the *Spanish Rose!*"

"I had it under lock and key."

"You should have been wearing it."

"I couldn't bear it any longer. It had grown restless. You know how it gets."

Beatriz knew what her sister was referring to, for when she had tried to take it from Peachy, it put up a great fight. It gave the girl more strength than someone with a cracked skull and broken bones should display, but Beatriz knew wresting it from its rightful bearer would prove a challenge. "Well, then we must talk about eliminating that little thing that stands in our way. Seriously, are we going to carry on this conversation on the porch like common folk or conduct ourselves like ladies over proper tea?" She pushed past Adèle.

"They are not permitted inside."

"I shan't be gone long, boys. Do not stray too far." She left her mindless warriors to stare at the front door of the *Spanish Rose*. She smirked as she removed her sunglasses, making a show of looking her sister over. "My, my, don't you look a marvel. These past near forty years have been easy on you. You don't look a day over six hundred and forty-two," she laughed.

"I see your sense of humor has not gone dormant with your abilities as I hoped it would."

"Seriously, Adèle. Tis all in jest. Your skin appears wonderfully supple and your style impeccable."

"What good is immortality if you can't also be beautiful?" They gave each other a peck on the cheek.

"I do wonder, though, if the only reason you want the amulet back is to ensure that you don't start to get wrinkles, rot, and die," Beatriz said as she circled her sister, taking her in from all angles.

She was breathtaking. Unlike Beatriz and her twin, Adèle was a petite woman who stood five foot five. There was one feature Beatriz loved about her little sister—an enormous appetite for blood. Last time she had seen her was in the early eighties. Then her hair was a feathery wave of swirls and wisps. She was all shoulder pads and pastels. Now her hair was coiffed and her lustrous locks sat atop her head as if in a crown. She wore a long-sleeve, ivory-colored draped blouse. The color complemented her olive skin, as did her exquisite taste in jewelry. It was also clear that her sister still took precautions to avoid revealing the marking of her skin, which Beatriz knew to be more pronounced on Adèle's torso and arms. She wore tapered black dress pants, and when she studied her shoes she asked, "Are those Valentino Rockstud Caged Leather pumps? Heavens, I just purchased those exact ones. Can you imagine how embarrassing it would have been if we were to have worn the same shoes upon our first meeting in nearly forty years?"

Adèle shifted her weight from one leg to the other and placed her hand at her waist. "Did you come to talk about fashion?"

"Oh, now. Can you blame a girl for wanting to make small talk with her favorite sister?"

Adèle sighed and rolled her eyes.

"Aren't you going to tell me how breathtaking I look?"

"Thanks to the cash and credit cards you stole from my safe."

"Oh now, tis in the name of fashion. I simply love the styles of this time." Beatriz lifted one of her feet and pointed to her Louboutins. She purposely shook her hand to draw attention to the Cartier love bracelet she'd bought earlier that day. "There's a full carat of diamond chips in it. It came with a screwdriver. Isn't that fancy." Beatriz had spent almost twenty-nine thousand dollars on a new wardrobe since she'd resurfaced, making up for lost time, delighting in the joys of spending money. She knew she looked as though she walked off a photo shoot, and she walked in that same manner as well.

"I am surprised that you look as good as you do for being buried for so long."

"Why didn't you look for me?"

"Did my lack of concern hurt your feelings?" Adèle made a show of concern and knit her eyebrows.

"Of course it hurt my feelings, you fool. I was ever lonely."

"Well, then you can also blame your twin, for she would not disclose your whereabouts, and believe me I tried to find out."

"Apparently your efforts were not applied with appropriate determination, and as a result, my disappearance is the least of our worries. We are positively devastated if we do not get the amulet back."

"Here we are yet again, us against her. Tis nothing we can't negotiate, I assure you." Adèle led her through the house. "Would you like tea?"

"As if tea would lessen the decades of loneliness I suffered."

"Tis all I have." Adèle rang a bell and shook it like a wet rag. A woman arrived. "Sabine, fetch us Jasmine Pearls and be quick about it. We'll take it in the atrium," she said before the woman retreated the way she had come.

"How do you keep staff when you treat them with such regard?"

"You're one to talk," Adèle blurted and laughed.

"Oh, my boys? They are very well cared for. Besides, they are programmed not to care. Yet another risk you are taking in leaving your help to minds of their own. I can create a boy for you if you'd like."

"I'm quite capable of manhandling others on my own. Come, this way."

"I know the way to the atrium, Adèle." Beatriz followed her through the *Spanish Rose*. The clicking of their heels echoed through the marble corridors. Beatriz smiled as she walked, reliving her time there, all of the memories, all the blood spilt, all of the fun she enjoyed under its roof. They settled in matching armchairs.

"Tell me what you know," Adèle said.

"That night I was able to determine that the girl is clueless about her lineage. Her powers are weak, almost nonexistent. She had no idea what she was stealing. Our only consolation is that it buys us time, but not much. She is beginning to awaken. It's only a matter of time before she is fully aware and has her own ideas about what to do with her newfound power. She could undo everything we've accomplished."

"That is unthinkable."

"Tell me, when did she meet Lisette?"

"Ten years ago, maybe? I don't remember. Last time I saw her she was a kid."

"She's twenty-five now and extremely intelligent, though it's her spirit—her heart—that we have to contend with. She holds inside herself more wildfire than her mother. Why she aligned herself with Lisette over us is beyond me, and it's most curious that Lisette hasn't told her a thing about who she is."

"My guess is that the girl was immature and not ready to grasp our reality. I saw her name come across the court system many times during my business affairs. Unfledged children like that are stubborn and difficult to wield."

"The fact that Lisette sent her on the job means she is ready, willing, and able. I believe that Lisette wanted to train the girl, and I think she wanted to send her home."

"Send the girl home *with* the amulet? That is suicide, and surely our people won't like having another one of us on their soil, though it's been a long time. I do wonder if they still care or remember three ancient Heathers."

"Three murderous Heathers."

"Our powers are diluted. We're hardly a threat to them anymore."

"I'm counting on the fact that they are a proud people with long memories and that they're insistent on ensuring justice."

"I still don't understand why Lisette would want to rid us of our power source except—"

"Except to kill us. My other guess, based on what I see inside her, is that she is tired of wrestling with her inner turmoil. She's riddled with guilt."

"And sending the amulet away with the girl will help ease her guilt how?"

"She sees something in her that's special. Different. She thinks Peachy can redeem her."

"How will she ensure that Peachy won't follow our path and inspire destruction greater than we ever did? She is of our blood and of her mother, who commanded a destructive appetite as well."

"It's a risk she's willing to take," Beatriz said. "Make no mistake, Adèle. Lisette is powerful and stronger than I remember."

"She's been out of the picture ever since you disappeared. I rarely give her a thought these days. Pity is the only reason I haven't killed her."

"I am glad to be back. I can bring you to your senses and help you remember that pity accomplishes nothing. Are you getting soft?"

"I had three men killed today and it isn't even noon." Adèle tapped her nails against the glass top end table.

"We have this world in our iron grip, don't we? Dear me, Adèle, what if our time is up?"

"I have several hundred million reasons for assuring you our time is not up."

"Then quit thinking with your pity and more with your insatiable appetite for carnage. There's a creature, a fiercely protective Seer and Shifter no doubt, with other abilities. She walks with Peachy in her mind, protects her. There is an intense love blossoming between them. The good news is they are both young, scared, and clueless."

"We should let this creature seek guidance, let that play out, let it come to the attention of their rulers."

Beatriz nodded. "I agree that we should let the creature do our bidding, ensuring us a willing ear for negotiations."

"How is Peachy? I saw the videos. She was positively broken."

"Healing at a remarkable rate. Confused. Wonders if she should stay or return home. She knows what's waiting for her here, and I take great pleasure in knowing that when the time comes, I will be the one to make that decision for her."

"And Lisette?"

"She is in hiding somewhere near the bayou. I cannot get a clear reading. I only see woods and water."

"Let her be. In fact, let her train the girl; it will only help us in the end. I have an old friend of the realm, one that I used to trust, even at my lowest."

"Is that right?" Beatriz asked. "Do tell me about this friend? Is she willing to negotiate?"

"Let us find out."

Sabine entered the room with a young woman following. She wore a red crew shirt. *Security Advisors* embroidered onto the lapel. "I'm sorry, Madame Blanque. They need to get into a basement. There's an issue with the wiring."

"Then show her the basement," Adèle replied. "Come, Beatriz. Let us take this into my quarters."

CHAPTER SIXTEEN

Lisette filled her basin with water and herbs, created a swirl with her index finger and gazed into the whirlpool. It came alive, took shape, became a celestial orb, and pulsated with life. She closed her eyes and thought of Peachy, looked for her, let time and space guide her to where she existed. She found her. She sat at a table in the home where she lived. Lisette felt no sign of Noomi. Only Gabin sat with her, along with the two mice sleeping inside a basket on the table. Lisette looked over the girl's shoulder. Peachy held a pen in her hand. She had written of the night her life changed. It appeared those memories took up several pages. She appeared stuck. She kept underlining the same word. *Mother.* Lisette placed her hand on Peachy's shoulder, wanting to know more of what the girl seemed unable to commit to paper.

Confusion and grief bubbled at the surface and blurred her thinking, caused her to doubt if she really did want to know her mother for fear of learning who she actually was. Instead, Lisette saw that Peachy had immersed herself in every precious memory she could conjure of her old world. The colors of the great baskets of Bougainvillea in full bloom, the swaying of the Spanish moss on the limbs of massive oak trees. How much she loved the pride her city took in dressing the French Quarter storefronts during the holidays, especially Halloween. How everyone would scramble to shut their windows and doors upon the *thought* of coming rain. The sounds of live music that spilled from the cafés, the impromptu parades, all the crazy tourists in awe of the sights and in search of magic. She also had written of the excitement in her heart when she and Lisette were planning a job. That memory made Lisette smile too. Peachy worried about Minette and prayed that she was safe. Peachy dropped her pen and rubbed her chest as if in pain.

Lisette rounded the table and sat in the chair opposite her. She placed her hand on Peachy's, willing her to sleep.

"Child tis me, Lisette. Do not be scared. You are safe."

The girl shook her head and moaned, wanting to wake up. Lisette tightened her hold.

"Listen to me. Don't fight it. I am so sorry for your pain. I sent you here with nothing and with no explanation. I know you are confused, and for that, I am sorry. Soon I will be able to tell you more, but it is not always safe for me to make a connection. Please know that I love you. Minette loves you and we are safe. We're learning everything we can in order to protect you from my sisters. They look for you day and night and seek to bring you back against your will. I do what I can to keep you hidden. I'll do what I can to ensure that whatever choice you make is yours alone. I am sorry that I am not always able to intervene and for the damage my sisters cause to your beautiful spirit. Soon you will be able to protect yourself far better than I."

Peachy knit her brow and moaned again, this time louder. The mice and cat watched her with great concern.

"What I tell you next will only confuse you further, but you need to know. People will want you for what you possess inside. You are of these people, as I am of these people, as your mother was of them, as Noomi is of them. Within you, within the amulet, are the keys you need to reach your potential. Learn from Noomi, but be cautious. Trust no one, and in the meantime follow your heart, follow your love for her. I leave you with this: your mother loved you more than anything. When she knew she was pregnant with you, she realized that nothing else mattered but you. She was a beautiful, powerful woman, and you look like her. Her name was Rahimah. Rahimah of the Sky."

Peachy roused herself awake, breathless, holding the amulet against her chest as if to still it. She looked about the home, over her shoulder and then straight ahead, as if she could see Lisette sitting in that chair. But Lisette knew that was impossible. Peachy got up and left, the giant cat and mice following her. Lisette ended her connection and prayed that Peachy found peace in her message.

Minette would be home soon, and she would be hungry. She would fix her a stew. As she worked, she caught a glimpse of herself in the mirror that hung on a wall. She stared into it, unable to recognize her reflection. She was too old a creature for this world. Death should have claimed her an age ago. She ran her fingers along her cheeks. Cavernous lines, bottomless trenches brimmed with guilt and doubt marred her face for single-handedly sending Peachy to an unfamiliar place with no training, no tools, or explanation. She regretted that she had been unable to see that Beatriz had surfaced, and she was equally responsible for the pain Peachy endured that night. She was culpable for the blows to her body, her broken bones, and damaged spirit. She felt suffocating shame for finding Minette and playing on her crushing love of Peachy, for putting yet another innocent in the way of harm and in the same room as her two ruthless sisters. The girl drank too much, didn't sleep, and was spiraling in a depression so deep that Lisette worried Minette wouldn't be able to climb out.

She wished she could have served her sentence in the Realm of the Heathers. She had made her own choices and earned a spot in that cell. After hundreds of years, she still remembered Rahimah's death—the smell of her spilled blood, the fear in her eyes as she was torn apart, and how time and space had scattered her body and spirit across the celestial expanse. Moments before

Beatriz had killed her, it was as if Rahimah had known what was coming. She made Lisette promise to find her daughter and raise her as best she could.

"One day," Rahimah had said, "show her love and send her home to redeem our kind."

CHAPTER SEVENTEEN

Minette did everything in her power to focus on the task and not bore the six-inch drill bit into the skulls of Lisette's sisters. Not that she could get past the three-hundred-pound linebackers that Lisette's twin had brought with her. She reminded herself that there would come a time when she would witness revenge. In the meantime, she focused on her work, outfitting the *Spanish Rose* with video cameras.

"It's the most up-to-date home invasion prevention technology on the market," she'd told Adèle when she'd sold her the service. "It comes with a comprehensive assessment of your home. Then we make recommendations about camera placement so all of your precious treasures are protected."

She had told Adèle it would be expensive, to which Adèle replied that money was no object. Minette felt some satisfaction in taking her money, triple what it would cost for a real job. Lisette spoke the truth when she said that her sister was technologically stunted.

It worked like a charm and landed her inside the *Spanish Rose* wiring the shit out of the place. She used the blueprints she had sourced at the library to find all of the hidden areas Lisette had described—walls within walls, hidden floors, false bookcases, and the corridor to get to and from the carriage house and the big house. Soon her little shack on the bayou would stream live sights and sounds, everything that went on inside the walls of the *Spanish Rose*.

Her timing couldn't have been better. She heard most everything the sisters discussed. She felt a pang of jealousy when she heard Beatriz say that Peachy was conflicted about returning home and that it was because of a woman, a Shifter and Seer for whom she was developing feelings. Minette was unable to fathom anyone else touching Peachy in *that* way, loving her more than Minette did. It hurt. She only wanted Peachy to be happy, but she hadn't realized that meant happy with or without her. She didn't know how much longer she'd be able to endure the weight. It threatened to overtake her and send her into a bottomless pit.

She found herself staring at walls, unable to eat, sitting idly on her motorcycle. Only the sound of someone's blaring horn pulled her from her inner torment. She'd taken long reckless rides in the middle of the night, searching for that bottomless pit, hoping to face it head-on and wrestle with what she found in its depths. Still, Minette would do everything she could to ensure Peachy was safe and free from the two demented women who were, at present, talking about murder, as if they were reviewing the latest movie they'd seen. She would do whatever Lisette needed to protect Peachy. Maybe along the way Lisette would talk some sense into Peachy, tell her that she was loved and needed at home.

"Yo," Rosa said. She was Minette's recruited helper, another person with whom Minette and Peachy had run jobs with, had a huge cargo van, and more importantly never asked questions.

"What?" Minette looked below from her spot on the ladder.

"I asked what's next."

"Sorry." Minette shook her head.

"You okay?"

"Totes. I think we're done for today. Let's pack up and get the hell out of here."

"They know where you are," Minette said, upon arriving home. She found a towel and began drying herself of the rain that drenched her ride. Lisette had started dinner and Minette looked into the pot, a savory-smelling soup simmered but failed to warm her soul as she had always expected a hot pot of soup to do.

"Tell me everything," Lisette said.

"They don't know your precise location. They know you're on the bayou, but I don't think they're going to try and find you."

"Did they say why?"

"They're going to leave her alone and stop getting in your way. Said it would be better, in the long run, to have her already trained for later use."

"What else?" Lisette wiped her hands on a dishtowel before joining Minette at the table.

"Adèle seems to think she had a friend there, someone who was loyal to her that might be interested in negotiating. That's all I got before they took the conversation upstairs. I'm far from having that part of the house wired."

"This is valuable intel, Minette. I can't imagine what we will learn when you get everything set up."

"Your sister Beatriz is moving in."

"Good. They will be under the same roof."

Minette nodded. "She looked pretty good for being buried for thirty-seven years. Like really good. More than she's had work done. Both of them actually looked like they'd seen the same plastic surgeon and paid a shit ton of money to take decades off."

"They have mastered the art of preservation."

"And not you?"

Lisette gave her a look.

"Sorry." She laughed. "That didn't come out right."

"I take no offense, child." She smiled.

"Well, for what it's worth, you look pretty darn good for six hundred seventy-three. Never thought I'd hear myself say that. Not because you don't look great; it's more that you're so old. Damn. Sorry. Not what I meant either. You look great." She gave Lisette two thumbs-up and a wink.

"Thank you, child. Tell me what else you heard."

"At points, they also called each other different names. Terezi and Emeli."

"We had to assume the names of this world when we assimilated. Terezi is Beatriz's given name and Adèle is called Emeli."

"And you?"

"I am Thala."

"Do you want me to call—"

"I am no longer that person."

"Does Peachy have a given name?"

"Peachy is a nickname for Prudence."

"Eh."

"She felt the same way. Tell me what else."

"Beatriz said that her abilities had suffered."

"I wondered. She isn't as feisty as I remembered."

"I don't think it's permanent."

"Regardless, her real damage comes when she speaks. Beatriz has an uncanny ability to get people to do what she wants without inflicting physical damage. She's brilliant with words."

"So she hurts people for fun?"

Lisette nodded.

"That's fucked."

"As a gifted Protector, it does not surprise me that she aims to negotiate with those from our old world rather than incite war, though I do imagine it will come to that eventually."

"Do you think she will regain her full capacity?"

"I don't know. Speaking only for myself, being away from the Realm of the Heathers for so long has altered my abilities. I've ceased to evolve and learn. I've not been applying my gifts in the way they were intended. I imagine that my sisters have experienced this as well."

"Will the Heathers know that you're different and that your powers have diminished?"

"I pray they don't. Our people will not have forgotten the destruction we caused when we lived among their kind. For all they know we could wage war once again. They will want to avoid confrontation at all costs."

"It seems farfetched that any of this will go our way or even your sisters' way. They have Peachy and the amulet. Why talk? If I were them, I'd take the amulet, and I hate that I'm even going to say this, and kill everyone off."

"It doesn't quite work that way. They need Peachy or another Teller to possess the amulet."

"What if they turn Peachy? Tell her about how you and your sisters were going to be sentenced to death because of what you did. Do you think she would turn?"

Lisette hesitated before responding. "If she does, then this world stands only to lose three old women who weren't supposed to be here in the first place."

"I don't think she could do that. She loved you. I can tell from how you talk about her and the lengths we are taking to protect her. She's not a traitor."

"She knows nothing of my ways or the ways of her mother. She has this beautiful image that she carries deep inside, and I fear one day when she learns the truth about Rahimah, her heart will fill with pain."

"She has too much love inside her. That pain won't stand a chance."

"I pray that you are right, child. I am ashamed every day I draw breath. Sometimes I can't bear to look at myself. If it weren't for Peachy, if it weren't for you, I do not know how I would have lived as long as I have. Tell me what else you saw today."

"Beatriz showed up with these huge men. I couldn't tell if they were the same ones that almost killed Peachy, but they looked similar. They looked like you could knock them over by blowing on them. I know that's not true, but they looked hollow, dumb and huge, *huge* dudes." Minette motioned with her arms. "They just stood there, staring into space. They were so creepy, wearing sunglasses, even inside. What are they?"

"They're dead."

"What?" Minette felt the blood drain from her body.

"They're dead."

"I heard you, but what?"

"Beatriz rewires their brains to do basic functions and obey what she commands. These puppets don't last long, maybe a month before they die for real. It's—"

"Gruesome as fuck. I'm not sure if I want to know what's under the sunglasses."

"They wear them because they have no eyes or tongue. She removes both as they are needed to raise them back to life."

Minette grimaced. "Great so they're zombies?"

"In a way."

"Well that's fucking freaky. Can she do that to anyone? Could she do that to me?"

"Technically yes—"

"What?"

"You are not her type. She prefers big men."

"What do you mean 'technically yes?' I'm the one who has to go back there tomorrow and get up close and personal with Adèle for her training session. They'll be there."

"You have my word. I will not permit them to harm you."

"How?"

"I have my ways, child. Trust that I will protect you."

Minette wondered if she could back out right this second.

"You have one more day there. Then we can watch from afar. Now take off your coat and stay a while."

"I'm not staying." She found her keys on the counter, jingling them in her hand.

"You don't mean to take another night ride. It is too dangerous with the rain and wind."

"Fine." She did as Lisette asked. She was cold and too drained to go for a ride anyway. She hung her coat and sat at the table. Lisette served her a bowl and set a spoon beside her. Minette only stared at it, picked up the spoon, then set it down again. "I'm not hungry."

"Tell me why."

"They don't think Peachy wants to come home."

"'Tis not the entire truth."

"It's entirely true, Lisette, and you can quit pretending. I guess it's me that needs to quit pretending that Peachy is in love with me, because I know she isn't." Minette pushed her bowl away and hunched her shoulders, unable to find a cleansing breath. She hated that tears threatened, but she was unable to stop the hurt.

Lisette pulled a chair next to her, rested her hand on her shoulder and rubbed. "I know that she loves you. I see it in her heart when I reach out to her. She is conflicted because she loves you."

"What is this creature they mentioned?"

"Her name is Noomi. She is a Shifter and a Seer."

"Great. So she's powerful? She's probably hot, huh?"

"She found Peachy when she arrived and she nursed her back to health. She is a good person. She's what Peachy needs right now, and she's helping her as much as us. She wants Peachy to have a choice too."

"Peachy's in love with her?"

"She is dealing with an array of emotions that are new to her."

"So she's in love." Minette grabbed her coat, put it on and faced the door. "This is hard, Lisette."

"I know it is."

"Why doesn't she love me?"

"She does love you."

"Not like that."

CHAPTER EIGHTEEN

Noomi's house felt hollow without her. Her walls, which boasted vibrant colors and hues, now appeared lacking in luster. Noomi's fires, which usually roared, crackled, and sounded like the company of a good friend, didn't seem as cheerful. Noomi brightened every room with *her* warmth and *her* light. It illuminated Peachy's world when Noomi spoke, smiled, and created with her hands. Her spirit existed in everything that filled her home—the baskets she made, maps she painted with her steady hand, and her lovely books, some of which she wrote and illustrated herself. Peachy held one in her hands.

She felt the leather spine against her fingertips, unbending leather that stretched her mind with each turn of the page. She hoped to absorb its meaning through her touch, through smoothing her fingertips over the images, letters, and handwritten notes Noomi had left. These great volumes were similar to the ones that Lisette and Adèle had in their possession, but Noomi's were different, full of magic and wonder. They weren't filled with words that, when appropriately strung together, poisoned, controlled, warded, conjured and filled empty and begging brains and bodies with things that people wanted or desired, badly enough to trade their souls.

Peachy returned the book to its shelf and eyed her journal that lay on the table, afraid to touch it—unnerved by it. She had been writing about her mother when Lisette had come to her. This time it felt as though Lisette was there, sitting across from her, holding her hands and telling her all the answers to all the questions she wrote within the pages. "Rahimah," Peachy whispered. "My mother's name was Rahimah of the Sky." She touched her own face. "I look like her."

Lisette had told her that her mother was of Noomi's world. That she herself was of Noomi's world. Lisette didn't outright say they were Heathers. The way she spoke, her allusions, never stated anything and nearly drove Peachy off a cliff. *Soon answers, soon. Listen, don't fight.* So enigmatic. Was Peachy a goddamn Heather? Did she have abilities? Could she see between two worlds, feel Lisette in her mind, and communicate with Noomi through her touch? Was it real or a byproduct of a crack to her skull? Peachy felt as though she sat atop a merry-go-round, spinning in circles, accomplishing nothing.

Lisette's other advice, *trust no one*, felt more like a warning. Everyone wanted to possess Peachy, to use her. *But everything would be okay.*

Nothing would be okay ever again. It most certainly would not. She wasn't angry or resentful that Lisette had sent her on a cosmic journey to a world with beings who held mystifying abilities. Should she trust Noomi? Lisette had told her to love her and learn from her. Should she still be cautious? She closed her eyes and rubbed her chest. How could she be untrusting of the woman who had pieced her together little by little, starting with her body and ending with her heart?

Peachy felt Noomi's promises everywhere, in her mind, against her lips, through her touch, and with her expressive eyes that changed like an animal before claiming its prey. *I will not let anythin' bad happen to ye. Listen to me heart. Feel me promises on me lips.* Noomi's words of encouragement that last night they were together. Along with the comfort Noomi's promise also brought trepidation. Noomi's words were meant to be tested, which meant that harm would need to threaten. If it did, Noomi would need to be there to fulfill her promise. If Peachy were to return home, she would be there alone. Noomi's words only meant so much and were only applicable in Noomi's world. The thought of facing *that* life again—alone—brought anxious palpitations against the weight of the amulet. For now, she felt safe…cared for…self-sufficient…in love.

She managed to cook for all in the house. While Missy and Sissy carefully selected scraps of cheese and fruit, Gabin didn't display signs of hunger. If she did, she didn't *say* as much, preferring to sleep, watching all the goings on with one eye open and the other closed. Peachy wanted Noomi's pipeweed, but she worried she'd burn the place down. For now she'd satiate her clouded mind with thoughts of Noomi and the night they shared.

It didn't help that every time Peachy got a scent of the healing salve, it pushed her toward a climax of the mind. She felt as though she'd explode if she didn't do something. The idea of doing *that* in Noomi's steaming hot pool, sounded amazingly appropriate and overdue. "Um, Gabin? I'm going to take a bath."

The cat stared at her, blinked a few times, shook her head, scratched herself behind her ear, and sent a wisp of fur floating through the air.

Peachy moaned when she settled into the steaming hot pool, letting the steam soothe her mind. She closed her eyes and ran her fingers along the inside of her thigh, thinking of Noomi, as if the woman were there with her. She was already close, already wet with her thoughts for her. She encouraged herself, she was almost there…

"Hello." A woman entered and promptly turned her back. "Oh, apologies."

Peachy jolted forward, surprised. The striking woman wore a hooded velvet robe and spoke near perfect English. "Hello?"

"I'm sorry for interruptin'." The stranger turned toward her and held her gaze. "I'm Nefertari. I come in peace. I'm a friend o' Noomi's. Was hopin' we could talk? I can...I'll wait inside." She pointed. "Here let me help. That cast looks a bear." Nefertari handed her a towel. "Ye must be Peachy o' the Sky. I am sorry to arrive unannounced."

"Where is Noomi?" Peachy climbed the three steps from the pool, feeling the woman's gaze linger on the amulet around her neck. Peachy covered herself with the towel, sensing as though the woman had taken something from her when she grazed her fingers against her own.

"She's involved in a research project, back at the Realm o' the Keepers. Please, I mean no harm. I only want to talk. I'll be inside. Take your time."

Nefertari retreated to the house as if she had been there before. She probably had. She remembered Noomi saying this woman was five hundred and something years old. Likely she'd seen every corner of their realm. Peachy hurried to their room, dressed and found Nefertari seated at their dining table. With her hood off, Peachy saw her long and lustrous white hair shimmering down her entire back. Her skin radiated a beautiful deep bronze. She looked to be about Lisette's age, but after everything that had occurred, Peachy questioned how old Lisette really was. Noomi's kind appeared youthful. She eyed Gabin and saw that the mice were up, the lot awaiting her grand entrance. It was now or never. She took a deep breath before making her presence known.

"Again, I am sorry for bargin' in on ye. The door to Noomi's cottage, used to be, the way I entered." The woman held out her hand. "Let's start over. I am Nefertari and ye are Peachy. I understand that a handshake is how your kind greet each other."

Peachy knew enough from her interactions with Noomi to know to avoid touching her. "It is how *some* people say hello, mostly businessmen, and since neither of us are businessmen, I'll settle for a *how do you do?*" Peachy joined her at the table and folded her hands. Nefertari eyed her hands as if she debated reaching for her. Peachy felt Gabin's tail thump against her leg. She ran her fingers through the fur on her head and held it there for support. "What can I do for you? Would you like tea? Fair warning. I haven't quite mastered the art of boiling water."

"No. Thanks. I am here mostly out o' concern."

"Mostly?"

"Noomi was distraught when she arrived this mornin' seekin' me counsel. I only wish to put her mind at ease."

"I hope I can help alleviate all of your concerns."

Nefertari gave her a curt smile. "Forgive me if I come across as intrusive. I'm merely curious."

"Concerned and curious? Are you also cautious?"

"'Tis not every day a visitor makes her grand entrance to our realm by fallin' out o' the sky."

"Then your realm and mine have something in common." They held each other's gaze for what felt like an eternity. "Well," she said, causing the animals and Nefertari to startle, "have I satisfied your curiosity, alleviated your concerns and given you cause to relax the cautious way you are interacting with me?"

Nefertari chuckled. "Ye are an interestin' spirit, Peachy."

"I'll take that as a compliment." Peachy gave her a toothy grin.

"May I ask ye questions?"

"May I ask some in return?"

"O' course," Nefertari said. "Mind if I go first?"

"Shoot."

Nefertari narrowed her eyes.

"That means you can begin."

She nodded. "Where are ye from?"

"A tiny, mostly blue planet in the Milky Way Galaxy, hot, full of plastic. Where exactly is the Realm of the Heathers?"

"We belong to a system o' seventeen planes o' existence. We reside in the third level comprised o' bein's that attract energy from elements, animals, and emotions. What are ye doin' here?"

"I don't know. What are you doing here?"

"I wanted to make sure ye were who Noomi said ye were. What were ye doin' before ye arrived?"

"About to fall to my death. Don't you trust Noomi?"

"I only wanted to ensure that ye were not ill with intent and out to take advantage o' her kindness. Tell me about your latest dream."

"I dreamt of a friend who offered me advice. Where is Noomi?"

"She is safe in the Realm o' the Keepers and will be released when I am sure that she is safe. How old are ye?"

"Twenty-five."

"Twenty-five…"

"Twenty and then five."

The woman blinked a couple of times. "Is that—"

"It's my turn."

The woman nodded. "O' course."

"What keeps you up at night?"

"The protection o' me people. I ensure that our times are peaceful and free from conflict. I apply justice when appropriate. What was the advice your friend from your dream left with you?"

"To not worry so much. When was the last time your people saw war?"

Nefertari leaned back and crossed her arms. "More'n four hundred years ago. What is your mother's name?"

The door opened, startling everyone and saving Peachy from having to answer that. She felt the warning in Lisette's message come to life. It was Noomi. She was breathless. A handful of men entered moments after she did and pushed her to her knees. Peachy stood wanting to go to her.

The look on Nefertari's face said she was as surprised as Peachy. "Guards, please!" Nefertari helped Noomi to her feet. They spoke so fast in Noomi's language that Peachy didn't understand a word. Noomi made eye contact with Peachy before following Nefertari outside. When all had left, Peachy collapsed into the chair and wrapped her arms around Gabin. "What the hell was that?"

CHAPTER NINETEEN

"Ye defied me orders. This is most unlike the Noomi that *I* know," Nefertari said.

"I had no choice, no explanation. I have nothin' to hide to warrant keepin' me prisoner."

"Then ye still aim to tell me that the amulet is a trinket? That ye did not recognize the script o' our realm imprinted upon it?"

"I am sorry I was not forward. I was scared. She asked me to keep it between us. I am only as good as the promises I keep to those I love. I had planned to tell ye when I understood more. I prayed to the Heathers for their guidance and understandin' for the choices I made today. I felt they supported me actions."

Nefertari crossed her arms. "I am disappointed but understand the value ye place upon keepin' your word. I hope that ye too can understand why I did what I did. For the protection o' the realm."

Noomi nodded.

"There is no doubt in me mind that I made the right decision for I learned she possesses no trinket. I also sense that she has no idea what it is, which causes the confusion and turmoil you've described to me."

"'Tis true. She doesn't understand. Neither do I."

"I know that ye are pure hearted and that ye know where your alliances rest. I also trust that ye know o' the line between loyalty and treason and understand the consequences o' crossin' that line."

"I do." Noomi bit her lip and looked to her home, seeing Gabin's silhouette in one of the windows. She wanted to go in there and hold her family and pretend this day never happened.

"I still trust ye, Noomi, as does the realm. Together we will be reliant upon ye for the part that ye will play."

"What part would that—"

Nefertari held her hand up. "She is not who she claims. I don't mean to suggest that she has been untruthful with ye. I believe she is unaware o' what, exactly, she is."

"What *is* she?"

"From me brief interaction, from the abbreviated brush o' me touch upon her, along with the amulet she wears, I conclude she is a direct descendant o' a line o' Heathers that nearly drove our realm to ruin."

"I don't understand."

"She is a Teller."

Noomi shook her head. "How is this possible? They were sentenced to death. Their line ended and with 'em their gifts."

"That's not entirely true. Before they were sentenced, they escaped. Vanished. Our attempts to locate 'em were unsuccessful. They haven't been heard from in more'n four hundred years. The fact that a livin', breathin' Teller is inside your home is beyond me comprehension."

"But our history has told us o' their demise."

"Sometimes our history is presented in a way that benefits a particular narrative."

"A cover-up?" Noomi held her face in her hands and shook her head unwilling to believe.

"Call it what ye want. It happened before me rule and now that I am ruler, I will do what *I* see fit. She will be made to atone."

"She is to be celebrated."

"Oh, no. Their kind were murderous. Their hearts corrupt. They were traitors and greedy with power. She is here to incite war."

"Ye know nothin'."

"And ye forget your place, Noomi."

"I aim to say that her soul carries not war but a message o' peace."

"Tell me how ye explain the evil that lurks inside her?"

"They want the amulet. They fight inside her mind. She means nothin' to 'em. They torment her for it. They aim to kill her at all costs. Let us give it to 'em and be free."

"When I took me oath to keep our people free o' harm, I made a promise to do everythin' I could to ensure peace and avoid war at whatever cost. I promised I'd uphold the law, be fair and ensure justice."

"Ye don't mean to tell me that ye plan to hold her accountable for what has happened prior to her existence. She had nothin' to do with anythin' before her!"

"Easy, Noomi. I will not ask ye again to mind your temper in me presence."

"I'm sorry."

"I don't aim to punish her for acts she did not commit. No, that is not how I want to play this."

"Play this? Play what?"

"A Teller walks among us. She presents an array o' possibilities. The fact that Peachy o' the Sky, Peachy the Only, does not comprehend her powers means a clean slate for our people. As ye can imagine, this is most interestin' and worthy o' exploration."

"Tis exploitation. What gift could she possibly possess worthy o' that?"

"Gift? More like gifts. She possesses 'em all for her kind bestowed 'em upon themselves, gifts in abundance and then some that we are unfamiliar. However, tis not the fact that she bears powers beyond comprehension. Tis the amulet she possesses that is o' most use."

"Where did she get it?"

"I don't know. The original amulets were confiscated, and before me departure from the city, I verified they were still in our possession. The words on her amulet read *daughter*. If she is a daughter o' one o' the original Tellers…" Nefertari rubbed her hands together like a greedy child with a treat she wasn't going to share. "The power within her is like nothin' we've ever seen."

"Why not take the amulet for your own?" Noomi suggested. "Store it with the others, be free o' it, or better yet, wield it yourself?"

"It does not do for me what it will do for her. Tis meanin'less in me hands, your hands or anyone else's. Tis her hands that we want."

"Ye aim to use her?"

"For the betterment o' the realm and to ensure our safety and protection."

"Are we not safe now? Do we not live in peace?"

"We've lived in peace because her kind is gone. If she is permitted to stay and live out her years here, there is no guarantee that peace will endure. With the amulet under me protection, we all but ensure our people will live in peace. What are ye failin' to understand?"

"We are talkin' about a woman's life. She should have a say as to her own fate. Let her exercise free will. If she wants to go home, let her go. If she wants to use her gifts for the betterment o' our people, she should have a choice and decide how to use 'em."

"Ye should hear yourself. 'If she *chooses* to contribute to our realm.'" Nefertari laughed as if Noomi's comment was ignorant. "And if she decides to take us down in a ball o' fire?"

"She won't."

"I will not risk it."

"If she truly means us harm, she should be sent back to her world."

"This *is* her world."

"No."

Noomi hadn't imagined this outcome when she embarked on her journey that day. She went in search of answers to illuminate Peachy's pathway, to bring her options and now she had none.

"We are done talkin' about this, Noomi. Here are your orders. Ye will get her ready for me. Teach her how to use her gifts. One day I will return, and ye will turn her over to me. Peachy the Teller, Peachy the Only, is destined for greatness. The fact that she is in love with ye couldn't have worked out more in our favor."

"What does love have to do with this?"

"She trusts that ye are doin' everythin' for her because ye love her and that ye are teachin' her because ye believe in her."

"And when I turn her over, all that will shatter. She will shatter. She won't trust me or ye or anyone else for that matter and then what?"

"Let me manage that when the times comes."

"No."

"Or I take her now and train her meself and ye will never see her again."

"No."

Nefertari walked into Noomi's personal space. "Tell me no one more time and I will strip ye o' your gifts. The realm will treat ye as a traitor. Ye will live out your long days in a dark cell under lock and key. No books, no art, no sister. I will only share with ye in great detail o' Peachy's glory. How she's moved on and taken new lovers, and I'll describe her life each year that she is with us. You've already put us in danger by not bein' forthcomin' with me. I should take ye both captive, but I am a gracious ruler and don't want it to come to that. I care about ye Noomi. I care about her too. Do I make me wishes clear?"

"Do I have a choice?" Noomi knew she was walking a fine line between loyalty and treason and was prepared to cross it.

"Ye always have a choice. Your life or hers."

Noomi fell to her knees.

"I shall take your silence as your willin'ness to cooperate."

"How am I supposed to go in there and keep this from her? Tis a betrayal o' me heart and o' hers."

"The fact that ye are concerned with betrayin' her and not the people o' your kingdom along with your inflexibility is most concernin' to me and will be dealt with in time. For now, ye have your orders. Train her. Ye will know when tis the time to turn her over to me custody. Oh and one other thing Noomi, I will be watchin'.'"

Noomi watched Nefertari and her guards transform into a flock of birds and disappear into the trees. She jumped up and ran home.

"Where is she?" Noomi asked upon opening the door.

"I knew this would happen," Gabin said.

"Not helpful!"

"She's in the loft," Missy said.

Noomi parted the fabric separating her main room from the under construction library and in her rush, completely pulled it from the ceiling. She climbed the ladder leading to the observation loft, stopping short of going the entire way, crossing her arms on the ledge and resting her chin on her arms. "I am sorry from the bottom o' me heart," she said, catching her breath.

Peachy sat with her knees drawn to her chest and her arms wrapped around them. She didn't move from holding her eyes on the moons.

Noomi saw tears on her wet cheeks. "May I join ye?" she asked, but Peachy said nothing. "Please. I've thought o' nothin' but gettin' back to ye all day for the void in me heart."

Peachy finally made eye contact. "What happened?"

She shook her head. "I was not careful. I allowed her to take from me without me consent. She knew ye possessed an object that caused uncertainty that might be dangerous. I was unable to deny it. I made it worse by tryin'. I would have come sooner, but she did not tell me o' her plans to find ye. I wasted most o' the day doin' nothin' before I realized what was goin' on. The city guard would not permit me to leave the city. T'was under her orders."

"But that did not stop you, did it?" Peachy smiled and wiped her cheeks.

Noomi nodded. "I am sorry I was unable to keep me promise. The one secret ye asked o' me and I failed." She shook her head and closed her eyes. "I am weak."

"That's not true. You've given me more strength than I know what to do with. You are the opposite of weak."

"What is the opposite o' weak?"

"You." Peachy smiled. "I don't blame you. She brushed my fingers for like two seconds, and it felt as though she took half of my memories with her. It was such a bad feeling."

"I'm sorry that she frightened ye, that she arrived unannounced and took from ye without your consent."

Peachy shrugged her shoulders.

"What were ye doin' when she arrived?"

"I was in the pool, thinking about you."

Noomi smiled and climbed the rest of the way up and sat opposite Peachy. "Then what?"

"She asked me a bunch of questions. Wanted to make sure I wasn't dangerous. Asked if I was taking advantage of you, your kindness." Peachy nudged Noomi's leg with her own. "Am I?"

"No. Never in a million years would I feel that way. When I found your poor broken body, even before ye woke up, before ye spoke, before I saw your heart, I knew ye were sent to me for a reason."

"What reason?"

"To love ye."

Peachy smiled and took Noomi's hands in her own. "I am sorry you got in trouble."

"T'was not your fault."

"It's entirely my fault."

"No."

"Did you get any information? About me? About the amulet?"

"Yes." Noomi took a deep breath and scooted herself close until their foreheads touched. She took Peachy's hands in her own. "I know who ye are, Peachy o' the Sky." *Peachy the Only. Peachy the Teller is destined for greatness.* Nefertari's words felt like barbed wire that strangled the life from her.

"Tell me. Please."

"The reason why ye are able to communicate with me, include me in your dreams and cross time and space is because ye are a Heather. Ye are like me, like Gabin. Your people, this Lisette, Beatriz, Adèle, are of me people as well." Noomi watched her reaction. Peachy bit her lip and looked at their intertwined fingers. Noomi expected Peachy to recoil, to push her away in disbelief. "Do ye understand what I say?"

"I do."

"And ye are not confused?"

"Oh, I'm confused as fuck, but not entirely surprised. Lisette came to me today. I was writing in my journal, thinking about my mother, writing about you and being here, my life. It was *so* real because it was real. She was with me. Right down there. Sat in the chair directly across from me, held my hands and told me that I was of this world. As crazy as everything is, I know I'm not crazy."

"Ye are the opposite o' crazy."

Peachy let out a gentle laugh.

"Did she give ye any more details about what ye are capable o', your gifts? Ye have several."

"No. I don't think she had enough time. It was all very rushed. I woke up shortly thereafter," Peachy explained. "Do you know?"

"Ye are o' the line o' the Tellers."

"Which ones are they? The ones good at strategy?"

"Tellers were the ones who waged war against our people, the ones who are no longer among us."

"I thought they didn't exist anymore."

"Apparently before they were sentenced to die, they escaped. Your family, Lisette, her twin Beatriz, Adèle, and your mother escaped, she could still be alive."

"She isn't."

"How do ye know?"

"Because I know."

"I'm sorry." Noomi brushed her thumb against Peachy's cheek.

"What about the amulet?"

"The amulet ye possess is different'n the ones they beheld. Nefertari said that the realm still has their amulets under lock and key."

"They had their *own* amulets?"

Noomi nodded. "They were taken from 'em, which is the only reason our people were able to get the advantage. That's why they are lookin' for ye. For that." Noomi motioned with her eyes to Peachy's chest.

"Whose amulet is this then?"

"Yours."

"How?"

Noomi only shook her head.

"Should I be worried?"

"No." Noomi held Peachy's hands tightly in her own.

"Your people aren't going to let me live here without wanting something, without making me pay." Peachy began hyperventilating. "They must think I'm like them, corrupt and evil. I'm not, Noomi. I'm not." She placed her hand upon her chest and winced as if the amulet pained her. "Nefertari must think... I got to hide. I don't want to die."

"Listen to me." Noomi held Peachy's face in her hands, giving her strength, warming her spirit. "Breathe." She kissed her lips. "Ye are not goin' to die. Ye are not under threat. Nothin' bad will happen to ye. Ye need to learn. Ye need to learn how to use your gifts."

"Why?"

"For your protection."

"Protection from what?" Peachy pulled the amulet from her shirt. "From this, right? What is it? Is it like a portal between our worlds?" Peachy looked skyward and moaned.

"The amulet makes the future possible."

"I can see into the future?"

"Ye can create the future."

"What? How?"

"Through writin'."

Peachy's eyes grew wide. "I've been writing, Noomi. A lot. I've wished for things, for stuff to happen."

"It's not as easy as it sounds. Trainin' must come first. They work together."

"Nefertari wants it. I know it. She could have easily overpowered me. Why didn't she? It's a weapon."

"The amulet only works in your possession. Or another Teller's."

"Like Beatriz or Adèle."

Noomi nodded.

"But Nefertari—"

"She wants me to help ye, protect and train ye."

"She does?"

Noomi nodded. "Let me be your guide and show ye how to use your precious gifts."

"Why not just get rid of it or send me home?"

"We don't know how to send ye home. Ye are here for a reason. I aim to help ye understand why."

Peachy nodded and groaned. "This is so fucked."

"'Tis a great amount to bear all by yourself."

"Lisette said something else to me."

"Tell me."

"She said to love you, to trust you. Can I? Trust you?"

Noomi straddled Peachy on her lap and wrapped her arms around her. She held her until Peachy's breathing slowed and she relaxed against her completely. "Ye can trust that I will always be true. I will put ye first, always and forever."

"And what if I take it off? Will it take me home?"

"I don't know. But if ye want to try, I'll hold ye. I'll go with ye."

"You will?"

"I'll go anywhere with ye. Please know that."

"I love you, Noomi. I can't imagine a day without you for the peace that you bring to my heart."

"I love ye more'n I thought I was capable o' lovin' another bein'."

"So now what?"

Noomi slipped her hands under Peachy's shirt and tickled her fingers up and down her back, causing Peachy to arch into her. Noomi rubbed her nose against Peachy's neck and began kissing her, licking her, feeling the pulse of blood in Peachy's veins against her tongue. Peachy moaned and squirmed but then pulled away.

"Noomi?"

"Hmm?" she said in between her kisses.

Peachy leaned back and took Noomi's face in her hands. She smoothed her thumbs across her cheeks before she kissed her. "I think it's best we take a step back."

"Like this?" Noomi leaned back.

"No." Peachy laughed softly. "I mean I need time to think. This news, these dreams, being here, this world… You forget that it's new and strange, so fucking strange."

"Even me?" Noomi kissed the palms of Peachy's hands. "Am I still so fuckin' strange to ye?"

"The fucking strangest," Peachy said. "I've fallen in love with you. Fallen head over heels. You are all I think about, when I sleep, when I'm awake. So much so that I don't think I've given myself time to digest the magnitude of any of this, of us. Do you understand?"

Noomi nodded. "I am here to support and love ye. If ye need time to think, ye can have all the time ye need. I'll be here." Noomi closed her eyes, knowing that time was most certainly not on their side. Again Nefertari's barbed words cut into her. *Ye have your orders. Train her. Ye will know when tis the time to turn her to me custody.* She began to cry.

"Noomi? Oh. Please, no." Peachy kissed her lips. "I need time. That's it."

"I know. I'm sorry. This day has been long and full o' stress."

"I know and *I'm* sorry for causing it. For being here, for falling into your world, turning it upside down—"

"Tis right side up remember?" Noomi smiled.

"Today sucked. It was a reminder of the danger I present to you, your family."

Noomi's tears weren't because she wasn't strong. They were because she was weak. Because she had orders to follow.

"So what about the sleeping arrangements?"

"Ye mean not to sleep with me?"

"If I do that, neither of us will sleep."

"We won't?"

"Noomi."

"Oh. Oooh. Please take the bed. Tis better, warmer. Ye are still healin'. I'll sleep up here."

"Are you sure?"

"Positive. At least I will always hold the memory ye gave me the night before everythin' came tumblin' upon us."

"That was the most beautiful memory."

"Wait," Noomi said. "What if ye need me in the middle o' the night?"

"I can take care of myself." Peachy smiled.

Noomi cocked her head and then smiled, understanding Peachy's double meaning.

They descended the ladder. Noomi escorted Peachy to their room and closed the door behind her. Noomi walked back to the dark and cool reading room and sat upon the stone ledge of her fireplace.

"Are ye okay?" Gabin asked as she and her mice friends entered.

"No," was all she managed before the tears came.

Sissy and Missy crawled into her lap, and she took them into her hands. *"What happened?"* Missy asked.

Noomi shook her head. *"I can't talk about it."*

"Can't or won't," Gabin said.

Noomi only hung her head and closed her eyes.

"She is a Heather?" asked Missy.

"I told ye so," Gabin said. *"I told ye she was a Seer. Didn't I? All o' her odd and dramatic dreamin' not knowin' how to control herself,"* Gabin said to the wee mice, who nodded in agreement.

"She is a Teller."

"Impossible."

"Possible."

"That explains Nefertari's visit," Gabin said. *"What are her orders?"*

"Not now, Gab. Please. Ye were right as usual. When we found her, I should have listened to ye and let her…"

"*Let her what Noomi, let her die? Cold, hurt, and alone? Unimaginable.*"

"*Me heart will never be the same.*"

"*If there's a reason she's here with us as part o' our family, then it will be known. Maybe not today or tomorrow, but soon,*" Gabin said.

"*Whatever happened will be okay,*" Missy said. Sissy nodded in agreement.

Noomi could only shake her head and vehemently disagree. "*Thanks for takin' care o' her while I was away. Your watch was better'n mine.*"

"*I can see that ye love her,*" Gabin said, nudging Noomi's leg with her head.

"*I love her more'n me own life.*"

"*I see her love for ye grow every day,*" Gabin said. "*When ye are ready to talk, ye have me help and guidance.*"

"*We can help too!*" The mice shouted and clapped their hands. Noomi picked them up. She rubbed her nose against their tiny faces before placing them into their basket.

"*With thanks,*" she said and stood. "I should reattach the fabric...No. I'm goin' to work." She nudged the fallen fabric aside with her foot. She lit a wax lamp, gathered her tools and worked into the night until she nearly collapsed with fatigue and became blind with anger for herself and her idiocy and willingness to go along with Nefertari's plan.

Nefertari's instructions were clear, but the thought of deliberately tricking Peachy, training her, turning her over for the use of the realm, made her sick. This would not have a happy ending and their love was forever doomed.

She spent the night in the loft alone, longing for her lover, wondering if she'd ever be able to touch her again. If she had to turn Peachy over, she'd make the most of every moment with her and cherish the feeling of her in her arms. She'd make her smile and make her laugh whenever possible to see the beauty reflected in her eyes. She held onto that image while she drifted to sleep; however, the image soon turned horrific when she imagined Peachy's eyes once she learned of Noomi's betrayal.

CHAPTER TWENTY

Lisette helped Minette transform their dwelling into command central. They covered the windows with blankets. The only visible light came from the screens of their electronics. Lisette counted twenty different feeds displayed on two laptops and one giant monitor. The feeds showed every room in the *Spanish Rose*, the marbled corridors, and every entrance and exit, including the hidden ones.

"They don't see *all* these feeds do they?" Lisette asked. She scooted her chair closer to Minette's.

"Adèle only sees what *I* want her the see." Minette waved her hand over a group of feeds on one of the monitors. "The rest are for our eyes only."

"What is that interesting device?" Lisette asked, pointing to the object Minette held. It looked like a video game controller.

"It's how I angle the cameras," she said, positioning one on a couple of Beatriz's bodyguards. "Behold. The walking dead. They're so creepy. I *really* hope I don't need to install more cameras to keep an eye on these fuckers. There's more of them every day. It's not like there are hordes of people threatening the *Spanish Rose*. Why are there so many?"

"Beatriz is paranoid. She wants to avoid another hiatus underground. There will also be a time when I will require a face-to-face meeting with my sisters, and she wants to be prepared."

"I dread the day." Minette shivered so hard she rattled the assortment of electronic devices littering their newly acquired card table.

"Let us take each day, child, and learn as much as we can about my sisters' end goals and go from there."

Currently Beatriz and Adèle were deep in conversation in Adèle's workroom, standing over a shallow basin.

"Looks like they're getting ready to do something," Minette said. She handed Lisette a set of headphones. "You'll notice a slight delay with the audio. It's nothing to worry about. I'll need it in the event I need to reuse a recording."

"Let us both show ourselves. Show our force," Beatriz said to Adèle.

"We'll look weak. Two ancient Heathers looking for an amulet that a twenty-five-year-old child took from them."

"They know the terror we bring doesn't originate inside the amulet," Beatriz said. "Besides, the girl arrived in their world beaten and bloodied. It's a taste of what's to come."

"It shows them that we can beat up the weak."

"Exactly."

"No. You're not ready. She will sense it."

Beatriz rolled her eyes. "I forgot just how dramatic you are, Adèle."

"Be my guiding hand until you recover your abilities. It has been an age since we've looked upon our old world. We risk identifying our whereabouts. If that happens, nothing will stop them from sending an army to retrieve us."

"Let them come. I want war."

"No one is going to war!"

"This long-lost acquaintance is a long shot, Adèle."

"It's our *only* shot right now. We have no other choice but to play it safe."

"I want to play it recklessly."

"Luckily, I am here to remind you of the things that happen when you play it your way. Cement coffin ring a bell?"

Beatriz set her jaw and growled. Lisette looked at a wide-eyed Minette.

"Well then I wish you the best."

Adèle let out a clipped laugh. "I know you want to go back to tormenting Peachy—"

"And using my twin against her will. I am still capable of causing Lisette great mental anguish, weakening her, thus weakening the girl. We should do both. Split ourselves up." Beatriz rubbed her temples.

"I'm not talking about this again. We do it my way to start, stick to the plan…"

Lisette took off the headphones. "They are divided."

"They seem nervous too."

"All to our benefit." Lisette stood.

"Where're you going?"

"I need to take advantage of their squabbling and connect with Peachy. Beatriz knows when I make contact and I don't want to draw her attention and further encourage her to split from Adèle."

"Good idea," Minette said, casting her eyes downward. Visible defeat settled upon her shoulders.

Lisette sat back down and put her hands upon Minette's shoulders. "You are worried?"

"Will you tell her hi for me?"

"I will tell her you love her and you have put yourself in great danger to ensure that she is safe."

Minette shook her head. "Just tell her hi or something."

Lisette stood and gathered her supplies. "I will relay the message."

"So while you're doing your thing…" Minette motioned toward Lisette's basin. "Is there anything I should watch for? I mean, it's not like I can record what goes on in their pretty little demented heads."

"Capture their follow-up conversations, and I'll review it upon my return. If it sounds like they've made contact with their long-lost acquaintance, get me. If what they say sounds alarming, get me. If they talk about going after Peachy, get me."

"Roger that." Minette put her headphones on. "Good luck."

Lisette settled in Minette's room. She readied her basin. The connection took life and she closed her eyes to search for Peachy. She arrived at Noomi's house and found everyone asleep. She went to their room and found Peachy sleeping alone. The fire's embers cast an amber glow and illuminated Peachy, making her look like bronze artwork. Lisette sat at the edge of the bed, placed her hand upon her hip, and closed her eyes. She learned that the girl knew who she was, that she longed for her lover, and she was more confused than ever before.

She also looked different—no longer the child that Lisette had sent on the biggest job of her life. Peachy was a woman who had emerged from a living terror, with both mental and physical scars. She was stronger than before, ready and able to learn who she was and what she was capable of accomplishing. Lisette knew she was a long way from knowing the truth and that her pain, confusion, and worry were only beginning.

"Peachy wake."

Peachy jolted upright. She rubbed her eyes and looked around the room, gasping when she saw Lisette. She held out her hands and backed away. "Easy, child. It's me, Lisette. You are safe."

"Lisette? Are you really here? Can you really hear me?"

"I can hear you loud and clear. This is a safe connection."

Peachy nodded, swallowed hard. "Jesus." She looked Lisette over.

"Are you okay, child?"

Peachy nodded. "When you came to me last time, I felt trapped. I couldn't move, talk, or do anything. Why is it different now?" She looked at her hands.

"You are aware. I know that you have learned who you are. That's the first step."

"I have so many questions, Lisette."

"I will answer everything I can." Lisette hoped Peachy found peace in their connection instead of more confusion and pain. "It's okay to be scared. First, I need to show you something."

"What?"

"Take a deep breath and look at your body."

"What do you mean?" Peachy held her own hands in front of her, inspecting both sides.

"Your body." Lisette motioned with her chin.

The girl looked behind her and saw her own lifeless form. She wasn't sure whether she should sit next to herself or the apparition of Lisette. "Jesus, am I…"

"This is how Seers walk. You leave your body behind when you make a connection; that is how you know it's true. If you do not see yourself, if you can't find yourself in your mind's eye, then you are dreaming. When you walk, you are here and there, as my body is here and there, and I can see myself in both places."

The girl appeared petrified with fear.

"Move freely, child. Both your physical being and your spirit are safe."

Peachy shook her head before meeting Lisette's gaze. Peachy looked like she wanted to hug Lisette. She tentatively reached for her hand, but Lisette pulled her into a long hug. Eventually Peachy pulled back, keeping hold of Lisette's hand.

"Why didn't you tell me anything?"

Lisette sighed. "You were not ready. You were being a carefree child. I didn't want to rush you. The lessons you learned along the way—"

"You mean the court fines?" Peachy smiled.

"All of that shaped your beautiful heart, and I still see that beauty inside you despite the horror you endured."

Peachy cast her eyes downward.

"I did not mean to thrust you into this world. I did not intend any of this." Lisette looked around. "But I couldn't have imagined a better, safer, place than with Noomi."

"Me too." Peachy nodded. "Why did it happen that way? One moment I was in the *Spanish Rose* about to die and the next I woke up here. If I take off the amulet, will I go back?"

"No. Something happened, a chain reaction. I am trying to piece everything together."

"I'm sorry I put the amulet on. I had no other choice."

"You did what you thought best in that moment. I am sorry that you endured pain and heartache. Can you ever forgive me?"

"There is nothing to forgive, Lisette." Peachy hugged her again. She sniffled and wiped her tears with the cuff of her sleeve. "I understand why you did what you did."

"Your spirit never ceases to amaze me. You've grown so much since we were last together."

"I feel like a different person."

"You are a different person. You are Peachy of the Sky."

"How long have I been gone?"

"Three and a half months. The times between our worlds move along the same continuum."

"And what about your sisters?" Peachy rubbed her chest as if thinking of them caused her pain. "Why didn't you tell me you had a twin?"

"It had been thirty-seven years since I had seen her. I thought she was dead. I thought if I told you about her, I'd have to tell you everything. I knew you would have a million questions and that I would not have satisfactory answers."

Peachy nodded.

"Is Beatriz still tormenting your dreams?"

"It's stopped. Noomi's been helping me. She walks with me in my dreams. I felt you there too." Peachy met Lisette's gaze.

"Why are you sleeping alone? Why aren't you under her protection?"

"I needed time to think after everything that's happened. She's right upstairs if I need her."

"Learn from her; she is good-hearted. You will continue to need her, for my sisters are plotting against us and are growing more powerful every day. They will not rest until they have you or the amulet in their possession. Ideally, they want both. They're planning as we speak a way to bring you back—"

"But I don't want to go, at least not yet. I don't know…"

"I know, child, and we are working to ensure that the decision to stay or leave is yours and no one else's. I can't guarantee that I will be successful."

"I understand. What about Minette? I saw her in a dream."

"I had to leave our home, for it is no longer safe for me. I found Minette and she has graciously let me live with her. She has proven quite useful. She is amazing at her work. She's outfitted the *Spanish Rose* with cameras. We are able to keep better track of my sisters because of her."

"She's brilliant." Peachy smiled. "Is she okay?"

"She knows everything."

"Everything?"

Lisette nodded. "Her heart is strong. I see why you included her in the biggest job of your life."

"Does she know about Noomi?"

"She does and she is okay, child. She is a remarkable spirit with strength beyond measure. She's put herself in harm's way on multiple occasions, just so you and I can talk safely and figure out what my sisters are planning. We don't know much yet, but we're working day and night to find out."

"Thank you. Please tell her thank you and that I do love her. I am sorry I didn't express it very well. I just…I never deserved her."

"Her love for you guides her every step. Do not feel bad because your heart needs something else."

Peachy shook her head. "What was your plan had I returned with the amulet?"

"I was going to tell you everything, train you, show you this world. Your home."

"And we had to have the amulet to do so?"

"Once you became aware, you would have been visible to my sisters. I did not want that target on your back. The amulet needed to come first, then training, then your choices, one of which was returning here."

"Our kind isn't quite respected here. I know the story, well, part of it."

"I'll tell you the rest, but first, tell me how you became aware."

Peachy recounted her meeting with Nefertari the Only, how Noomi had gotten in trouble, and how they were under watch. "Nefertari wants Noomi to train me."

"Go along and be cautious. I'll find out more about this Nefertari the Only and her intentions. What else have you learned?"

"Basic stuff about the realm, the land, reading maps, memorizing towns, their customs, stuff like that."

"And the gifts?"

"At a really high level. Noomi tries to help me, but I'm stuck."

"It's still early and your mind is only now beginning to open. I also think I have something that might help clear your mind."

"What?"

"I can tell you about your mother."

Peachy nodded. "Please. She's all I think about."

"By telling you I am risking your love for me, but I'm ready to accept your reaction and will still provide you protection and love."

"I could never stop loving you, Lisette. Trust that I will understand."

Lisette took a deep breath. "Your mother Rahimah, my sisters, and I, were among the race of Tellers. We could conjure anything we wanted and we abused it. With our amulets, we ensured that our kind would reign forever because we ensured that we could live forever. We didn't pass our gifts to future generations as the founding Heathers had intended. We were the past, the present and the future. We created a world so corrupt, so void of good, that hope had no chance. This next part of the story will be difficult for you. It is difficult for me, and I've had an age to understand why she did it."

"Did what?"

"Your mother betrayed us. She conferred with the realm elders and agreed to put a stop to our domination."

"How?"

"She agreed to negate the wrongs that our collective had caused by turning us over and agreeing to obey the rules of the Heathers. She made good on her promise and relinquished our amulets of power, even her own. They melted them into a single rod of metal and crushed the jewels into powder. Fate was again wild and free."

"Why would she do that?"

"Love makes one commit the unexplainable. Sometimes understanding comes years after, sometimes after several hundred."

"Love?"

"Your mother learned that she was pregnant. She did not want to raise you in the war that we created. She did what she thought was best and that meant betraying her own kind."

"Why didn't she talk to you first? Give you the option to change?"

"She thought we wouldn't listen to her."

"But to not give you a choice?"

"Beatriz, Adèle, and I asked ourselves that same question as we sat in a cell, awaiting our death. Your mother came to us and explained that she had a plan. She did not intend to let the realm put us to death. She had found a new world to send us to, one where we would fit in and live as powerful immortals.

"Beatriz and I share a unique bond, much like Noomi and Gabin. Beatriz had her own ideas of how this would end. She told me to go along with her plan. She was going to overpower your mother, kill her or die trying. We had nothing to lose

"While Rahimah said the words and we floated free in an abyss with only the twinkling of distant stars lighting us, I was the one who got to your mother first. I wrapped my hands around her neck, choking the life from her. In our struggle, I saw a glimmer of silver at her neck. Rahimah bore another amulet—a different amulet, one that she forged in secret. We fell into a rage. I don't know where Beatriz got the knife, but the next thing I remember was Beatriz stabbing her, spilling her blood across time and space.

"After the attack, we fell to Earth. Rahimah was not with us. We knew that she had died. Beatriz had spared no restraint. We were lost, evil, more bitter than before. Rahimah had decided our collective fate, giving us no choice to decide if we wanted to join her in living free of evil. I can't say now if I would have joined her, but I wanted that chance. We've walked an eon trying to find solace within blood, riches, and greed."

Peachy bore no tears as Lisette thought she would. She didn't display anger in knowing that Lisette had killed her mother. She looked at her hands and closed her eyes.

"I am sorry I killed your mother, that I robbed you of a life with her, exchanging the hardships you've known for one of peace among your kind."

"You are my kind, Lisette." Peachy took Lisette's hands in her own. "You are not that woman anymore. You showed me kindness as you have shown countless others. I've seen it. What changed for you?"

"I grew tired, always ill and carrying hatred. Part of it happened when we arrived at a small island, La Española, Haiti, where we fought alongside people who readily exchanged their lives, not for their own freedom, but the freedom of their unborn children. Before your mother died, as I looked into her eyes and saw the light dying inside her, she expressed regret. She asked me to look out for her unborn child. She said that one day you would appear to me, but only when the time was right. All she ever wanted was a life for you that was free of evil. Our victory in Haiti brought us to New Orleans, where we helped inspire others looking for that same freedom for their future generations. We weren't successful, but we liked it there. We felt magic that reminded us of home. We stayed and I began looking for you."

"I am not sure I would have done the same if my family had betrayed me."

"Child, I've had hundreds of years to come to terms."

"Where have I been this whole time?"

"I do not have those answers. You appeared to me when you were a child of twelve. I only knew you were twelve because you said so. I knew immediately that you were of Rahimah. I can't explain how."

"I hate that she betrayed all of you."

"Love brings out the best and the worst, and there's no telling which is right at the time."

"And all because of this?" Peachy pulled the amulet from her shirt.

The glint of the jewel caught Lisette's eye, much as it had that first time she saw it hanging around her sister's neck. She had wanted it then and killed her for it. She had shed the blood of innocent people because of it. It looked appropriate—right— as if it had found its home and would no longer be used to incite ill will in Peachy's possession. "All because of her love for you."

"Why didn't it work for my mother? As I understand it, this thing all but ensures a happy ending."

"It betrayed her."

"It can do that?"

Lisette nodded. "My assumption was that it did not find your mother's heart pure and betrayed her for its rightful owner. You."

"Can it turn on me too?"

"You have nothing to worry about. Your heart is good."

"Just because I've been raised a certain way doesn't mean I won't turn."

"Do not worry about that."

Peachy closed her eyes and sighed. "Jesus Christ, Lisette."

"Tell me what's in your heart, child."

"What am I supposed to do here? Learn my gifts and then what? It's not like I can be myself. They hate us here and for good reason. I'm not going to be accepted with open arms…" Peachy put her head into her hands. "Tell me what to do."

"I can no longer tell you what to do, child. The time has come where you make those decisions and find your own answers. Your heart is good, pure, and sweet. It has always been and ever will be. Learn everything you can. There will come a time when you will apply what you know. I may or may not be successful in preventing my sisters from getting to you first. Should that happen, you need to be ready."

"How?"

"Listen to Noomi. Write everything down. The more you write of what you need, the faster your abilities as a Teller will develop." Lisette hugged her. "I will not be able to see you for a long time. Don't be alarmed. I am up against several powerful forces."

"I understand."

Lisette stood.

"Wait," Peachy said. "What do I do?"

"What do you want to do?"

She looked at her sleeping body. "Uh, go there?"

"Then go." Lisette watched her crawl over her body and mirror its position. She closed her eyes and was asleep. "Be good, child."

CHAPTER TWENTY-ONE

"Relax your mind," Noomi whispered.

"I am."

"No, you're not. I need not touch ye to tell that your mind is full o' this and that."

Peachy took a sharp breath in and out. They were sitting on the ground next to the warmth of the freshly tiled fire pit in the new library with their legs crossed, facing each other, atop pillows and blankets. Peachy worked to learn as much as she could every day since the shock of Nefertari's visit and the revelation learned from Lisette's message. Noomi didn't press her. She was patient beyond measure and continued to work at Peachy's pace. Since Lisette's visit, Peachy's abilities as a Seer came easier.

"Don't force it, take your time. Everything else will happen when the time is right."

"I want to learn everything at once."

"Well ye can't. Hold me hands and close your eyes and be easy on yourself. Ye are testin' me patience."

Peachy obeyed and felt the surge of power transfer from Noomi to herself. She felt the wind against her face and opened her eyes. Still in the library. She popped up. "What the hell is my problem?" She ran her hand through her hair, strands catching on her cast. "Damn it. This thing needs to come off." She held out her casted arm and turned toward Noomi who was still seated on the ground, next to her physical self.

"I did it," she whispered. "Shit." Her voice sounded muffled, as if she were wearing earplugs. She walked toward herself and leaned closer, fearful to touch her own body. There appeared to be a haze over everything, nothing like when Lisette visited her and everything was crisp. She rubbed her eyes. It didn't help. She went to Gabin and the mice, who were sleeping in a cove. She almost touched Gabin but thought better of it, not knowing how the cat would react.

"*Noomi?*" She placed her hand upon Noomi's shoulder and closed her eyes. Her senses felt different. She could *see* feelings and *anticipate* words, as clear as if they were written on paper. Noomi was an overwhelming array of emotions bundled tightly—desire, hurt, worry, and regret. She backed off and looked at her own hands, unbelieving of what she felt. She remembered Lisette's instructions for coming back. She sat down mirroring her physical body and closed her eyes. A transfer of energy came to her as strong as the last pass between them. Peachy gasped when she opened her eyes, she met Noomi's rings of copper and gold.

"Did you see that?"

"I was there. Observing ye. I saw everythin'!" Noomi leaned in and hugged her.

Peachy felt shy when she met Noomi's gaze again, now slivers of black surrounded by vivid color. "I'm so proud o' ye."

Peachy cleared her throat. "I can't believe I was able to do it." She realized her hands were shaking. "Where were you?"

"I was there. Ye just didn't see."

"Why?"

"It takes time."

"How will I know if someone is with me? I mean anyone could spy on me, on us."

"Any *skilled Seer* can spy on ye if they know where to find ye," Noomi reminded her. "Over time ye will be able to sense the presence o' others. Over time ye will be able to also protect yourself from unwanted visitors."

"Why was it cloudy? I couldn't hear very well."

"It will get clearer the more ye practice."

"Can we try it again? Can you show yourself to me this time?"

"How about I hide in the house and ye find me?"

"Hide and seek?"

"Tis how the young ones learn to gravitate toward a presence."

"Okay."

They practiced well into the evening. Peachy didn't feel like she was getting any better. The last time she found Noomi by pure luck. Her stomach grumbled. "I am ravenous."

"Wakin' as a Seer takes an enormous amount o' energy. Once your body adjusts, ye will level out."

"In the meantime can we have that stuffed bread thing you make?" The wee mice clapped their hands, and Peachy picked them up and kissed their noses.

"O' course."

"I have one other request."

"What is it?"

"This needs to come off." Peachy held out her casted arm. "I think it's time."

"Tomorrow."

"Thank God."

"What is it?" asked Peachy.

"Do ye hear that?"

"Hear what?"

"The wind has stopped."

Peachy shielded her eyes when the clouds parted and a spot of sun shone on her skin. "I hear dripping."

"Tis odd. Very odd."

"Can we go outside? Please, Noomi."

Noomi alternated looks between the window, Gabin, the girls, and Peachy. "Aye!" Noomi said, her eyes wide with excitement. "We have to dress warm, for tis still winter, still cold."

Peachy picked up a map that she'd been studying. "Can we go here?"

"The lake. Yes. That will be a manageable walk. I hope ye don't aim to think we can go swimmin'." Noomi laughed at her joke for there was still a great amount of snow on the ground.

Peachy shook her head and thought about her skinny-dipping wish that she had written about. A short while later they were suited for their adventure. Noomi led the way with Gabin in step with Peachy. The air felt wonderfully crisp, clean, and freeing.

"Are ye with pain, Peachy?"

"No," she wheezed. "This is just a lot of…phew…lot of cardio right now. Jesus, I'm out of…" Peachy didn't say anything else. She couldn't. It pained her to breathe from the small amount of walking they had done so far, but she kept it to herself and kept apace, enjoying the peace and scenery that she'd been dying to see for so long.

Noomi must have sensed that Peachy was tiring, because they stopped twice to let Peachy catch her breath. There was only so much heart-healthy exercise Peachy was able to do in the house. Jumping jacks did not adequately prepare her for trudging through knee-high snow, but the burning in her lungs felt marvelous, so they kept walking. Gabin allowed Peachy to grasp her coat, and she thanked Gabin for her help since the cat seemed to be doing most of the work.

"Careful." Noomi reached for Peachy, preventing her from taking another step. "This tree marks the edge o' the lake. Tis covered with snow and ye can't see it, but look there, in the middle is water."

Peachy fell onto her knees, catching her breath, high on endorphins. "It's so beautiful!" She drew a cleansing breath of crisp, cold air.

"I'm surprised we are able to venture at this time o' the year. Gabin, is this not strange?"

"Given these past few months, nothin' is strange anymore."

"You can say that again," Peachy said.

"What did ye say?" Gabin asked. Noomi and Gabin both looked wide-eyed at Peachy.

"I said," Peachy rubbed her gloved hands on her face, "I don't know, what did I say?"

"Ye responded to me."

Peachy felt Gabin's words again, faint but there.

"Her lands, Peachy!" Noomi picked her up and held her in her arms. When she set her on the ground, Peachy took Gabin's head in her hands and held her forehead against the great cat's.

"This is amazing! Will I be able to communicate with the girls too?"

"Let's find out." Gabin purred.

"Do you think I can shift?" she asked Noomi. "How do I try and what will I be? Can we do it now?"

"Slow down. This all takes time. Tis yet to be seen and believe me, we don't want to rush your Shiftin' abilities. Take it slow and know that it may come and go and will get stronger every day."

"This is crazy."

"Tis a Winterberry bush in full bloom around that bend there. Doesn't a pie sound like a delightful way to celebrate?" Noomi asked.

"Oh yes, please," Peachy panted.

* * *

"I didn't think it would work! Everyone's telling me to write, write, write. I'm simply following orders," Peachy said. Her written wishes for an early spring had come to fruition, which caused the snow to melt at an alarming rate.

The entire chain of events caused Noomi a great deal of heartache. "All me precious trails. I know not how we will keep up with the changes."

"I will help you," Peachy offered.

"I correct a map today and tomorrow it's erased from the formation of a new creek." Noomi wouldn't stop pacing. "I have to update scores o' maps and forget me credibility. Everythin' I've done in the past is no longer accurate. No one will believe me now."

"Hey. Come on," Peachy encouraged. She placed her hands upon Noomi's tensed back muscles, and began kneading her shoulders. "I imagine you're not the only one going through this. Things change, people see it happening, and they will rely on you for their new maps. Think of all the talents you'll make selling these new maps. Now, chin up." Peachy hesitated before she gave Noomi a kiss on her neck.

The more Peachy practiced her gifts, the more in tune she became with her body and Noomi's. She felt like Noomi was a magnet at times, always wanting to touch her, always fighting her urges. "Don't worry, okay? You have my help. We will document every little change. It'll be a fun outdoor adventure. Did I ever tell you in my old life I had a knack for finding alternate routes to places that were difficult to enter?" Peachy left her with another kiss and followed her out the door for another day of mapmaking.

"What are you doing?" Peachy asked as Noomi plopped her bag of tools against a tree.

"I'm goin' swimmin'. Want to join?"

"It's way too cold!"

"The water will be refreshin'—"

"Refreshingly cold!" The idea of swimming sounded amazing after their long hike. "There's still snow in places." Peachy didn't care if the entire pond was filled with snow. Nothing would stop her from getting in there with Noomi, but her overwhelming desire caused her trepidation.

"It will feel wonderful. I promise," Noomi said. "Besides, I have thought o' nothin' but dippin' me toes in fresh water all day."

"Then let's dip only our toes in… What are you doing?"

Noomi flung her clothes off.

"Come on!"

Peachy tried not to stare, but Noomi's body proved too delicious. Her winter of building her library and going to and from on her snow blades, made her a wondrous sight to behold—toned muscle, flawless golden skin, and full and heavy breasts. Peachy closed her eyes.

"Tis wonderful!" Noomi's laughs echoed off the water. "Her lands, this is splendid." Noomi splashed, plunged underwater and reappeared a few yards away, laughing all the while. "Maybe an early spring isn't bad aft' all."

"No, nothing bad will come from this," Peachy whispered to herself. "Is it deep?"

"In places."

Peachy set her bag down and sat on a large stone. She removed her shoes, her top, her pants. "Fuck," she muttered and slipped out of her undergarments, instantly aware of the gentle wind upon her skin. She wrapped her arms around herself and tiptoed to the shore and to Noomi.

"Come on Peachy, tis wonderful." Noomi held out her hand. "Hold on to me. Don't be scared."

She reached for Noomi, who pulled her in too fast. "Noomi!" she yelled, falling into her.

Peachy wrapped her legs around Noomi's waist, feeling Noomi's warm stomach against the most intimate part of herself.

"Tis better to jump in all at once."

"It's f-f-freezing," Peachy huffed, finding basic breathing difficult.

"Tis not," Noomi disagreed, looking straight at Peachy, her eyes cat-like, near slivers, hidden within her molten gold irises that held copper and green in the sun. "Lean back."

"Like this?" Peachy asked. She let go of Noomi except for her legs, which she kept wrapped tightly around Noomi's waist. She immersed herself in the water, the sound of her own breathing intensified when her ears submerged. The white silhouettes of the three moons felt closer than ever. She spread her arms out, feeling Noomi's gaze on her body.

"Do ye feel like ye are dancin' amongst the moons?" Noomi whispered through her thoughts, while she floated in circles and took them deeper into the lake.

"I do," Peachy croaked. Noomi's hands ran from her back, down her stomach, grasped her waist, and pushed her away.

Peachy let go and floated. She closed her eyes and let the sound of gentle water lap against her body, helping her forget everything. She sank and then bobbed up and shook her hair out, ready to play. "Noomi?" She saw nothing. "Noomi! Not funny!" She felt a hand around her foot and she screamed.

Noomi popped up next to her, laughing at her little joke. "I am here!"

"Don't do that!"

"Did I frighten ye?" Noomi pushed off and floated on her back.

Peachy shook her head and swam away—diving and twisting, splashing, getting Noomi back for scaring her. Their playful romping turned into more touching, pressing against each other and offering lingering, blistering looks despite the cold spring lake. Peachy's breasts pressed against Noomi's back, her arms around her neck, her legs floating behind as Noomi swam them around the lake, listening to the sounds of spring.

"We should get out, dry off, and then make for home," Noomi said, facing Peachy.

"Already? I don't want to." Peachy's words held several meanings. She didn't want to lose her excuse to touch Noomi or be touched by Noomi.

"Did I not tell ye this would be refreshin'?" Noomi swam to the shore and climbed out, finding two pieces of cloth from her bag. Instead of drying off, she set hers on a patch of grass in the sun, and lay down on her back. Diamond-like beads of water glistened in the sunlight and rolled off her body.

"Her lands," Peachy muttered.

She made her way to the shore, found her towel, and placed it next to Noomi's, where she joined her in the sun. Swimming proved a wonderful idea and basking in the sun was equally wonderful. Enjoying Noomi's body would also, no doubt, be a wonderful idea. Peachy closed her eyes, imagining devouring her.

Noomi turned over and lay on her stomach.

Peachy followed suit, turning her gaze to Noomi's perfect backside, audibly sighing.

"Are ye still cold?"

"I am fine."

"Wasn't it fun?" Noomi faced her, opening one of her eyes.

"One of the best ideas you've had." Peachy smiled.

"Next time we can stay longer. I don't want to risk our good luck and sunny day, for a cold front could move in at any instant and freeze us all together."

Peachy doubted she would ever cool off, not with a naked Noomi in arm's reach.

"Look around. The blossoms o' the flowers and trees are fat with buds, which means tis time."

"Time for what?"

"The tellin' o' The Bestowin'."

Peachy jolted upright. Her eyes widened. She smiled at the thought of an adventure to their city.

"We shall journey aft' a week's nights. Besides, now that we know that ye are gifted, tis only fittin' that ye attend."

"I can't wait."

Noomi propped herself up and smiled at her, but Peachy wasn't looking at Noomi's radiant smile. Instead, she focused on the droplets of water on Noomi's stomach. She followed a trail of water, wishing she could catch them with her tongue.

"Are ye ready to go home?"

"Not yet. You're still wet."

Noomi looked at herself. "I guess we wait." She lay on her back and rested her arm over her eyes.

"Or…"

"Or what?"

"I help you dry off," Peachy croaked. "Do you want help?"

Noomi nodded. It was the first time Peachy had seen her act shy. Peachy took the invitation and crawled toward Noomi. She licked a bead of water from her stomach, and then she found another and another yet. She lapped the droplets of water from her chest, neck, and shoulders. Then she eyed the beads of water at the tips of Noomi's breasts. She grazed them with her tongue, filling her mouth.

What had Peachy been thinking, trying to find clarity on her own? Noomi was a ray of clarification, Peachy's only illumination. She cursed herself for the time she had wasted attempting to find something that was right in front of her. She met Noomi's gaze and covered Noomi's body with her own, pinning Noomi's arms above her head. She took from her a blistering kiss, hotter than fire and so deep that it elicited a growl from Noomi that nearly took Peachy's breath away.

Noomi flipped them over, and with Peachy lying on her back, she ran her nails down Peachy's body, raising faint red lines. She spread Peachy's legs and grazed her lips along the inside of her thighs before bending them back and running her eyes where Peachy wanted them. She felt Noomi's determined mouth on her burning center, coaxing and encouraging her liquid essence from her body. Noomi plunged her fingers deep inside her. Hard and fast, over and over, just like Peachy needed, eliciting labored cries and shallow breaths. Noomi showed her the intersection of magic and mayhem.

"We are long overdue for a celebration," Noomi said as she presented Peachy with a green bottle that same night.

"Was I *that* good?" Peachy smiled through her well-earned daze. Every action she took was slow, taking all her effort after their lovemaking at the lake.

"Better'n ye know." Noomi lifted Peachy's chin, getting lost in another kiss. Peachy stood, backing Noomi up against a table, causing a cup to clatter to the floor.

"What is this that we need to celebrate?"

"Your birthday."

"My birthday can wait." Peachy nibbled at Noomi's neck, feeling her body tense, feeling the anticipation emanate from her mind. A popping sound against her stomach caused her to yelp in surprise. "You have champagne!" Bubbles fizzed out of the bottle in Noomi's hands.

"What did ye call this?" Noomi said before placing her lips around the liquid fizzing out the top, laughing, getting it all over her hands and her face.

"Bubbly!" Peachy licked it from Noomi's lips. "It's amazing, so smooth…" She took the bottle from Noomi and took a drink. "So good," she said and set the bottle on the table. She lifted Noomi's top and tossed it on the floor. She reached for the bottle and drizzled the liquid down Noomi's chest, lapping at her breasts. Noomi shuddered. "Was this a gift for me or for you?" Peachy asked in between her licks.

"For both!" Noomi growled. She picked Peachy up and set her on the table, removing Peachy's clothing and then the rest of her own, as if it were a race against time. She picked her up, and Peachy wrapped her legs around Noomi. "Bring the bottle," Noomi ordered. Peachy reached for it, taking a swig, while Noomi carried her to the library, setting her onto one of her polished shelves meant for books. Noomi reached for the bottle, took a drink, and poured it on Peachy. She began licking it off her breasts, her chest, getting on her knees and savoring the juice that had made its way between Peachy's legs. Peachy felt sweet and wet—perfect. The aroma of her own scent mixed with the wine and Noomi infiltrated her senses, more intoxicating then she could bear.

CHAPTER TWENTY-TWO

Adèle's contact had long ago passed, so they milled through the Realm of the Keepers in search of a willing mind, not entirely surprised that they were so easily able to wander undetected. They had the run of the realm and floated about the city, learning of their vulnerabilities. The more time Beatriz spent in the realm, the greater her urge to gut something and watch it bleed, as if the place awaited her return and urged her to pick up where she left off. Kill more and torture longer. Be a better version of herself. Her mind swarmed with images of blood-fueled insanity.

"They have grown lazy and are no longer paranoid," Beatriz said upon a visit to their weapons store, which functioned more like a museum filled with ancient relics instead of implements of war. Everything was polished and arranged like a display, complete with placards describing their uses with a profile of the last Heather who had brandished it in battle. The Keepers talked little about their defenses. Rather they spent their time dusting spell books, artifacts, amulets, and rings used once upon a time. They reminisced with each other about the old days, hypothetical outcomes and unearned glory. To their credit, they held mock tournaments, though the Protectors seemed more concerned about their attire than making improvements.

"You know as well as I that they don't rely entirely upon physical tactics," Adèle said. "It's their minds we need to worry about."

"Their minds are as dull as a window painted with wax."

Adèle tapped her finger on the edge of a battle blade. "Ouch!" She looked at a drop of blood on her finger. "At least their blades are still sharp," she said and put her finger in her mouth, licking the blood.

"If only they knew how to use them."

"Do you miss it here?" Adèle asked.

"No."

"I see the way you smile, and I hear the hum in your heart when you look upon our old ways and these people."

"My improved disposition comes with greater ease because I'm imagining the fun I will soon have at the behest of my homegrown army and you, my dear sister."

"Always the ever-cheerful outlook. Let's go back to the reliquary and find that peculiar woman."

"After you," Beatriz said. She motioned for Adèle to pass through the stone archway and up the stairs to the promenade.

They walked the short distance, their apparitions only visible to each other. They'd observed this peculiar woman over the span of several days, a regal woman in blue velvet robes with long white hair—old, but not as old as them. She walked heavy in a restless way, as if she carried a great weight inside her heart. Beatriz knew of only one enigmatic device that would cause a person such a burden. They only needed proof before they showed themselves to this woman, Nefertari the Only.

"There's our potential willing mind," Adèle said.

Nefertari sat at a wooden table nestled in one of the many coves in the great hall in which the sisters often saw her. A fire roared behind, providing heat and light. She conferred with a small council. They spoke with hushed voices that grew in volume as the sisters neared, but then they stopped talking altogether when the sisters were within earshot. The group dispersed and huffed off, as if they didn't like the outcome of the conversation.

"What was that all about?" a woman in black said.

"Let us talk in private," Nefertari stood and gathered loose sheets of paper that surrounded her.

Beatriz and Adèle followed the Keepers through several corridors and descended a staircase to what seemed to be Nefertari's chambers, judging by the way she settled in one of the chairs and fished for a cloth from a drawer of a small table next to her.

"I am concerned, ye appear with unease o' late. Ye are constantly comin' and goin', early hours and late. Always mutterin', never fully attentive."

"I was not aware that me whereabouts were under scrutiny, Rona."

"If it weren't for the visible burden that ye bear, I would not give it another thought. Let me help ye bear the load. As a fellow Keeper and lifelong friend, I come only with concern."

"I am tellin' ye with the understandin' that I have your discretion and loyalty."

"Ye ever will have it."

"What I am about to tell ye will forever change our realm and our people." Rona leaned toward her. "A traveler has been brought to me attention. All signs indicate that this traveler is a long-lost Heather and from the line o' the Tellers."

The woman gasped. "Not in several hundred years have we seen or heard... Tis impossible."

"Tis possible and not only is this traveler a Teller, but she also arrived with a powerful weapon, an amulet."

"How? Legend has it their amulets were destroyed."

"Tis the truth, however, the amulet this Teller possesses is a different one."

Rona shook her head. "Which Teller has returned to us?"

"This one is the blood daughter o' Rahimah o' the Sky."

"Her lands." Rona's eyes widened, and she leaned back in her chair and stared at the wall behind Nefertari. "Where is she?"

"No one will know until I deem otherwise."

"Ye are willin'ly placin' our lives in danger while she walks free."

"I keep a very close eye on her. Hence me seemingly random comin's and goin's. I am havin' her trained as we speak. One o' me trusted mentees works with her. This girl is more powerful a Teller, more powerful a Heather...I've not seen such potential before."

"Ye fail to remember the days when Tellers walked among us. They drove us to ruin, murdered scores. No good can come o' this."

"Me actions ensure that our people can at last benefit from the Tellers as the foundin' Heathers had intended. With her under me rule, I all but ensure our peaceful longevity and then some."

"Ye cannot possess a Teller."

"But love can."

"What are ye takin' about?"

"This traveler and me mentee are deep in love. Both are with youth, easily manipulated and will do anythin' for each other."

"Ye are playin' with unpredictability. Ye must bring this to full council o' the elders. Your secrecy does not bode well."

"Ye forget your place, Rona." Nefertari stood. "All will be known in due time."

"When?"

"When I say so. There is still much to do and I am settin' the stage, gettin' her affairs in order, guidin' the Teller toward her gifts, and ensurin' that all her loose ends, a couple in particular, are dealt with." Nefertari hinted a slight look over her shoulder.

"Do you think she knows we're here?" Adèle asked.

"Without a doubt. Let us retreat and come up with our terms. It looks like we found our willing mind."

"Ye will be permitted to keep your amulet, but the Realm o' the Heathers will retain the girl," said Nefertari the Only.

"No," Beatriz said. She wanted more. She wanted the girl. She wanted revenge.

"She belongs here. She has no business in your world."

"She's more part of my world than yours."

"Your desire for revenge clouds your ability to see that ye are comin' out on top. I'm outnumbered. The realm elders insist that your blood be spilled, tis owed to us."

"It was not our fault that the elders failed to see our sentence to fruition."

"Your kind had no intention o' fulfillin' their part o' the bargain. The agreement is null and void. Take this way out. We will forgive and forget, and ye can continue the lifestyle that ye have grown accustomed to," Nefertari said with a smirk.

"Let us take this under advisement," Adèle said.

"No. The girl needs her family," Beatriz disagreed with a smirk of her own.

Nefertari laughed. "I saw what her family did to her. The girl arrived broken, at the brink o' death. Ye want revenge and ye think me a dalt."

"That's not why I think you're a dalt. You're a dalt because you're leading your people to an unnecessary war," Beatriz said.

"Watch your gawf mouth, Teller."

"Please. Can we just…We mean no disrespect," Adèle said. "Let us think about this."

"Ye would be wise to listen to your sister Terezi, or do ye prefer the name Beatriz? In any case, ye do not give her the credit she deserves. These are good terms. Even she can see that any other way means a long overdue death for your kind."

"You forget that Peachy is our kind too," Beatriz said. "Peachy is as bloodthirsty as we are, if not more. It's a matter of time before the girl recognizes what's inside her heart. The more time she spends in your world, the louder it calls to her."

"I saw her heart. Tis nothin' like yours."

"You saw what she wanted you to see. She is a young, new plaything. Her shine blinds you. You think you will exploit her, when it's the other way around."

"As much as I'm enjoyin' playin' this little game with ye, I think we're done."

"Wait," said Adèle.

"No." Beatriz shrugged her sister's hand from her shoulder and leaned toward Nefertari. "I think we shall pay your kind a visit in the flesh, along with my glorious army, and show you the meaning of blind rage. We are thirsty for blood and meaningless war, and your kind will more than quench our thirst."

"Ye would die the moment ye physically crossed into the realm."

"Is that an invitation to try?" Beatriz threw back her head in laughter.

"By all means. I can tell ye what will happen—"

"As can I, for my sister and I spent considerable time learning about your defenses. Inadequate isn't quite the word I'm looking for."

"Beatriz..." Adèle shook her head.

"Tell us," Beatriz continued, "do the other Keepers of your realm know what goes on in their weaponries? Do they know that you single-handedly let your realm's defenses suffer?" Beatriz refrained from shattering Nefertari's mind with her siren's call for battle, but instead she leaned back, crossed her legs and folded her hands across her lap. "Your Protectors are old in the mind, lost in books, with lazy tongues. You've long ago forgotten the ways of war, while we have spent hundreds of years perfecting our techniques. We shall leave a lasting impression that will scorch the land so nothing will grow ever again. It will take eons to forget, that is, if there are beings left to tell of the horror."

"Ye forget one thing," Nefertari interjected. "We have the girl, who by the way, has grown tremendously powerful. Her powers far exceed yours and mine. We also have five amulets in our possession, which ensures a favorable outcome."

"You forget that four, only four sisters brought this realm to their knees. We can do it again. We don't need the amulet to do so," Beatriz said. "It's...how should I put this? The icing on the cake, a garish bow on an already lavish gift."

"Ye will lose."

"We have absolutely nothing to lose and don't care if we die. Imagine what that must feel like. Imagine the power of that." Beatriz laughed. "For the safety of your people, do your job as Keeper of this realm. Give us the amulet and the girl, or we wage war."

"Or," Nefertari leaned toward them when she spoke, "I could sentence the girl to death, punish her in lieu o' ye. Upon her death I'd destroy the amulet, negating everything you've done these past few hundred years. Do ye like that deal better?"

"We will agree to your terms," Adèle said.

Beatriz growled her displeasure.

"Unfortunately, your gawf-jawed sister has caused me to rethink me terms. This offer is off the table," Nefertari said. She stood and began fixing herself a cup of tea. "Before I go, I have to know, are ye still usin' the Mirror o' Time and Space to make contact? Ye might want to exercise caution, for those connections are easily traced. I know where ye are and threats o' war go both ways." She ended the connection.

"Gawf-jawed?" Beatriz roared with laughter.

"What the hell were you doing?"

"It's been an age since I've heard that." Beatriz stood and paced the room. "Negotiating with her brings me indescribable joy."

"Are you listening to me?"

"We have her where we want her, Adèle."

"And where is that?"

"We know she's willing to risk the lives of her people for the girl."

"That tells us nothing."

"It tells us everything. She is as blind as we are, blinder with want of her. Her decisions are no longer fueled by reason, rather by her desire to use Peachy, exploit her and gain power. This is good."

"Nefertari is right. Your need for revenge is clouding your ability to think clearly."

"So maybe my thinking is slightly obstructed."

"You are sick of being weak. I know this, but toying with Nefertari, pushing her to her limits, will get us nowhere."

"I fear that I may never regain my full strength. There isn't enough anger and pain in this world to fuel what has been depleted while I wasted away underground. I need the girl. She's my only solace in all of this."

"We're better off taking the amulet and rebuilding your strength. We can start over somewhere new."

"This isn't about the amulet anymore," Beatriz said. "Now that it has found its rightful bearer, it'll be worthless in our hands, and it's only a matter of time before it betrays us. Let us negotiate for the girl, and let me have my revenge."

"Then it's over? You're going to make this choice for me as our traitor of a sister did for us all those years ago?"

"I would never do that to you, Adèle. Never." Beatriz shook her head. "I spent almost forty years alone in the dark, thinking through every memory of my life in Heatherton and on Earth. Vengeance for me, for you, even for Lisette, is what kept me sane down there."

"The girl has nothing to do with the decisions that were made before her."

"I don't care. The fact that she looks like her mother, is of her mother, will cause our demise. She will make decisions on our behalf just like her mother. I can't let that happen again."

Adèle sat in the chair facing Beatriz and took her hand.

"Please. You've stuck with me since the very beginning of our time in this world. You've been more of a sister then my own twin. Please, stand with me again, like you always have."

Adèle closed her eyes and shook her head. "Okay."

"Thank you." Beatriz placed her hand over her heart.

"We have to play Nefertari's game. Let's go to her hat in hand, grovel for forgiveness and see where that takes us. Hopefully, your gawf jaw didn't permanently take the offer off the table. We agree to take the amulet and leave the girl alone. Nefertari won't know that the amulet is powerless in our possession."

"Let's tell her that the girl must hand it over herself and then figure out a way to replicate the portal between our worlds."

"Brilliant. Tell me again what happened. Tell me everything that was done and said in the moments before the girl disappeared."

They settled in and Beatriz recounted her side of the story.

"You were right," Beatriz concluded. She stared at Nefertari and added, "my rage clouded my ability to think clearly and for that I ask your forgiveness and the opportunity to discuss your terms again." She loved placating others, putting up a false impression that she would later tear down with her bare hands. She could almost feel her success in the vision of Peachy's neck in her grip, her knuckles white with rage, suffocating the life from her. She cast her eyes downward.

"Ye are doin' what's right."

"We merely needed to come to our senses."

"It takes thought, doesn't it? Inner searchin' to come to that realization," Nefertari said. "Then the amulet is yours and the girl stays with her people."

"If it will please you," Adèle said.

"I assume that ye have talked about how to orchestrate a non-violent transaction."

"We have," Beatriz said. "For this transaction to be successful, the girl must relinquish the amulet herself in the physical realm."

"Do ye think I am dalt?" Nefertari's laughter caused Beatriz's brain to wrench and her neck to throb. Beatriz felt her sister's hand upon her shoulder.

"As the rightful bearer," Adèle said, "it is Peachy who needs to release it to us and free it from her rule. There is no other way. This I promise. It's how amulets work and why the amulet betrayed her mother all those years ago. The amulets of the Tellers are beholden to one person only. If it does not happen this way, it will only be a matter of time before it makes its way back to her. Do you not want a clean break?"

"Then I must insist that it takes place on our soil."

"Whatever you think is best," Adèle said. "We will need time to bring about a secure portal."

"Ye have no more'n three months. Then ye will await me further direction as to when such a time will permit this trade. If ye are not ready in three months, then the agreement is null and void. Have I made meself clear?"

"Crystal," Adèle said.

CHAPTER TWENTY-THREE

"That pain in the ass job was so worth it," Minette said. She counted her share of the money, fanning herself with it.

"Didn't I tell you it would pay off?" Peachy threw her portion into the air before wrapping her arms around Minette and tackling her on the bed, laughing, their kissing turning more heated. "Want to know what's more fun?"

"Our eight-inch friend?"

"Are you a mind reader?"

"Only with you." Minette kissed her hard before popping up. "I get to wear it first!" She rummaged in her bag for their new toy.

"Why you?"

"'Cause I said so and I know how much you like getting fucked with it."

"True and true."

Peachy removed her clothing. The last item she took off was her bra, and her gorgeous breasts spilled out and her nipples stood at attention. Minette could hardly concentrate on affixing the buckles of her strap-on. Peachy crawled to her on all fours and wrapped her arms around her, pressing the hard appendage against Minette's stomach as *she kissed her. Peachy's hands squeezed her backside before Peachy lay on her back, her legs open.*

"Get me ready," Peachy said.

A knock at the door startled them.

"Child, it's urgent," Lisette called.

Minette shot awake at the sound of gentle rapping at her door. She was so deep in sleep that when she awoke, her heart beat out of control and she didn't know where she was. Then the depression of her reality set in.

"I'm awake. Gimme a sec." She cursed Lisette's piss-poor timing. She consulted her phone, noting the time. 4:20 a.m. She had overslept and missed her shift. The past month of keeping odd hours was pushing her to her physical limits. Excessive caffeine was messing with her digestion. She was never hungry and always felt guilty for barely touching Lisette's wonderful meals. When she slept, she had crazy dreams where she was either on a job or reliving sex with Peachy. She squeezed her legs and moaned her disappointment. She pulled a sweatshirt over her head, donned a pair of lightweight sweats, and sluffed her way into the living room, still aching from her dream.

"Why'd you let me oversleep?"

Lisette held a finger to her own lips, silencing her. She held the headphones to one ear.

Minette put on her headphones in time to hear the sisters shuffling out of the workroom and headed to their respective bedrooms. "What happened?" Minette dropped onto the folding chair at her command center and covered her mouth when she yawned. She began rewinding the recording to see what she missed.

"They figured out the portal and will soon plan the exchange."

Minette's stomach lurched. Their nightmare had come true. Her mind filled with horrifying images, all the ways in which the sisters had described how they would hurt Peachy if they ever got their hands on her again. She stared at the floor, her tears spilled from her soul and onto the ground along with her broken heart.

"Look at me, child. This is far from over. We still have a plan, different than what we had intended, but one that ensures she lives and is not used against her will."

"How?"

Lisette rubbed her hands together and paced their small living room. "Let me make us coffee and I'll tell you."

Minette watched Lisette fill their teakettle with water and set it to boil. The woman looked all her hundreds of years at that moment. She never slept anymore. She spent all her time plotting and planning, thinking about everyone but herself. The dark circles under her eyes reflected as much.

"Let me finish," Minette said. "You sit. It's the least I can do for missing my shift." She forced a smile before she took over. She found two mugs, retrieved the milk and sugar and served them both steaming mugs.

"Thank you, child." Lisette took a sip. "Oh. That is amazing. Are these new beans?"

"No. They're the same ones."

"What is different?"

"Want to know my theory?"

"Tell me."

"It's always better when someone else makes it."

"That's it." Lisette laughed softly and took another sip. She closed her eyes for a moment and her shoulders relaxed.

"So. The plan. The portal. Peachy…" Minette coaxed.

"How easily can you get back into the *Spanish Rose*?"

"Very easily. I crash Adèle's home security cameras. She makes a maintenance call, and I show up."

"How long does that take? Can you do it now?"

"Now?"

Lisette nodded.

Minette tapped at her keyboard and the *Adèle only* feeds flickered before going black. "Boom," Minette said. "Now we wait for her to notice and call."

"Perfect."

"Now what?"

"Everything we do from this point on must be precisely timed with their planned exchange with Nefertari."

"But now that we know how to create the portal, can't we just create our own?"

"The creation of the portal involves forces that have already been set into motion. We don't have time to mastermind our own re-creation."

"So we'll use their portal?"

"To intercept her before they do. My hope is that by the time my sisters figure it out, Peachy will have arrived and will be far away from them. In the meantime, Nefertari will think the sisters have broken their agreement, making her more likely to join with us against them."

Minette held her face in her hands. "How will Peachy get out?"

"That's where you come in. We need to leave her clues."

"Will she arrive as she left, hurt and injured?"

"No. She will arrive as she is today. Healthy, but dazed. She will not expect this; she will be confused and angry, and she'll need guidance."

Minette consulted the blueprints. "She disappeared here, right?" She circled a staircase with her finger.

Lisette nodded.

"Where's the safest place for her to exit?"

"The underground corridor, as far away from the big house as possible."

"Okay." Minette rummaged for a sheet of paper and began taking notes. "I know the perfect route." Minette studied the blueprints. She tried not to sound overjoyed about Peachy coming home, but she was. She had thought of nothing since that night at the *Spanish Rose*. Her mind filled with images of seeing her after almost six months of missing her. She knew that Peachy was happy there and head over heels in love with Noomi, but one way or another, all that was going to come to a painful end for both she and Noomi. It was a three-way tug of war that either Minette and Lisette, Lisette's sisters, or Nefertari would win. Up till now, it was anyone's game and never Peachy's game to play. Peachy never had a choice to begin with. All these decisions about her life were at the behest of other people.

Peachy was innocent—clueless—and for that, Minette hoped she would forgive them for doing what they needed to do in order to protect her.

Later that morning Minette sat in her borrowed cargo van with her plans. Her goal was to leave clues for Peachy to find a route out. She'd also lock a few of the hidden passageways, creating only one way in and out. The excitement of the early morning was replaced by anxiousness. She watched the feeds from her cell phone. Adèle woke up, consulted her phone, freaked out and made the phone call.

Minette's phone lit up and she smiled. "Security Advisors."

"Why am I paying for a security service when it does not work when I need it to?"

"I'm sorry, ma'am. Can you please explain what happened?"

"As I stated, my security system is down. All the video feeds are broken!"

"I'm sorry that happened. Just one moment. Let me look at your account. Yes. I see. There was a system error. A technician will need to inspect your cameras. Likely they will need to swap out some equipment. A technician will be there in under twenty minutes. Our apologies."

"Thank you."

"No, thank you." She ended the call, started the van and drove to the *Spanish Rose*. She cringed when she saw Beatriz's zombie boys milling about by the carriage house.

Minette rang the intercom. "Hi, it's Jan with Security Advisors." She heard the buzzer and the gate rolled open. She texted Lisette who was watching everything from home base. Minette's hands were shaking, her fingers stiff.

I'm in.

I see the van now.

Zombie boys everywhere!

Deep breaths, child. Stick to the plan. Good luck.

Roger.

Once inside she received a verbal berating by Adèle, a warning that if this happened again, she'd switch services. "You have our money-back guarantee, ma'am," Minette said, and that seemed to appease Adèle.

"Find me in the atrium when you are done."

Minette listened to her retreat, the clicking of her house slippers, more like house stilettos, her overly dramatic nightgown billowing behind her.

She wrapped the tool belt around her waist, shouldered a large canvas bag that held cameras, wires, and locks, and made her way to the staircase where Peachy would make her reentry. No way Peachy would have survived if she'd fallen the entire fifty-foot drop. Minette shoved the image from her mind and began working.

First, she placed a gold star on one of the spindles on the banister, one that Peachy would see upon reentry. They had used gold stars in the past to communicate when either of them needed to lay low after a wayward job. Once Peachy reached the landing, she'd know to start looking for more gold star clues. The next star would be placed on the middle panel of a wall which, when depressed, opened into a dumbwaiter. Once inside, Minette left a note that would instruct her to lower herself until she reached the bottom and the old slave kitchen. She would then need find the next gold star located on the floor that opened into the underground corridor. Hidden behind a gold painted rock set into the dirt wall would be Minette's last clue telling Peachy to make her way to the carriage house where she would find clothes in a brown paper bag and await the midnight tour bus.

After the clues were placed, Minette locked the selected hidden entrances, and then she was ready to get hell out of there. She gathered her equipment and began to leave when she heard a thud. It wasn't loud but it worried her. She turned this way and that, unable to pinpoint its location. She followed it until she came upon an odd wooden panel and a new sheet of plywood inset among the aged paneling. The thudding stopped when she neared it.

She placed her hand over it, feeling the splintered wood. She gasped and jumped back when something pounded against it, harder this time followed by grunts and more thuds, more pounding, more grunting. She backed off, trying not to make a sound, when the force behind the door pounded through it. She fell on her back. While the sheet of plywood covered her and protected her from the horde of zombie boys who barreled out, she was suffocating and being trampled. Everything hurt. Every part of her body felt crushed. She couldn't protect her head from the blows, and she tasted blood in her mouth. She knew she would die there if the men kept coming.

She struggled out from under the board and backed away. In her pain, she couldn't remember which way she had come. She couldn't see for the fog in her brain. She yelped when she smacked into the back of one of them. It turned around and reached for her, but she jumped away—into another one. Their eyes were gone and dried blood caked to their cheeks, their mouths and necks. Some of them were naked. She had to get out. She pushed through them. It was like running blindly through a field of corn. They were never-ending. She whimpered, not knowing what to do because she couldn't see over them. She dropped to her knees and crawled through their tree trunk-like legs. Their grunting grew louder and more frantic. Minette didn't know if she was screaming along with them.

She kept crawling, knowing her choices were to escape or die in the bowels of the *Spanish Rose*. She finally made it to her feet, but there was no way she'd be able to face Adèle in her present state. She stowed her tools in an empty room filled with draped furniture. She needed Lisette's help. "Damn it." Her phone was gone. No way she could go back and get it. She wandered until she found a window that she could open. She crawled out and ran to the van. She fished her keys from her pocket, and despite her quivering hands, she managed to turn over the engine and back down the long driveway, crunching into one of the stone columns as she angled out.

She pulled over a short while later, remembering Adèle's feeds. She opened her laptop and popped them back online. She opened another program and cut the service to both her and Lisette's burners. She filtered through the video feeds. She saw Adèle sitting in the atrium, drinking something and staring out the window. Just then Beatriz entered the room. Minette was about to adjust the volume when the van was showered by pebbles—no, gunfire. They were coming from a sportscar behind her. Her adrenaline kicked into action. She put the van in drive. Her tires screeched. She shook her head. There was no way she'd lose the tale with her behemoth of a cargo van that maxed out at fifty miles per hour.

She led them to where she stored her motorcycle. She increased her speed and headed for the building, bracing herself for impact. She crashed through the aluminum garage door, skidded to a halt, crawled out of the van and made for her bike, revving it to life. She rolled through boxes, old junkers, and equipment before speeding out the back door and heading home.

Minette struggled to prop her bike into its kickstand because she was shaking so badly. She ultimately decided to leave it on its side, not bothering to hide it using the canvas cover. She tried to nudge it under foliage and brush. In a dazed state, through blurred vision and a murkier mind, she headed for her house.

She knocked on her own door and Lisette opened it and gasped. Her eyes were wide, her mouth hung open and her hand lay upon her chest. She reached for her. "Child, what happened? Get in, hurry. I couldn't reach you."

"I fell off my bike." The words echoed in her brain. The blinking lights of their electronics worked their way through the fog. The faint humming threatened to shatter her eardrums. "It's over. All of it. We're done." She began closing laptops and pulling wires. "We need to shut it down."

"What are you doing?" Lisette took Minette's trembling hands in her own. Minette realized her own fingers were a bloody mess, scraped skin with bits of embedded gravel. Her jeans were torn and she wore only one shoe. "Tell me what happened?"

"I fell off my bike."

"Come here, child. Sit down." Lisette guided them to the couch.

"We don't have time to sit. Didn't you see what happened?"

"They said nothing out of the ordinary. Adèle sat in the atrium all morning. Beatriz joined her a short while later, about the time you left. They're still drinking coffee. Look."

Minette gazed at the screen. "Well, someone fucking followed me." She jumped at the sound of rustling outside. She closed her eyes, trusting that when she did so, she'd drown out the images of the lidless, crying zombies. Instead, they gathered their strength and mobbed her mind and crushed everything that had held her together over the past six months—the radiance of Peachy's smile, the feeling of her soft locks in her hands, the sound of her voice, her laughter, the taste of her. Everything erased. Minette hunched in her chair and sobbed.

"Easy, child," Lisette said. "I got you." Lisette held her in her arms and whispered things to her.

"I fucked up. I deserve to die."

"No."

"Yes! They'll know it's us. They'll figure everything out—the cameras, the clues. I killed her. I killed Peachy. All our work down the drain. Do we have a plan B? What's our plan C?" She started hyperventilating and felt light-headed. She hid her face in her hands and screamed into them.

"Take a deep breath, child." Minette felt Lisette's hands upon her own and then felt a calming sensation wash over her like an infusion of warmth and safety that helped her swim through the frightful depths to the surface for air. "You okay?"

"Yeah. I am. What did you do?" Minette breathed deeply, placing her hand over her chest. Her pain subsided. She felt as though she could think clearly again.

"It is what I do and not important right now. Tell me what happened."

Minette told her about being tailed and her run-in with the zombies.

"Where were you when this happened?"

"Maybe south of the slave kitchens. I don't know. I was confused."

"How many were there?"

Minette shook her head. "Fifty, seventy?" She hung her head, and an overwhelming shame washed over her. "It's over. All the work we did, the clues, everything. I'm a fucking idiot."

"Enough of this. You are among the greatest, most fearless people I've known. That should mean something coming from someone who has lived hundreds of years."

"But I failed." Minette dried her tears with her hand.

"No you didn't."

"But the clues! If they find those, they'll know we're planning something too."

"The work is not over, Minette. It's just about to begin and you've done more than your part. It's my turn now. I've put you in too much danger already. I see that today." Lisette handed her a piece of paper. "Take this."

"What is it?"

"It's a safe place. There you will find a hundred thousand dollars, a passport, a new life."

Minette only stared at it.

"Take it, child. Tis freedom and safety."

"No." Minette ripped apart the paper and threw it into the air. "I'm finishing this job. I'm not walking away now."

Lisette held her face in her hands. "You do not know what you're asking."

"I am willing to do whatever it takes to ensure that Peachy is home and safe. Tell me what to do."

"We should assume they'll find the cameras and will have them removed. What about the sound?"

"The cameras were our eyes *and* ears. But…" Minette popped up and opened one of her laptops.

"What are you doing?"

"My phone." She started typing. "I hope to God she finds it."

"Why?"

"I'm hacking it, so we can use it as a camera."

"Brilliant, Minette. Not all is lost."

"What is the new plan?"

"Break down everything we don't need. Throw it in the river. If you were tailed, we need them to believe that we're scared and on the run. That we've abandoned our plan."

Minette nodded. "And then what?"

"We lay low for a couple of days, hope that Beatriz finds your phone and it's business as usual. Everything rides on the portal and the forces already in motion."

"What if they find the clues?"

"We need to assume that they will."

"How will she get out?"

"You will have to guide her. Can you do that?"

"Yes."

"Are you certain?"

"I won't let her die. What will you do?"

"I need to get to Noomi."

CHAPTER TWENTY-FOUR

Gabin pulled their sled that Noomi had outfitted with earth blades, for there was no longer snow covering the ground. Their load included baskets and maps for trading, as well as Peachy, and Noomi, who steered.

"Tis difficult to describe," Noomi said. She felt as if she was falling short of preparing Peachy for all they would see when they arrived at Heatherton. She knew her words were no match for the vision of her town's beauty, bounty, and festive halls decorated with elements of spring. Garlands of fresh blooms would be strung together and draped everywhere, and all would be fragrant and colorful.

"Tell me what you look forward to most," Peachy asked.

"The massive cherry trees. They'll be covered in pink and white blossoms awaitin' their leaves. The smell is almost better'n the sight."

"What's Gabin's favorite?" Peachy asked. Even though Peachy's Shifter abilities had awoken, it was hit or miss if she could communicate.

"Takin' a break from your constant kissin'," Gabin said.

"She's lookin' forward to seein' a long-lost lover cat." Noomi laughed. "They'll chase each other for hours and then end up fightin' over a pinecone!"

Peachy laughed along with Noomi.

"Tell me more."

"Yes, do tell her more Noomi!" Gabin said. *"Shall we tell her about your crush, Isl?"*

"Don't ye dare!"

Peachy looked between Noomi and Gabin. "Not fair! Tell me what just happened?"

"Me sister is threatin' to tell ye all me mysteries."

"Sound's salacious." Peachy scooted closer to her. She lifted Noomi's shirt and tickled her stomach, causing her to laugh. "Tell me more."

"There's the smell o' the bakeries, and cheese shops, and frozen milk with sweets mixed in, and the smell o' the great halls dedicated entirely to books. There's nothin' better'n that. Oh, and all the different wonderful and unique people and creatures. I can't wait for ye to see 'em," she said as a family pulled alongside on a sled like theirs, full of children with two great wolves pulling them. They waved to each other as they passed.

Peachy smiled, but then it faded as quickly as it appeared.

"Are ye scared o' that family?"

"It's not that."

"Ye are scared o' seein' her aren't ye?"

Peachy nodded.

Noomi put her arm around her and told Gabin to slow down and pull to the side of the path. "Look at me, love."

Peachy focused on her hands. Peachy held her breath and knitted her brows, and her chin quivered. "Tis okay, love. We probably will see her there. N'fact, I am certain that we will." Noomi had felt Nefertari's presence growing stronger in recent days, as more ravens would flock around her cottage and at all hours. "But let's not think about that right now. Let's think o' all the beautiful sights we'll see and food we can eat. We're going to hear one o' the greatest stories o' me time. Five Heathers, one of whom hasn't been seen in over four hundred years until ye. Tis somethin' to celebrate. *Ye* are a wondrous bein' to be celebrated. Later when we get there," she whispered, "I intend to celebrate all o' ye with me lips and tongue." Peachy smiled and Noomi pulled her into a hug. "Let's not allow her to ruin our good time."

Noomi tried to take her own advice but failed. Nefertari was a constant threat, but she wouldn't let her intimidation overtake the joy she felt witnessing the beauty and wonder painted on Peachy's face when they arrived.

"Let's do a bit o' tradin' before we settle in," Noomi said when they arrived close to dusk. She guided their sled in between two others at The Forge.

"How about this early spring?" asked Mer upon seeing them enter. "Tis somethin' for the history books?"

"Tis a rarity," Noomi said. "Mer, tis me friend Peachy. Peachy, tis Mer, the fairest trader in all o' Heatherton, in all the Realm o' the Heathers I presume."

"With thanks, Noomi. Tis a pleasure to make your acquaintance, Peachy."

"With pleasure," Peachy said in her best dialect of their language before laying her hand atop his.

"I will assume by your great canvas bag that ye are here to trade?"

"We have baskets and maps. Revised maps."

"I was wonderin' about that. I imagined they needed updatin' with the changes the early spring has brought. I heard from a trader before ye from Heather's Edge, floods have damaged his large crop o' flower bulbs. A total loss."

"Tis a shame." Noomi placed her hand over her own heart. "We understand the pain. We've spent countless hours mappin' and remappin'."

"Tis a lot o' unexpected work for a lot o' us," he said. "Speakin' o' Heather's Edge, how'd ye like the bottle o' spirits I sent with ye the last time?"

Noomi locked eyes with Peachy and they both erupted into laughter.

"That good?" he asked.

"Amazin'. So good I aim to trade for a couple more bottles if ye are in stock."

"Tis your lucky day. Let's see what ye got for me today, and then I'll take your order and we'll go from there?"

"Perfect." Noomi unloaded her baskets and maps on the counter.

After trading for springtime garments, paper, pipeweed, and jams, they found a festive hall filled with spirit and laughter. They settled on two seats at one of the hall's several long tables where they could sit and eat dinner.

"What we're about to do tonight is customary. Necessary. A very important tradition at every Bestowin'," Noomi said.

"What is it?" Peachy asked.

"Drink ale!" Noomi laughed as she waved over a woman carrying a tray of frothy ales. "Two please," she said and gave the woman three of her fresh-earned talents.

"Cheers," Peachy said and she held out her mug.

"What are ye doin?" asked Noomi.

"Cheersing you. We tap our mugs together and say cheers."

"Oh! Scroof."

"Scroof?" Peachy laughed.

"Like this," she said. "We hold out our mugs, place our other hands over our hearts and nod. Scroof!"

"I like my way better," Peachy said, clanking their glasses together. Other people found her actions amusing, and by the end of their dinner, the entire hall was clanking mugs and saying cheers. After a hearty meal and two mugs of ale, they were tired and secured a room at the Heatherton Arms. They bathed in the community pools and headed to their room.

"I'm not tired anymore," Peachy said.

"Ye aren't?"

"Nuh-uh."

"What do ye have in mind?" Noomi asked as she tugged the towel off Peachy and claimed her mouth with a kiss.

"Are you a mind reader?"

"Yes. I am." Noomi threw Peachy on the bed and settled upon her. They spent the night making love, smoking pipeweed, and listening to the celebration and music that filled the streets and filtered into their room until the late hours of the night.

They woke up the next day well before dawn and made their way to the grove to listen to the telling of The Bestowing. They spread a blanket and sat down, surrounded with others from the great village that gathered for the anticipated event. Gabin took her leave, preferring to spend her time with a pack of other mountain cats. Noomi smiled, watching them wrestle with each other.

"If ye need me to explain anythin' ye don't understand, tell me," Noomi said against Peachy's ear.

Peachy sat between her legs. "I will." She placed a kiss upon Noomi's neck, and Noomi nestled against her and nearly fell asleep. Noomi startled when the crowd erupted in cheers at the coming of the sun that illuminated the great tree, fat with buds. Upon the sun's warming, they burst into bloom, one by one, and an intoxicating fragrant aroma drifted in the air. This was the moment they had waited for. The Elder, Manon the Only, appeared and all fell silent.

"Gather 'round young and old, wise and stupid, those who are gifted and those in waitin'. There are lessons to be learned this day. If ye heard me story once before and have learned nothin', then listen with your heart. If ye heard me story once before and found what ye searched for, listen again for *new* wisdom. The tellin' o' The Bestowin' comes but once, when the moons are languid on the horizon and appear as one, for in that moment is the comin' o' life and bounty. This winter is over, early but on time. The first blooms o' this tree confirm it. Do not fret, do not question. Instead let us rejoice and give respect, for with these blooms means also death. Remember always that death is a beginnin' to an end that has no end. When death is at our doorstep, we must embrace her with open arms for tis a beginnin', your beginnin'. The Bestowin' o' gifts.

"In the beginnin' were Heathers. Sisters born unique and powerful. Glorious and beautiful. Compassionate and fair. One born through creative thought with the ability to see and know, to walk across time and space, to anticipate, aid, and counsel. A Seer. Another born from the jaws o' the wild, her gift to shift, to learn and understand from the perspective o' creatures great and small. She would ensure that our realm was safe for even the smallest and for those with no voice. She was a Shifter. The third was uprooted from the earth, covered with clay, fragrant with bloom, and metallic for the minerals that clung to her. Her gift is healin' through touch and mastery o' plants. A Healer. The fourth, shaped through strategic thinkin', a great strategist, highly witted, a warrior and a leader. A Protector. The fifth sister born last and great, o' the sky, o' the infinite. Her gift? To conjure, not to foresee, but to shape. A Teller.

"Together these Heathers brought peace and structure. Their rule ensured our thrivin' realm. Through us, their spirits endure, for each o' us bear their gifts, and those who do not, soon will. With your gifts are responsibility and freedom to manifest your abilities in your own unique way, for the benefit o' the realm. That is how our foundin' Heathers intended and how they ensured their immortality. Look 'round. We are proof. We are the past, the present, the future.

"Now comes the time. I call from the air, the sky, and the earth, from the water and from the wild beyond. To all the souls o' the Heathers we have known, we have loved, and we have learned from, to those who have crossed into death this past cycle o' our moons, now is your time to pass into peace and legend. But before ye leave us, if tis your will, bestow upon your chosen your gifts that ye have spent your long life shapin'. Bestow 'em upon us. Live forever!"

After a moment of silence, the crowd erupted in cheers, the moment punctuated by the magic of the sky, a fire of brilliant, intricate colorful patterns and shapes that painted the horizon with sparkle.

"Amazing." Peachy clapped and shouted with the others at the display.

Noomi held her tighter. She reveled in the warmth of Peachy's neck, placing kisses there, loving the moment, loving her. But the moment was cut short. Across the grove she spotted Nefertari and heard her as clear as if she were speaking in her ear.

"*Now's the time, Noomi. The time has come.*" Noomi closed her eyes and held Peachy tighter, unable to imagine the loss to her life, heart, and mind. "*She is not ready! I am not ready.*" Those words were meant for Nefertari; however, when Noomi opened her eyes and scanned the grove, she had vanished. She doubted if she truly saw her.

"The way she told the story, with the blossoms opening around her, and the smell of the flowers…" Peachy inhaled several times. "Exquisite. Thank you for bringing me." Peachy stood, offering her hands to Noomi, who took them. "I'll always remember my first time," she said and leaned into her. The kiss that Peachy gave her almost erased the dread in her heart at Nefertari's reminder and her role in the whole thing. "Are you okay?"

"I'm fine. I just, I always forget how beautiful the story is." Noomi took Peachy in her arms and kissed her, not stopping until Peachy grew breathless, restless, and greedy. "There is a great feast. Do ye want to go?"

"I'd rather devour you," Peachy said against Noomi's lips.

"Sounds perfect," said Noomi, scanning the grove for a sign of Nefertari before they headed to their room at the inn.

A few hours later they rested in each other's arms. "What are you thinking about?" Peachy asked.

"Always ye." Noomi grazed her fingers along Peachy's back. She kissed her sweaty brow and held her closer.

There will come a time when I will take her. Peachy the Only is destined for greatness. Do I make me wishes clear? Ye always have a choice. Her death or yours.

Her death or yours. Those words ran amuck inside Noomi's head like a swan song, over and over. She couldn't *not* hear the words no matter how hard she tried to focus on other things.

"Do ye want to make for ByHeather tonight?" she asked, hoping they might be able to leave Heatherton without bringing attention to themselves. A dalt thing to do but worth a try.

"No. Not yet. There's still so much I want to see and do and eat and drink and smoke! Don't you?"

"I'm only checkin'." Noomi kissed Peachy's forehead and held her closer. She couldn't avoid the inevitable, or could she? Could she and Peachy run away, remain hidden forever, until she discovered the way to be free from everyone who wanted to take her? She played through the scenarios in her mind and they always ended one of two ways: Peachy's death or her own. She wanted to tell Peachy everything so they could devise a plan together. There were several times she almost did. The only thing stopping her was the threat of Nefertari. She watched them day and night. If they were to encounter her, Nefertari wouldn't ask for permission to take their thoughts from them. "We will stay and celebrate."

"I want to celebrate you, your body, and your magical fingers," Peachy said as she climbed on top of Noomi, smoothing her hair from her eyes. Noomi kept her eyes shut, hoping that in doing so her tears would not be free, but she failed.

"Hey?" Peachy kissed her falling tears. "Where is this coming from?"

"I don't know."

"Yes, you do. Talk to me please."

"Do ye miss your old life, your friends, Lisette?"

"At times."

"Tis all I think about."

"Come here," Peachy said, flipping their positions, wrapping her arms around Noomi. "The more I think, the clearer it is. There's no place I'd rather be than here, with Gab and the girls, surrounded by your love. When I dream, you're there. When I'm awake, you're there. I'm inspired by your creativity, your brilliance, your tenderness, your beauty, the way you mix paint, your steady hand when you draw…everything else about you. You said it yourself. There's a reason I'm here. There's a reason I endured all that pain, my broken body, the confusion, the horrible dreams. It wasn't for nothing. I have to believe that, and I'm staying to find out."

"There may come a time when ye won't have a choice."

"I know."

"It haunts me always."

"The thought of leaving you is the most unbearable thought in the world." Peachy smoothed her hand over Noomi's chest. "Let's not think about it right now. Tis the celebration of The Bestowing." Peachy kissed Noomi's head and rolled her onto her back. "Let's celebrate."

"Ye know that I will do anythin' to help ye find peace."

"I'm at peace," Peachy said against Noomi's lips.

Noomi lost herself in the feeling of Peachy's tender kisses. "I will miss ye…"

"I'm right here, my love. Feel my hands on your body and my kisses. Feel my breath upon your skin. This is my promise to you." Peachy drew lazy circles between Noomi's legs with her fingers, encouraging her until she was fragrant and wet. "Feel my promise inside you," she said. Noomi tensed, wanting to hold the promise of Peachy's words and actions forever. Peachy began a tortuous dance with her fingers and her tongue, and they feasted on each other until they were wasted.

They finally broke away, ravenous for food, onto the bustling streets, filled with music and laughter and the best stuffed bread and ales in the realm of Heatherton.

"I want a big one!" Peachy said after their meal.

"A big mug o' ale comin' up," Noomi said. She edged her way through the crowd, reaching the barkeep and ordering two pints of ale.

"You've been avoidin' me," Nefertari said.

"Her lands," Noomi gasped, almost dropping both pints.

"Do not turn 'round."

Noomi continued facing forward.

"Have ye not seen that I've been lookin' for ye?"

"We've been busy enjoyin' the festivities."

"Oh, I am quite aware."

"I don't aim to avoid ye."

"And I don't aim to startle ye. I just wanted to let ye know that I am pleased with your work."

"Each day that I trick her, me hatred for meself grows stronger."

"Well then, I shall put an end to your inner battle."

"What?"

"I am takin' her."

"No."

"Ye knew the terms, Noomi. This should come as no surprise."

"When?" Noomi turned around and came face-to-face with Nefertari in disguise. Instead of her indigo robes, she wore cream-colored robes, more befitting of a Heather in plainclothes and not nobility.

Nefertari motioned with her head. "Ye see that entertainer there next to her?"

Noomi turned to where Peachy was seated. She was laughing and clapping in time with the music, a beautiful smile on her face.

"He's one o' mine. Your thinkin' o' late has caused me major concern. I see that ye ponder the success of running away. I can't risk those kinds o' thoughts from ye."

"'Tis nothin' but wishful thinkin'. I would never defy ye. Ye have me promise. I won't let ye down." Noomi shook her head and tried to make her way back to her table and to Peachy. Nefertari's guards, disguised as servers, blocked her path.

"I'll give ye this last night with her, Noomi. Ye will leave tomorrow at midday, usin' the route ye used when ye found her. The rest I will orchestrate. Take advantage o' your last night together."

"Please no." Her plea fell upon deaf ears, for again, Nefertari, her men, and the entertainer had vanished.

Noomi hunched against the bar, trying to compose herself before facing Peachy, wondering how she'd ever be able to hide the pain in her eyes and mind.

"One more thing."

"I heard ye loud and clear," Noomi said as she raised her eyes, seeing that the voice next to her belonged to the spirit of a strange woman. "Who are ye?"

"No one can see me but you."

Noomi looked over her shoulder.

"Listen to me. I am Lisette, and we don't have much time. Peachy's life is at stake. Do as I say, if you want her to live and be free of Nefertari."

CHAPTER TWENTY-FIVE

"Her blood must come into contact with the blood of another. It must be mixed with tears of pain and dried with love. That's how it must happen," Beatriz said to Nefertari.

"I can assure ye that all o' those elements will be set into motion. It won't be long. Aft' the girl relinquishes the amulet and the rights, we shall never see or hear from ye ever again. Yes?"

"You have our word."

"Until we meet."

"I long for it," Beatriz said and ended their connection.

"So it begins." Adèle rubbed her hands together. "Let's get into position."

"And what position would that be?" Lisette emerged from the shadows.

"There she is," Adèle said as she stood. Lisette held her in place with a mere look, and with a flip of her wrist sent her sister back to her chair.

"Look at that fancy trick," Beatriz said. Lisette's power had grown in the years Beatriz had wasted away underground. Beatriz tried to summon her army but couldn't so much as lift a finger to do so.

"Oh, this?" Lisette said. She flicked her wrist again, causing Beatriz's brain to throb. Beatriz didn't give her the satisfaction of showing her the pain it caused. "There's more where that came from, as you know." She stopped and corrected herself. "Oh no, you don't. I almost forgot you are a shadow of your former self. Both of you. What's your excuse, Adèle? Really? Apparently, paying others to inflict bodily harm *for* you is all you can muster these days."

"You can trick all day long. It matters not, for I am sorry to say that everything is in motion. You are too late to play savior," Adèle said.

"Hush now, let me get reacquainted with my twin." Lisette approached and rounded their chairs. "It's been a lifetime, Beatriz. Goodness you look a fright." She ticked her tongue. "There's something about you. I can't quite put my finger on it. Are you getting enough sun?" She laughed. "It's the scarf. That's it. It's an ill color for your skin tone. It's more my color. Don't you think?" Lisette slid it from her neck. "Oh my, is that where the girl stabbed you? It's still red. You should have it looked at. If only you knew a good Healer." Lisette dropped the silk scarf into Beatriz's lap. "On second thought, you need this more than I do."

The air on Beatriz's scar caused her entire neck to burn, her shoulder to ache and her head to throb. Her expression remained neutral. She wouldn't give her sister the satisfaction of seeing her pain. "I wish I could praise your look, but you haven't changed since our last meeting. I wonder what the late great Marie Laveau would say if she knew you were still trying to pull off her look after all these years? It's like those magazines where they ask you who wore it better. Newsflash. Not you." Beatriz laughed.

"How I've missed your attempts at humor." Lisette strolled around the room touching this and that. "The memories we made in this house, in this room. It still smells like blood and decay." She leaned toward Beatriz and sniffed.

"Your attempt at buying time because you don't know what you're doing is as obvious as you are a haggard and feeble-minded old woman," Adèle said. "Let this play out and there might be a chance you will come out alive."

"Our sister is right, Lisette. You still have a chance. Join us. We can be a family once again."

"The plan is in motion, the wheels are turning, spinning so fast you couldn't keep up if you tried," Adèle added.

"What plan would that be?" asked Lisette.

"Oh, I think you know," Adèle tossed Minette's gold stars and clues onto the table. "These are cute, really cute. Make your way to the carriage house where you will find clothes in a brown paper bag and await the midnight tour bus… Shame on you for using another innocent, unsuspecting, and lovesick girl to do your bidding. Coward."

"Now, now. No need for name calling," Lisette instructed. "If you can't refrain from talking to your elder with respect, I shall turn you into a snake. On second thought, you might feel *too* comfortable in a snake's body. How about a toad?"

Adèle rolled her eyes, then began choking and sniveling. She grabbed her own neck and howled in pain as her body split open. She collapsed to the floor. She gurgled and spat blood as she morphed into her new toad form.

Beatriz knew of the pain that some Shifters endured when they transformed. For she had only done it once in her long life and only to save herself. She also knew that the pain was magnified if they were forced to shift and not always reversible in that case. She looked at Lisette before erupting into laughter. "I didn't think you had it in you!"

Lisette picked up their sister's toad body from the slop of blood and guts. She plopped her on the table and placed an empty glass over her. She held it in place as she sat directly across Beatriz. "Do not doubt me."

"I've never doubted you sister. I know what's in your heart."

"Then you know that love will prevail."

"What do you know about love?" Beatriz choked out her words. "You misled Peachy her whole life. You sent her on a mission that almost killed her. Then you used Minette, another innocent, as a pawn in our game. You sent her to me, knowing I could crush her. Those actions are the opposite of loving."

"I'm not talking about *my* ability to love. I know I have very little to give. I only know that the power of love is unrequited by anything you have to offer. Rahimah's betrayal made that point for all of us," Lisette said.

"And she died because of it."

"But her love didn't. Peachy is living, breathing, and powerful proof."

"Peachy is a byproduct of greed and betrayal, nothing more, nothing less. She's as prone to adapting that same lifestyle as we were, and I know for a fact she is headed that way. I felt it when I strangled her with my mind. She wanted to strangle me right back even harder."

"Do not confuse self-defense with blind rage, dear sister."

"I don't plan to kill her, Lisette. I have plans for her. Join me, join us. Let's be a family again and live under one roof. Imagine all that we could accomplish."

Lisette laughed.

"Or when I get my hands on her, I'll create her in my image, but more evil and destructive than any of us can fathom." She tried once again to summon her army, but her sister's hold had tightened.

"For that to happen you would physically need to get your hands on her, but you're stuck and you're down a player." Lisette tapped the bottom of the glass and the toad looked up.

"There's no doubt you're more powerful than me, Lisette. My time underground has ensured you the upper hand. You've had the upper hand this entire time. Brilliant move with the cameras. Your power is one of your finest qualities; however, this time you are wasting your energy."

"How so?"

"You've forgotten about my wonderful singing voice."

Lisette's eyes widened. Beatriz's scream tore from her lungs, emanated from her soul, producing her ferocious battle cry, shattering windows and glass tabletops, rattling pictures off the wall and obliterating the glass goblet that encased their toad sister.

Adèle morphed into a huge wolf and lunged at Lisette sending her to her back. She gnashed her teeth and snapped her jaws inches from Lisette's face, moments away from tearing her throat out.

"Leave her to me!" Beatriz ordered as she stood. "Go! Get in position!" Adèle crashed through the door and into the hallway.

CHAPTER TWENTY-SIX

"I can still smell the flowers," Peachy said. She leaned into Noomi's chest, riding upon their sled as they journeyed home. Peachy closed her eyes, enjoying their slow pace and the gentle rocking of the sled that threatened to induce sleep. All of them were tired, even Gabin, for their pace seemed slower, less urgent and more relaxed than their initial, eager trip to the city. "I can't wait until next year. I had too much fun. I'm beat."

"That's not why you're beat." Noomi kissed Peachy's cheek.

Peachy smiled at the truth in Noomi's statement. Peachy couldn't get enough of Noomi. No matter how hard she tried, she wanted more. "What was your favorite part of our trip?" she asked, but Noomi didn't answer. "You okay?"

"Ye kept me up till near mornin'. O' course I'm not okay." Noomi smiled, yawned, and shook her head. "Maybe we should stop for lunch and maybe a nap?"

"Good idea. I'm starved."

"Ye are always starved."

"You are always starving me."

Noomi laughed. "Gabin says if we don't stop our dirty talk, she refuses to pull."

"Sorry, Gab."

They found a grassy area in the sun, spread out their blanket and shared a meal of jam sandwiches. The three of them were content to lie on their backs, staring into the brilliant blue when Peachy felt a drop of wet on her nose. "Is it raining?"

"It looks as if it's startin' to," Noomi said. "Come on, we have to hurry." She shot up and began throwing their belongings into their bags. She tossed everything onto their sled and secured the canvas cover.

"It's just a bit of rain, sprinkling more like. Feels kind of good. Doesn't it?"

Noomi pulled their travel cloaks from her pack. "Ye never know. Sometimes these little sprinkles turn into dangerous flash floods. I don't aim for us to get caught in it."

Peachy followed Noomi's gaze skyward to a massive gray cloud. They froze when they heard a rumbling in the distance followed by a great shard of blinding white light.

"Wow," Peachy said.

"We need to move. Find a place to take cover till it passes. Come on!" Noomi yelled over the growing storm. Peachy's anxiety heightened at the confusion of the approaching deluge, strobes of light, and rumbling that shook the ground.

With Gabin again harnessed, they started in search of shelter. A split second later a bolt of lightning struck steps before them, hitting a tree, sending splinters their way and creating the smell of fire and smoke. "Holy shit! Gabin! Noomi! Are you okay?"

Gabin was the first to move. She shook herself, sending bits of small wood chips flying.

Peachy reached toward Noomi. "Are you okay? Your forehead is bleeding."

Noomi felt the area with her fingers. "Tis nothin'." Noomi reached for her. "Peachy? Come here." She held out her hands.

The look in her eyes worried Peachy. "What is it?" Her entire right side felt numb and warm. "I don't feel so good." Her words sounded slurred. She gasped when she saw a shard of wood stuck through her shoulder. She fell and Noomi caught her.

Noomi picked her up and set her against a tree. Noomi took off her travel cloak and wadded it around her wound. She directed Peachy's other hand to hold the padding in place. "I need to free Gabin. I need her help. Do not move, love. I'll be right back."

Peachy nodded. She heard the unbuckling of straps as Noomi pushed everything off their sled, sending their bags and boxes to the ground. "Gabin, help me push!" Peachy watched them angle the sled toward where she sat. Then they tipped its side and angled it against the tree, creating a lean-to shelter.

"Noomi…" Peachy moaned, feeling her blood spilling from her body.

"I'm here. And so is Gab."

Gabin nudged Peachy's leg with her head. *"Be brave."*

"I can hear you again, Gab. I can hear you!"

"Tis a good sign."

"I'm cold," Peachy chattered.

"Easy love," Noomi said. "Ye can let go now." Peachy dropped her hand from the padding. Noomi held it in place and used her knife to cut away Peachy's clothes.

Peachy gasped the moment she felt Noomi's hands upon her skin. Warmth and healing infused with the pain and became one intoxicating sensation. She closed her eyes and heard Noomi rummaging inside her bag.

"I always travel with me gut and needles. You'll be okay. This I promise," she said. "What I'm about to do will hurt, but it has to come out."

"No, no, no!" Peachy yelled an earth-shattering cry when Noomi pulled the shard of wood from her shoulder. The pain blinded her, stealing her breath until the only screaming left took place in the void of her mind.

"I know, love," Noomi cried, applying pressure to her wound now free of the wood. "Ye did so good. We're almost done, but ye are goin' to need to help me. I can't apply pressure and thread the needle at the same time."

Peachy lifted her uninjured arm to reach for the needle and gut that Noomi handed her. Through threatening double vision, and on the cusp of passing out, she finally threaded it. "There, there…"

"Ye did great. Just a little bit longer. Place your hand on me. Feel me love for ye. Take me strength, take it all now, or I am positive ye will not survive this," Noomi said through her tears.

Peachy watched Noomi's tears, fat and mixed with the blood from her forehead, fall upon her injured shoulder.

"We're blood sisters," Peachy said.

"We will always be bound by love and blood," Noomi said and leaned into her, giving her strength from her lips, from her kisses.

Peachy felt all her love in the single kiss. Everything combined—her blood, her kisses, and her love—helped Peachy feel anew, and her breathing became easier and more regular. By the time the storm had moved on, Noomi had sewn her up and helped Peachy into dry clothing. She and Gabin righted the sled and spread blankets atop and Noomi built a great crackling fire.

"Come closer to me." Noomi pulled Peachy into her arms. They burrowed under the blankets. "Peachy," she said against her ear. "I need to tell ye somethin' and ye must keep calm for we are bein' watched."

"By who?"

"Nefertari."

"What?"

"Listen to me. I've not been truthful."

"About what?"

"Remember when Nefertari came to see us?"

"Of course."

"She told me to train ye, to get ye ready."

"I know that already."

"For one day she would come for ye to be property o' the realm and to be used against your will."

"What are you talking about?"

"I am to turn ye over to her, tomorrow."

"What?" Peachy gritted her teeth both in pain and anger. "No. You can't. I won't go. I won't. Noomi…"

"I'm sorry."

"Why didn't you tell me?"

"I'm tellin' ye now. Please, we have to be quiet. There's more. Lisette came to me last night."

"When?"

"In the pub when I went for our ales. Beatriz and Adèle have found a way to re-create the portal. They're plannin' your return to your old world."

"I will die if I go back."

"Ye will die if ye stay here. Nefertari is hungry for the power ye hold in your heart. She will exploit it until there is no more love left."

"This fucking amulet." Peachy gritted her teeth.

"Is the reason I found ye, the reason our love exists. Ye are here because there is somethin' ye must do."

"And now I have to leave."

"'Tis not forever."

"I *will* not survive in the hands of those two demented women."

"They *will* not get their hands on ye. There is a way out. Beatriz and Adèle have negotiated an agreement with Nefertari. The sisters agreed to avoid war with our realm if the amulet was turned over to them. Nefertari agreed so long as she kept ye."

"But I am powerless without the amulet."

"Not entirely."

"I don't understand."

"Ye will in time."

"So, what's going to happen?"

"Tomorrow mornin' at sunrise, I am to turn ye over to Nefertari. From there, she plans to receive the sisters and make the exchange. Lisette and Minette plan to intercept ye before that happens."

"None of this was *ever* my decision was it?"

"These forces are bigger'n us right now, but I assure ye it won't be that way for long."

"What would you have done had Lisette had not come to you?"

"I would have exchanged me life for yours."

"Noomi…"

"I would have and still will."

"No."

"I am sorry from the bottom o' me heart that I was not truthful." Noomi's tears streamed down her face. "I feared for ye, for me life, for me sister, the wee girls. I am the opposite o' brave."

"You were scared. I understand but that doesn't mean you are not brave."

"There's another opportunity for me to prove me heart to ye."

"You don't have to prove anything to me ever."

"I have to stay."

Peachy's tears of anger turned to heartache. "I don't want to be without you."

"It won't be for long. I promise. I'll be with ye before ye know it. For this to work, I need to take your amulet."

"Take it then. Take it now. I can't lose you."

"Not now. Tomorrow, when it happens. I need to show Nefertari that I am as surprised as she is. She needs to see me savin' the mission by takin' your amulet. She wants ye more'n anythin'. The amulet will be her only way to bargain."

"I'm scared."

"Gabin is goin' with ye, for your protection and hers. Nefertari will not be able to threaten me with me sister's life if she cannot get to her."

"And the wee girls?"

"They have a role in this too."

"I hate this."

"Nothin' has changed."

"Everything has changed."

"I still love ye more'n I can explain. I will do whatever it takes to get to ye as quickly as I can."

"How? When?"

"There is somethin' I need to do here first, somethin' that Lisette needs if we are to have the advantage against her sisters and the realm."

"What?"

"The metal o' the other amulets."

"Too dangerous," Peachy groaned.

"It's the only way."

"What if Nefertari sees into your heart and she learns what we've done?"

"Tis a risk I have to take."

"What if you get hurt, you will have no one to help you."

"I will have help."

"The wee girls?"

"Believe it or not, they are ferocious little creatures."

"I love you, Noomi. I'll miss you more than air, more than water. I won't rest until I hold you again."

"Neither will I."

It wasn't yet dawn when Peachy stirred. She heard a rustling. Gabin and Noomi were in the same spots. "Noomi," Peachy whispered. Her lover didn't rouse. "Gabin," she said. The cat perked her ears. They both heard the sound again and looked to the distance. Peachy sat up and groaned, expecting her entire body to ache, but it didn't. Her shoulder felt mostly healed. "Noomi. Wake up, please." The commotion in the distance grew louder.

Noomi opened her eyes. "It's time," she whispered.

"Hello, sleepin' beauties." Nefertari emerged from a shadow along with several of her guards. "The time has come, and goodness, that was very well orchestrated, Noomi."

Peachy looked between Nefertari and Noomi. "What is she talking about?" Gabin bared her teeth, but she didn't move. "What's going on?"

"Ye have to go." Noomi's voice sounded far away and distant.

Peachy sat up straighter. "Go where?"

"I don't have all day, girls. Time to hand her over. Peachy the Only is destined for great things."

"I'm not going with you. Noomi, tell her. I'm not going anywhere. Gabin? Please. Someone tell me what's going on?"

"It has to be this way. I'm sorry I did everythin' I could," Noomi groaned.

"She tells the truth, Peachy. She did do everythin' she could to ensure ye were ready for today," Nefertari said. "Come now, we have much to do includin' a brief visit with some very old friends o' yours. Up. Let's go."

Peachy's hot tears blurred her world along with the blur inside her mind. Her heart thumped in her chest watching the scene unfold as if she weren't in command of her own actions.

"Ye did well, Noomi. The realm will forever be indebted to ye."

"What is she talking about? Noomi!"

"Goodness, why did ye think she was trainin' ye so hard and so fast? Ye are Peachy o' the Sky, Peachy the Teller, Peachy the Only, who belongs to and is indebted to the realm."

"I am indebted to no one, least of all you." Peachy alternated looks between Noomi and Nefertari and her guards. "Noomi, please. How could you do this?" Peachy got to her feet, and Noomi fell in step behind her.

"I'm sorry!"

"Get away from me!" Peachy shook her head. She didn't know if her conjured emotions, the anger and betrayal, were her acting the part or genuine because she never had a choice or a chance. She yelled into the sky. Her voice caused the earth to shake and everyone to cower and cover their ears.

"She is glorious, Noomi! Did ye know she could do that? Tis the cry o' the Protector! She is comin' alive! She's glorious!"

"Did you know about this?" Peachy yelled at Gabin. "All this time you pretended to protect me, both of you, pretended to love me only to hand me over to her like property? I'm not going with any of you."

"Guards, bring her to me."

"Please, Nefertari, give me a last moment with her," Noomi pleaded. "Let me say me goodbye. Ye owe this to me."

"I owe ye nothing. Ye owe me the girl."

Noomi didn't wait for Nefertari's permission before she grabbed Peachy's arm and spun her around, so her back was to Nefertari. She hugged her tightly and placed a kiss upon her lips. "Are ye ready?" Noomi held her face in her hands.

"I love you." Peachy felt crackling in the air. Electricity charged overhead, swirled through the trees, surrounded them, wove through their legs and crawled upon their skin. Everything happened in agonizingly slow motion.

"What is happening?" Noomi shouted.

"Don't let her get away!" Nefertari screamed.

"I love ye." Noomi said against her ear while she grasped the amulet from around her neck and broke the chain. She held it above her head. "I got it!"

The next thing Peachy registered was the swarm of Nefertari's guards overtaking Noomi and the vision of Gabin leaping after her. Then nothing. Then a million stars. Then black. Then she dangled from the upper floor of the *Spanish Rose*, but someone grabbed her, a firm grip around her wrist held her tight.

"Hello darling, remember me?"

"Minette?"

"We need to hurry. We don't have much time."

Peachy reached for Minette with her other hand. They struggled over the banister's railing onto solid ground.

"You okay?" Minette asked.

Peachy nodded.

"Then let's go." Minette pulled Peachy, leading her down the hall.

"Wait." Peachy stopped their movement.

The sounds of screaming came from somewhere in the house. "We have to go. Now."

"But, Gabin—"

Another flash from above and Gabin fell from the crack of light.

"Oh my God!" Minette yelled upon seeing the massive cat landing next to them. "What the fuck is that?"

"Gabin."

"What?"

"Noomi's sister."

"Holy fucking shit."

"It's okay. She's with us." Peachy ran to her. "*Gabin can you hear me? Are you hurt?*" Gabin shook her entire body.

"*She's not hurt. She wants to play.*" A voice from the dark filled Peachy's mind. The sounds of snapping jaws, low guttural growling came from a massive wolf slinking toward them.

"*Get out o' here.*" Gabin's fur stood on end and she slinked toward the approaching wolf.

"*Not without you.*"

"*Go! I will find ye. I see ye always.*" Gabin lunged toward the menacing wolf. They began tearing at each other. The horrifying sounds, the yelping and growling and gnashing of teeth elicited heart-throbbing agony inside Peachy's body.

"We have to go," Minette ordered, her eyes wide at the unfolding scene. She grabbed Peachy's hand and navigated them through the *Spanish Rose* until they arrived at the underground corridor.

"Wait. Stop." Peachy hushed, moments before Minette opened the door to the carriage house.

"What?"

"Beatriz's goons are in there."

Minette risked a peek. "Shit. How did you know that?"

"I don't know. I saw it." Peachy squeezed her eyes shut. She felt the goons' fists on her body, as if they were pummeling her. She slowed her breathing, trying to calm her growing anxiety. "How many can you see?"

Minette risked a glance. "Fifteen, twenty. We'll never get out of here."

Peachy felt Noomi's voice whispering in her mind. Her tender words helped her through the ache and generated a surge of energy. "I got an idea."

"What?"

Peachy tore off the cloth bandage from around her once injured shoulder. "Put as much of this in your ears as you can." Minette only stared at her. "Do it." Minette nodded and began ripping strips and stuffing them into her ears.

"What's going to happen?"

"Open the door. Stand back and cover your ears." Peachy closed her eyes and let her anger, pain, and love swirl inside her body. She felt a flaming orb of energy spread through her veins and burn inside her lungs. She opened her mouth and she screamed. Her cry tremored through the underground corridor, causing the bedrock to crumble around them and shook the carriage house, shattering the windows and upending the men.

Peachy pushed Minette through the small door. "Go!"

Minette stumbled out of the corridor and onto the ground. Her hands held tightly over her ears and her face was contorted in pain. Peachy helped her to her feet and together they hobbled through the stunned, cowering men. They emerged from the building into the cool, dark night. In the distance Peachy heard the unmistakable sound of someone's voice projected through a bullhorn. A tour group.

"That's our out."

"But Gabin."

"We *need* to get on that tour bus."

"Not without—"

The sound of something crashing through one of the upper story windows caused them to halt their actions. "What was that?" Minette alternated looks between the unfolding scene and the crashing sounds filtering from inside the carriage house.

Peachy ran to the lifeless form that lay on the ground. A naked woman, dark skin, light hair and covered in gashes and blood.

"Help."

It was Gabin. "Oh Gabin. Minette! Please, help me, help her!"

"Who is that?" Minette stood her mouth open.

"Please!"

Minette jumped into action. They were able to shoulder Gabin and make their way to the bus. The door opened and they climbed inside. The bus was empty and dark.

"Is that everyone?" the driver asked.

"Drive, Jean. Now!" Minette shouted.

"Where's Lisette?" Peachy asked.

"She knows where to meet us."

"Gab, I'm so sorry." Peachy supported Gabin's injured body against her own. *"Let me see if I can do this… Take the strength from my body."* She felt Gabin shift in her arms, felt her labored breathing come easier.

Peachy placed her hand where her amulet once rested. Thoughts of Noomi helped fill the cold, empty void. In her veins coursed a strange yet familiar energy, something once dormant and now alive. Peachy the Only, Peachy of the Sky, is destined for great things, but what was her destiny and how would she fulfill it?

Bella Books, Inc.

Women. Books. Even Better Together.

P.O. Box 10543
Tallahassee, FL 32302

Phone: 800-729-4992
www.bellabooks.com